Suddenly his arms closed around her

Alec groaned, or maybe Wren did. She splayed her hands on his chest. His head bent and he was kissing her. Not sweetly and gently, but so desperately she could probably tell he'd bottled up all his hunger.

He was kissing Wren.

What in hell was he thinking?

He wasn't thinking. Couldn't. This felt too good. Too right.

He cradled the back of her head so that he could angle it to please him. The other hand gripped her hips and pulled her tight against him.

He wanted her. That was all his mind could wrap itself around. Wanting.

But he couldn't have her. He knew that, too. He pulled away before he got so deep he wouldn't be able to.

She blinked several times in succession and took a step back. His hands dropped to his sides. He saw her swallow.

"You kissed me."

Dear Reader,

There's something irresistible about stories where nature traps the hero and heroine together to work out a relationship, survive and battle emotions they never expected to feel. In *All That Remains*, the intimacy is even greater, given that poor Wren is in labor and Alec must deliver her baby in the most primitive of circumstances. Makes you cringe, doesn't it? Is there ever a moment in our lives when we feel more vulnerable than when we're giving birth? Bad enough to have a doctor and nurses seeing all, but how about having to depend on a man who is a complete stranger? And, maybe worse yet, a really attractive one? Yep, irresistible.

I like it even better when those two people stuck with each other and no one else are both emotionally damaged. My daughters always wince when I enthusiastically tell them about any new plot. I'm told I really love to torture people. And I do! But my goal, always, is to write about the resilience I believe we all have, the ability to rise to challenges, to heal, to put someone else first. We never see so much heroism as during wide-spread devastation, like the flood in this book. People surprise each other...and themselves. What better time for love to complicate lives?

Happy reading!

Janice Kay Johnson

P.S.—I enjoy hearing from readers. Please contact me c/o Harlequin Books, 225 Duncan Mill Road, Toronto, ON M3B 3K9, Canada.

All That Remains
Janice Kay Johnson

TORONTO NEW YORK LONDON
AMSTERDAM PARIS SYDNEY HAMBURG
STOCKHOLM ATHENS TOKYO MILAN MADRID
PRAGUE WARSAW BUDAPEST AUCKLAND

Recycling programs
for this product may
not exist in your area.

ISBN-13: 978-0-373-71736-1

ALL THAT REMAINS

www.Harlequin.com

Printed in U.S.A.

ABOUT THE AUTHOR

The author of more than sixty books for children and adults, Janice Kay Johnson writes Harlequin Superromance novels about love and family—about the way generations connect and the power our earliest experiences have on us throughout life. Her 2007 novel *Snowbound* won a RITA® Award from Romance Writers of America for Best Contemporary Series Romance. A former librarian, Janice raised two daughters in a small rural town north of Seattle, Washington. She loves to read and is an active volunteer and board member for Purrfect Pals, a no-kill cat shelter.

Books by Janice Kay Johnson

* Lost…But Not Forgotten
† The Russell Twins

CHAPTER ONE

GRIPPING THE STEERING WHEEL with white-knuckled hands, Wren Fraser struggled to see the narrow country road ahead through sheets of rain. She'd lived in Seattle, for goodness' sake, and had *never* seen rain come down like this. The road was winding, the yellow line down the middle her only salvation. There seemed to be no shoulders wide enough for her to pull over safely, and she didn't dare stop where she was; if another car came along, it would slam right into her. She couldn't see ten feet ahead, which meant an oncoming driver wouldn't be able to, either.

Shifting in her seat, Wren tried to ease the pain gripping her lower back. She'd been in the car too long, that was all, and her tension wasn't helping. She needed desperately to get out and stretch, but even if she spotted a driveway she could pull into, stepping out to get drenched in cold rain wasn't very appealing. She didn't have rain gear. In fact, she had only one small suitcase. Given her state of pregnancy, she'd been afraid she wouldn't be able to handle more getting on and off the light rail train back in Seattle as well as through airports in Seattle and St. Louis.

Her baby was moving restlessly, kicking, stirred no doubt by her anxiety. The seat belt felt uncomfortably tight over her pregnant belly, but releasing and refastening it wasn't an option with her hands locked onto the steering wheel.

"We'll be okay," she murmured. "I promise, Cupcake. It's just rain. Before we know it, we'll be snug in a wonderful farmhouse, with a fire burning. And even if I've missed dinner, I'll bet Molly will warm a bowl of soup for me. And then we'll *both* be warm."

The pain in her back had temporarily eased, but baby wasn't reassured. Wren's entire distended belly gave a disconcerting lurch and the pressure on her bladder increased. Oh, great, now she had to pee.

Wren had no idea whether she was lost or still following the route MapQuest had laid out for her. She wasn't sure she'd be able to see a crossroad if one appeared, or street signs; the numbers on the few mailboxes she'd spotted were unreadable through the rain. However desperate she was, she'd probably been foolish not to find somewhere to hole up until she could talk to Molly. Unfortunately, turning back to the last motel she'd seen, an hour ago, was no longer an option. When she fled Seattle yesterday morning, she'd had only one focus: getting to Molly's.

The Ozark country was supposed to be beautiful. In November it was too late for fall colors, of course— what trees she'd seen through the rain had been skeletal—but Molly had rhapsodized about the quiet rivers and stark gray bluffs, the rounded mountains covered with gum trees and oaks and hickories, the winding green valleys and occasional farmhouses.

Wren had crossed a river a while back, but it didn't look that quiet to her. The water had been running high and turgid. No wonder, with this downpour. She'd been glad that the road climbed to meander along the rim of the valley. Now it was dropping again, perhaps to meet the same river.

Please, please, let me be close.

She didn't have a cell phone, not since James had convinced her that she didn't need one. Even if she'd had one—who would she call?

Oh, Molly, please be home. Please be glad to see me.

Wren wished she'd met the man her best friend from college had married. Molly had wanted her to be the maid of honor, but James couldn't get away that weekend and he'd hated the idea of her going without him....

Wren shuddered at the memory of how stupid she'd been.

She made herself think again about Molly's husband. Samuel. If Molly loved him, he must be okay. He wouldn't turn Wren away. She didn't need that much from them. The house had extra bedrooms, Molly had said it did. If they could give her even a few weeks of respite, she'd figure something out.

She just didn't know what that something would be.

A split-rail fence appeared to the right of the road then disappeared behind a burst of wind-driven rain that pummeled the car with new ferocity, making it sway.

Would she need gills to breathe outside? she wondered with momentary whimsy. The car had become her womb. She hoped the waters her baby swam in were warmer and more hospitable than the deluge out there.

The defroster struggled to keep the windshield clear. Suddenly she couldn't quite make out the yellow line ahead. A flare of alarm triggered a stab of pain in her lower back, and Wren lifted her foot from the gas. While her brain grappled with the realization that she could see nothing but gray ahead—driving, swirling, misting—momentum carried the car forward.

The next second, it plowed into something. Wren was flung forward against the seat belt, then back. Even as she cried out, water rushed over the hood and windshield and she realized she hadn't come to a complete stop. Oh, God. She must have plunged off the road into the river or a lake or pond. Absurdly, she slammed her foot down on the brake.

The car came to a stop. The wipers tried valiantly to clear the windshield. The engine was still running. Hand shaking, Wren tried to push open her door and couldn't do more than open the smallest of cracks, through which water rushed. She wrenched the door shut again. Through her panic, she made herself think. Keep driving forward? Try to back up? Molly's house was ahead, but…she knew there was bare road behind. Whimpering, more scared than she could ever remember being, she put the gear in Reverse.

The engine choked and died.

Frantically she shifted the car into Park and turned the key in the ignition, over and over, and began sobbing. The windows were electronic. How would she get out if she couldn't roll them down?

The next second, the engine caught and, gasping with relief and fear, Wren hit the two buttons to roll down the front windows. They were almost all the way down when the engine died again.

This time, nothing she could do brought it to life again. Finally she gave up and sat gulping in air, trying to think. Cold rain was slanting in the open window and she was already soaked. If she could wade to the road, maybe somebody else would come along. Maybe even somebody who knew where Molly Hayes lived.

No, not Hayes. For a moment Wren couldn't think. Roth something. Rothberg. No, that wasn't right, the name was longer than that. Rothenberg. Or even… Rothenberger? She couldn't remember.

"It doesn't matter," she said aloud. "It doesn't matter. If I can find the nearest house, we'll be all right. Anybody would take us in."

She tried the door again, but she was pushing against water that wasn't far below the window. Could it be shallower on the other side? Wren unfastened her seat belt, let the seat slide back and laboriously clambered over the console to the passenger seat. But when she tried to open that door, she had no more success.

Shaking from cold and fear, she realized that the interior would soon be underwater if she did manage to get either door ajar more than a crack. In fact, it was trickling in anyway. She looked down to see that her feet stood in several inches of water.

She had to get out the window. Surely—please, God—she could squeeze her pregnant belly through. Wren twisted first and pulled her small suitcase over the seat. She would take it and her purse, that only made sense.

Getting out a car window wasn't as easy as it ought to be. She poked her upper body out, and saw that she'd be plunging into waist-deep water, at least. It was moving, swirling and parting around the car. The river, then, not a placid pond. She didn't dare go headfirst.

Feetfirst. Pain squeezed her lower back and, gasping, she waited it out. She'd made it worse, climbing so awkwardly to this side of the car. But the spasm passed, and she maneuvered so she was very nearly on her hands and knees on the car seat, her cheek pressed to the steering wheel. She lifted one leg and stuck it out, twisting so that her hip and not her belly would take her weight on the frame once she got the other leg out, too.

She squirmed and pushed herself, grabbing at the emergency brake, the dashboard, the back of the seat. Anything she could use for leverage. She didn't think she *would* have fit had she been facedown or faceup, but sideways her belly just barely cleared the window frame.

For an instant she hung partway, and then her lower body dropped and she gasped from the cold as she plunged into the water.

No, definitely not a pond—current pressed her against the door. Walking in this wouldn't be easy, and she momentarily hesitated. Maybe she'd be safer if she stayed in the car. The rain would let up eventually, wouldn't it? And the rental car was bright red. Someone would spot it.

But she was chilled to see that the water level was still rising, lapping now into the car. She heard herself breathing, huge gasps, and grabbed her suitcase and purse.

She started back the way she'd come, but immediately realized the water was becoming deeper. Had her car nearly made it through a flooded dip in the road? Struggling against the current, she turned. She was bumped hard against the fender, then the door, but as she forged ahead the water seemed to be not quite as deep.

She moved, crablike, to protect her belly in case the current carried a branch or something even more dangerous to batter her. Once she was nearly knocked off her feet. Somehow she saved herself. She heard a keening sound that she knew, in a distant part of her mind, was coming from her. She pushed on, trying to hold the suitcase above the water.

Miraculously, the surface was only hip-high now, then thigh-high. As relief began to trickle through her, she was slammed from behind hard enough to pitch her forward. The suitcase was snatched from her hands and gone, her lunge for it too late. Her purse...no, it was gone, too. She pushed herself up and kept going, so cold her teeth were chattering, and she was convulsively trembling. But the water came only to her knees, and then her ankles, and finally she was shocked to see a yellow stripe ahead. She was still on the road. She'd never left it.

She plodded ahead, following the yellow line. Nothing she did was conscious, not now. She was hiding deep inside, knowing only the cold and the intermittent pain in her back. She walked on and on, with no sense of time or distance.

The road curved, and there was a mailbox straight ahead. It was rusting, the post it sat atop beginning to rot at its base so that the whole thing tilted slightly. Still, it was a mailbox. And where mail was delivered, there must be a house.

The driveway could hardly be dignified by calling it that. It was a muddy track, streams running in the ruts. She slipped once, wrenching her ankle, but she was so cold the pain hardly registered. All she knew was that she had to keep moving. She didn't dare stop.

No warm golden light appeared ahead. There was no welcome smell of wood smoke. But the shape of buildings appeared through the rain. One was a decrepit barn, the doors sagging half-open. The other was a house with a broad front porch. No lights, even though dusk had deepened the wet sky to charcoal.

She dragged herself up the steps. Windows were blank, dark. Wren knocked. Her hand was so numb she couldn't feel the impact. She hammered harder, and harder, until she fell against the door and beat on it with both hands.

If she didn't get inside, she'd freeze to death.

She tried the knob, which turned, but the door didn't budge. A dead bolt above it was shiny, newer than the original hardware. *Break a window, then.* She looked around for something to use. An old Adirondack chair sat at one end of the porch. Its paint was peeling. She dragged it, bumpety bump, to the nearest window. Wren didn't know how she'd find the strength, but she did. She picked it up and slammed it against the small-paned window. Glass shattered, and she lost her grip. The chair tumbled through the window. She paused for a second, waiting for lights to come on, a voice to call out in alarm, a home owner to appear wielding a shotgun. Nothing. At last, painfully, she climbed over the sill, stumbled over the chair, and fell to her hands and knees on the floor of some stranger's house.

ALEC HARPER KNEW even as he tied the rope around his waist, climbed over the bridge railing and dove into the torrential Spesock River that rescue was coming too late for the driver and any passengers in the car that had plunged into the water. But he had to try.

Crap, the water was cold. He let the current carry him to the small white car, curling his body when he slammed against it. He grabbed for the door handle and held on. Passenger side. He fought his desperate need for air and strained to look inside. Oh, shit, shit. He could see a man, hair floating around his face. A deployed air bag hid the driver from Alec's sight. The backseat, thank God, was empty.

Alec maneuvered his body over the hood of the car. His achingly cold fingers found purchase on the rim beneath the wiper blades. He was screaming inside for air, but he was almost there. The rope was pulled taut now, and, trusting the men who held the other end, he let go as he washed over the hood. There, in the driver's-side window... A second man, his face blanched as well, stared with sightless eyes.

Alec yanked on the rope then kicked and fought for the surface. His fellow rescuers dragged him in. At the shouted questions, he shook his head even before hands pulled him onto the bridge, where he lay shaking.

Somebody wrapped him in a blanket. They were a disparate group—two men he didn't know who he thought were National Guard and himself, a police homicide detective. They held some discussion and decided they had to bring the bodies up.

It turned out to be grueling. They took turns going down and hammering on the window with a tire wrench until they succeeded in shattering it and could unbuckle the bodies, one at a time, and drag them out.

In the complete exhaustion afterward, Alec wondered how long the two had been dead. He and the others could have been rescuing someone still living. He thought of the stranded motorists he'd earlier plucked from the roofs of their cars, each and every one of them sure they could drive through the river their street had become. Stupid, yes, but who had anticipated the speed with which the floodwaters had risen?

These two, he thought, as he helped heave the two drowning victims into the back of an army vehicle, wouldn't be the last he'd see.

The Spesock River flooded regularly, but not like this. There had been talk about the hundred-year flood levels, although no one really took it seriously. It was hard to in this era of weather as entertainment and forecasts that seemed more hyperbole than fact. But these past weeks of endless, drenching rains had saturated the ground. Flash floods came along every few years in Arkansas, but this time the water kept rising. There was nowhere for it to go. It swallowed houses and roads and farms. When Alec had last stopped briefly at the emergency operations center—set up at the redbrick Mountfort City Hall—he'd heard that nearly one quarter of the county was submerged. He could believe it. He'd spent almost thirty-six hours in a borrowed aluminum fishing boat, and it was hard not to pause and stare in disbelief at the dark, swirling waters turning a once familiar landscape into something his eyes didn't want to believe.

He waved goodbye to his helpers and returned to his boat. The aging Mercury outboard motor started with a cough and burst of oily smoke, but it obliged when he swung it in an arc that would lead him to Saddler's Mill. He was so damn cold he had to return to one of the emergency shelters and find dry clothes before he could do any more.

This one had been set up in a high-school gymnasium. Donated cots and bedrolls were packed closely together. After changing clothes, Alec stopped to talk to several people he knew.

Jim Hunt and his wife had celebrated their sixtieth wedding anniversary last year. Alec knew, because his mother had written him about it. Now they were in the shelter, and the couple of suitcases tucked beneath the pair of cots were all they'd been able to salvage. Not much from a lifetime.

"I suppose the whole sheriff's department is out there," Mr. Hunt commented.

A nod was enough answer. Alec doubted a single sheriff's deputy or detective had stayed home, not when the people they were hired to protect were in danger. Earlier, he'd seen a lieutenant, red-eyed with fatigue, delivering a woman and child to a shelter.

"Have you seen my sister and her family?" Alec asked, as he had every time he saw anyone he knew today.

Mr. Hunt shook his head. "They're probably at one of the other schools." His expression was kind. "Don't worry. Randy's a good man. He'll take care of his own."

Alec nodded his thanks, although he wasn't so sure. Randy liked his booze. What if he'd been at the tavern when the flash flood rushed down the river?

On the way out of the gym, Alec stopped to gulp a cup of coffee and eat a sandwich. It was the first food he'd had since…hell, he couldn't remember. Last night? He remembered a bowl of chili over at the Hagertown Grange Hall. He hadn't wanted to stop even that long; there were folks all over town waiting to be rescued from upstairs windows or roofs, some in even more desperate circumstances. But he had the sense to know he had to fuel his body if he was to keep on without sleep.

During the never-ending day, Alec brought a dozen more people in from outlying homes before he conceded defeat and slept for several hours at a fire station that was high and dry. Cots had been set up here, too, for rescue workers like him. Cops from a dozen jurisdictions came and went, as well as firefighters, paramedics, National Guard. He recognized some people, but most were strangers. Faces were furrowed and gray with exhaustion, as his undoubtedly was. He ran a hand over his chin and found two days' worth of stubble. He must look like hell. His last thought as he dropped into heavy sleep was of his sister.

The sound of voices woke him. He blinked gritty eyes, waited for full consciousness then dragged himself up. He pulled on his boots, then, carrying the bright yellow rain slicker and pants, followed the smell of coffee to a small kitchen. In the odd white light from a lantern, four people leaned against the wall and wolfed down food. Bacon and eggs, he discovered, when a woman thrust a plate into his hands.

"Thank you." No electricity here, he realized, looking around. She was cooking on a two-burner camp stove. The coffee was instant, but, under the circumstances, tasted better than the last latte he remembered buying at a Starbucks in St. Louis. Hot, strong and invigorating.

He exchanged a few words with other workers, then donned rain gear and the annoyingly bulky PFD—the life vest, or personal flotation device—and went out into the cold and wet. Dawn was lighting the dark sky with a first hint of gray. The rain hadn't relented at all.

He refilled the gas tank and felt a kick of relief when, once again, the motor came to life. There were too few boats, too many miles of countryside to be checked, for the aging Mercury to decide to be stubborn, something he'd already discovered it was prone to do.

He hadn't been out half an hour when he found a whole family roosted atop the peak of a farmhouse. The two kids were tied to the chimney to keep them from falling, the parents huddled around them. God Almighty.

Getting them down was a trial with the boat bobbing a good twelve feet below their perch. The father eventually used the rope to lower first the kids, then his wife, and Alec managed to fight the current and keep the boat in place while catching the two small bodies and the woman in turn and lowering them onto seats. The children were sobbing with fear and scrabbled to throw themselves into their mother's arms when she arrived, which nearly tipped the boat.

"Sit down!" Alec snapped then realized he'd sounded harsh. Damn, he was tired. He pulled several PFDs, including child-size ones, from a rubber tub and showed the mother how to put them on. As she strapped everyone into the vests, he maneuvered the boat into place.

The man gingerly backed down the steep roof like a mountain climber rappelling, the rope tied to the chimney above. But either he lost his grip or his feet skidded on wet shingles, because he started to slide. If he came down hard enough, he'd sink them. Alec shoved the boat away from the house and rode the wave when the man hit. He pushed the woman toward the tiller and yelled, "Hold it straight!" then leaned over the gunwale, waiting for the head to pop up. Where the hell was he?

She screamed and Alec swung around to see that her husband must have gone underneath the hull and was being swept away. He gunned the motor and steered in a semicircle, timed so he could lean over and grab the arms that were all he could see. The aluminum boat, too lightweight, swayed wildly; the kids cried and the woman sobbed and in the moments of intense struggle Alec was convinced they were going over. Somehow he managed to pull hard enough to drape the man over the edge while keeping his own weight as a counterbalance, and finally to roll the guy in. He felt as though he'd been in a war, and the family was in worse shape.

He took them to a designated landing, where volunteers waited to lead them to a shelter. He waited while they took off the life vests and offered incoherent thanks that he knew would mean something to him later, but not now.

WREN WOKE WITH A START and lay still for a long moment, trying to figure out what had penetrated the stupor of exhaustion. A sound? Yes, there it was again, an odd sizzle from the potbellied woodstove here in the parlor. As if water was dripping onto the fire she'd thankfully built. Rain coming down the chimney?

Drawing the comforter with her, she sat up on the old, dusty sofa to look. But when she put her feet on the floor, they plunged into water. Wren cried out. It was night now, and she couldn't see, but... She tentatively reached her hand down. Oh, God, oh, God. Water was a foot deep or more. In horror, she grappled with the concept. How could it have reached the house? She'd climbed several steps to the porch. It had to have risen four or five feet to have reached this high. It was lapping into the stove, putting out her fire.

She *needed* the fire. It had been her salvation, finding brittle old wood heaped in a copper bin beside the stove, a bundle of yellowed newspapers with a date two years past and a box of matches abandoned atop the newspapers. The only food in the cupboards had been in cans and she hadn't been able to find an opener. It was lucky she wasn't hungry. The refrigerator was unplugged, which told her no one planned to be back in the near future. In fact, either the storm had taken out a power line somewhere or the electricity to the house had been cut off. But she'd been able to build a fire, and she'd dragged the comforter from an old bedstead in one of the two bedrooms.

Her back hurt again. The pain had been coming and going unpredictably, waking her periodically. Each time, she'd added wood to the stove. Kneeling on the sofa, she waited this spasm out. It had occurred to her sometime in the past few hours that she might be going into labor, but the thought had been so terrifying she didn't let herself take it seriously. Early twinges were common, she knew that. Braxton-Hicks contractions. Except…were they felt in the back? She didn't know. Wren didn't think this pain was any more severe than what she'd had earlier—yesterday?—when she was still behind the wheel of the car. So she wouldn't worry about that problem—not yet.

She laughed, and heard her own hysteria. Oh, yes. She had bigger problems.

She hadn't seen a staircase, which meant there was no second story. But, frowning, she seemed to remember the house rearing higher above her than the single-story ranch houses she'd lived in. Old houses like this often had attics, didn't they?

By the time she put her feet back on the floor, the water level had risen to her knees. Wren left the comforter on the back of the sofa and fumbled in the woodpile for a piece of kindling. When her fingers found one, still dry near the top of the heap, she opened the door of the stove and poked the kindling in to the coals, which sizzled as water inched in but remained alive. When the wood was alight, she went exploring, holding her torch high.

In a bedroom, she found the square in the ceiling

she'd been looking for. A rope hung down, and when she pulled on it, she was rewarded with a creak and some movement. Not for the first time, she cursed her petite size, but being pregnant helped. She hung from the rope, and with a groan a folding staircase dropped.

She climbed the narrow, steep stairs and poked her head up. She was relieved to see a floor rather than open joists. Dusty bits of unwanted furniture and heaps of boxes. The glint of a reflection from a window. At least she'd have daylight when the sun rose. She'd be able to signal for rescue, if anyone came.

She eased down the steps, holding tight as she went, then waded through the house looking for anything she could salvage from the rising waters. More bedding. The matches, and some dry firewood, although she'd only be able to start a fire upstairs if she could find a flame-proof container like a metal washtub. Clothes—nothing that exactly fit, but the voluminous flannel nightgown she'd found in her earlier exploration was wet now, and she was beginning to shiver again. She grabbed armfuls and thrust them upstairs.

The piece of kindling burned down quickly and she replaced it. She grabbed a knife from the kitchen—just in case, although she didn't know in case of what—and found her way to the staircase right before the flames reached her hand a second time. She cried out and had to drop the burning wood into the water, which quickly drowned it.

Climbing in the complete darkness was scary. She felt her way once she reached the attic. Her hands encountered cloth. Flannel, maybe a shirt, she decided, as she lifted. Denim beneath. Groping, she located the blankets and her comforter and an old quilt she'd found.

She crawled toward the window, dragging the bedding with her, then went for the clothes and the knife.

She shook out the comforter and spread it, then folded it twice to make a pad. Sitting on it, she scrabbled among the garments for something, anything, that might fit her, settling finally on a flannel shirt. She tugged the nightgown over her head and discarded it, then hurriedly pulled on the shirt, rolled the sleeves half a dozen times to free her hands, then buttoned it. If she stood, she thought the shirt would reach near to her knees. Right now, she wouldn't worry about putting anything else on. All she did was pull blankets and the quilt over her, and lie down facing the window. Praying for a pale tint of dawn that might allow her to see out.

ALEC HAD GOTTEN STARTED at first light and had rescued a dozen people by the time the sun was seriously up in the sky. He guessed it was about ten o'clock, and he was reaching his limit. He almost skipped the old Maynard house; he knew Josiah had gone to a nursing home in Blytheville a couple of years ago, and the house had been empty ever since. But Alec's conscience wouldn't let him. It was possible travelers had taken refuge there. There weren't many options on that stretch of the Spesock.

All he could see was the roof of the barn and the upper portion of the house. The water was nine feet deep or more. He swung the tiller to circle the house. That was when he spotted a white sheet hanging, sodden, from the attic window.

Even as he steered closer, he saw a figure behind the glass, struggling to push the casement up. He was bumping the side of the house before he got a good look.

Oh, hell. Oh, damnation. That woman was pregnant. Her belly huge. As he tried to edge to position the boat beneath the window, her mouth opened in a cry of distress and she dropped from sight.

Alec swore then yelled, "Ma'am! Ma'am? Are you all right?"

She didn't reappear. A gust drove rain between them and in the window. Swearing some more, he swiped his arm across his face, trying to clear his vision.

Finally she returned to the open window. She said something. He shook his head and gestured at his ear.

"I'm in labor!" she screamed.

"Are you alone?" he called, and she nodded.

His silent profanities intensified. There was no way a hugely pregnant woman in labor was clambering out of that window and lowering herself to the boat, then hunching beside him in the bitter cold and rain for a forty-five-minute trip to the nearest shelter.

Could a helicopter reach her? He knew how few were available. If eastern Arkansas had been alone in flooding, rescue workers would have had more resources to draw on. But the Mississippi and all its tributaries had gone over the banks, and the National Guard and army were spread over Ohio and Tennessee and down into Mississippi, too. Alec had had the impression rural Arkansas was low on the list of priorities.

Not seeing any other choice, he lifted a grappling hook on the end of a rope that was tied to the seat of his boat. He waved her back and she seemed to understand, disappearing again. Alec gave the hook a toss and watched it catch over the windowsill. He tugged on the rope until the boat was snug against the house and below the window. He thought he could reach his fingertips over that sill.

All right. What would he need? First-aid kit…although he couldn't imagine what in it would be of any use for a woman in childbirth. Nonetheless, he slung it in the window. Big rubber flashlight in case this went on into night. He had a cache that held some clean drinking water and energy snacks; he slung that in, too, hoping she'd had the sense to get out of the way and he hadn't knocked her out. Finally he killed the motor, reached high and just got his hands over the soaking wet sill.

He was hanging there when something big hit the boat. The whole seat that anchored the rope ripped free with a groan, and the boat swung away. His fingers began to slip. He had a cold, clear moment of knowing he was going to fall. Vest or not, he wouldn't have a chance in the bitter floodwaters.

Small strong hands grabbed his wrists and held on tight.

CHAPTER TWO

ALEC KNEW SHE WOULDN'T be able to hold on to him for long. He was a big man, his considerable weight hanging by his fingertips and her grip. But she'd arrested his slide toward the floodwaters, and he inched his right hand toward the rope and grappling iron. A second later, he'd managed to grab the iron above the knot.

His shoulders were screaming. As he tried to pull himself upward, he cursed the bulky flotation vest that caught on the clapboards. With his toes he scrambled for purchase. Any tiny toehold. His booted feet kept slipping. But the woman was exerting steady upward pressure, too, and he got a better hold on the windowsill with his left hand. He closed his eyes, summoned the memory of doing that last pull-up in P.E. so long ago, and with a guttural sound put everything he had into one try.

He was almost shocked to find his shoulders over the edge. She wrapped her arms around him and held tightly as he tried to clear the window.

The damn vest snagged. He had to maneuver a half roll, which meant he tumbled into the attic and fell hard onto one shoulder.

As he lay there, winded, muscles shaking from the exertion, the woman uttered little cries interspersed with "Are you all right? Oh, God. I didn't think you'd make it. Please. Are you all right?"

A grunt was the best he could do. She turned abruptly and shoved the window down as far as it would go with the iron grappling hook biting into the wood.

Alec flopped to his back and stared up at thick cobwebs festooning open beams. He'd left the goddamn radio, he thought, stunned at his stupidity. It was gone with the boat.

"Shit," he said aloud.

"You're all right."

He rolled his head to look at the woman. The extremely pregnant woman. It was hard to see anything but that gigantic belly.

"I'm alive," he conceded. "Thank you."

"For getting myself stuck here? You should be cursing me."

Alec gave a grunt of laughter. "Thousands of people have gotten themselves stuck somewhere or other. Nobody expected a flood of this magnitude, or the waters to rise so damn fast. Trust me, you're not alone."

"I didn't know there was going to be a flood at all," she admitted. "I'm not from around here. I stopped for the night before I headed into Arkansas, but I didn't even turn on the TV or see any newspaper headlines. The rain was scary, but I didn't have a clue until I drove into the water."

"Car still there?"

She nodded.

He shoved himself to a sitting position, his back to the wall beside the window. With clumsy, cold hands, he unbuckled the PFD and yanked it over his head. It landed with a splat on the attic floor. It was bloody cold in here, but he unsnapped his raincoat, too, and finally stood to strip off the coat and yellow rain pants. Beneath, he wore jeans and a thick chamois shirt under a down vest. Wool socks and boots.

His cell phone was in the pocket of his vest, which would have made him feel optimistic if didn't know damn well there would be no coverage here in the valley. Cell phones were notoriously unreliable through-out the Ozarks. He turned it on, in case.

No bars.

"Doesn't it work?" Her voice was barely above a whisper.

Alec shook his head. "Doesn't matter anyway. It would take a helicopter to get us out of here, and there aren't enough of those to go around."

She went very still for a long moment, as if absorb-ing the undoubtedly terrifying knowledge that he was as good as it was going to get. At last she said, in a briskly practical voice, "Your hair's wet. Here." She offered a piece of clothing—a pajama top, maybe Jo-siah's?—and he used it to scrub his head.

Then, finally, he sat and really looked at her.

She was a small woman. Hard to judge height, given her girth and with her kneeling, but he'd be willing to bet she didn't top five foot three or four. Small bones. Tiny wrists. Feet encased in enormous wool socks. Her legs were bare beneath what he guessed was a man's flannel shirt. Probably Josiah's, as well.

His assessment moved upward. She had a small, up-turned nose, nice lips that were neither thin nor pouty and brown eyes that dominated an elfin face so thin it looked gaunt. Medium brown hair that had gotten wet and dried without seeing a hairbrush. Stick-straight, it was shoved behind ears that poked out a bit, adding to that fey affect. Not a pretty woman, for sure, but... something.

"Are you here alone?"

She nodded. "Except for…" She gestured at her belly.

"You're having contractions."

"Yes."

"When did they start?" As if that would tell him any-thing. He sure as hell was no expert on childbirth. His wife's first labor had been dizzyingly fast, and Alec had missed the birth of his younger daughter entirely.

"I don't know," this woman said softly. "I think now…almost two days ago. When I was driving, my back kept hurting. It would come and go. I thought it was because I was so tense. You know, with the rain coming down so hard, and hardly any visibility, and not really knowing where I was going."

"Where *were* you going?"

Those big brown eyes sought his. "Um…to visit a friend. Molly Hayes. No, Rothenberg. She got married. Do you know her?"

Alec shook his head. "I haven't lived in these parts that long. I'm sorry. If I haven't encountered them on the job, I probably don't know them."

"Oh." Then, in an entirely different voice, she groaned, *"Ohhhh."*

Galvanized, Alec shifted to his knees, gripped her shoulder—so fragile his hand felt huge—and guided her as gently as he could to her makeshift pallet. "Lie down. That's it." She clenched her teeth, her body bowed so that he doubted anything but her shoulders and heels touched the pallet. Alec unpried the fisted fingers of one hand and took it in his. She grabbed on so hard it hurt. Hell, maybe she *could* have pulled him in the window on her own, especially in the grip of a contraction.

"You're doing great," he murmured. "That's it,

honey. Ride it out. It'll pass. That's it. You're doing great."

He listened with incredulity to his own drivel. For God's sake, how was that supposed to help her? As if she didn't *know* the contraction would pass.

When it did, she collapsed like a rubber raft with the air valve opened.

"Do you have a watch? How often are they coming?"

"I don't know," she whispered. "No watch."

"I have one." The glass was slightly fogged, but the second hand still swept around. "We'll time you." Her lips were chapped, and he saw a streak of blood. She'd bitten down too hard, he guessed. "Did you take a childbirth class?"

"I got books."

Alec didn't waste time discussing what she'd read. "Here's what you're going to do." He demonstrated the breathing technique he'd been taught in the medical part of the police academy. He remembered that much, thank God. "Breathe in through the nose, out through the mouth. Four pants, then blow. Got that?"

She nodded, those brown eyes fastened on his face as if nothing and nobody else in the world existed to her right now. "Yes. Thank you." She hesitated. "Have you… Are you a paramedic?"

"Cop. But we have some training, too. I've delivered a baby."

Hope lit her face. "You have?"

He hated to dampen that hope, but admitted, "A long time ago. I was a patrol officer. Woman was trying to drive herself to the hospital. She didn't make it." His mouth tilted into a rueful grin. "Scared me, but we managed."

"Do you think…" She bit her lip, then winced. "I mean, that we'll manage now?"

"Of course we will." He found himself smiling and meaning it, although something complicated was happening inside him that he suspected was partly fear. Yeah, they'd manage—if nothing went wrong. If the baby wasn't breech, or her placenta didn't separate. If she dilated fully without drug intervention. If the baby didn't suffer distress, or get the cord wrapped around its neck, or… Alec didn't even want to think about the myriad nightmarish possibilities.

Most childbirth was uneventful. Cling to that.

Okay.

"You're cold," he said gruffly. "Let's tuck you in."

He wrapped a hand around one of her feet and found it icy. Swearing, he gathered blankets and bundled her in them.

There was a chimney at one end of the space, he saw, but no opening for a fireplace. At some point, a floor had been laid up here, but rooms were never framed in. Alec didn't think the Maynards had children, which meant they'd never needed to add upstairs bedrooms.

"I had a fire downstairs," the woman said. "It felt so good. But then water started coming in. I brought the matches up and even a little bit of wood, but…"

"The bedding was smart. We can keep you cozy. The baby, too, when it comes." He paused. "Do you know whether it's a boy or girl?" *Or, from the size of that belly, both.*

She tried to smile, but it trembled on her lips. "A girl. I haven't named her yet. I guess I'm superstitious."

"You call her *it?*"

Now a tiny laugh escaped her. "Cupcake. She's Cupcake."

"Ah, that's more like it." He laid a hand on her belly. "Hi, Cupcake."

Beneath his hand, muscles seized and her belly became rock-hard. Cupcake's mother groaned. Alec glanced at his watch. Five minutes, give or take a few seconds. Too bad he didn't know how long it took to get from contractions five minutes apart to the actual birth. Assuming there was any norm.

He turned her face so she had to look into his eyes. "Breathe," he reminded her. "One, two, three, four, *blow*. One, two, three, four… That's it." He counted and praised until the tension left her body once again.

"Better?" he asked.

She closed her eyes, but whispered, "Yes. Better."

"Now I've met Cupcake—" he touched her belly again "—you and I might introduce ourselves. I'm Detective Alec Harper, Rush County Sheriff's Department."

"Oh." Her eyes opened. "My name is Wren." She studied him warily. "Um…will you need to put my name in a report or anything like that?"

He went on alert. "Is someone looking for you?"

After a moment she gave a small nod. "Cupcake's father. He's…" She swallowed. "I'm running away," she finished, with an air of finality. "For Cupcake's sake. And mine."

"There's not a warrant out for your arrest?"

She stared at him. "For my *arrest*?"

"You're not in trouble with the law?"

"For heaven's sake, of course not!"

"Then I promise Cupcake's father won't find you by any doing of mine."

Those eyes, as soft as a Hershey's bar melted for

a s'more, kept searching his face. "Okay," she said. "Fraser. My last name's Fraser."

"Ren? How do you spell it?"

"Like the bird. *W-R-E-N.*" She sighed. "I suppose that's how I looked to my mother. Small and brown-feathered and sort of plain."

He'd swear he heard a lifetime of sadness in words she said lightly.

"It's a pretty name," Alec said. Somehow, he hadn't let go of her hand, which lay trustingly in his rather like the small bird they were talking about. "Wrens may not be colorful, but they're quick and cheerful and full of life."

"Still, it would be rather nice to be a blue jay. Or a cardinal."

He grinned at her. "Blue jays are thieves, you know. Lousy characters all around. Cardinals are in bad taste. Too flashy."

Wren gave another tiny giggle that warmed his heart ridiculously. His hand tightened on hers, and she looked down as if bemused to see where it lay. But she made no move to remove it from his.

Another contraction came. Gaze fastened desperately on his, she breathed her way through it. When it passed, she said, "Do you mind talking to me? You said you're a detective?"

"Major crimes," he said. "Homicide, rape, assault."

"Do you like what you do?"

He felt his mouth twist. Funny she should ask him that. He might still be married if he'd been willing to give up what he did. He wouldn't have lost India and Autumn, the two people he loved most in the world.

"Yeah." His voice came out hoarse. He cleared his

throat. "Yeah, I like my work. I never wanted to be anything but a cop."

"Then that's what you ought to do," Wren said firmly. "You're lucky."

Lucky. That was one way of putting it.

"You?" he asked.

"Nothing special." Her voice brightened. "I did graduate from college." The brightness left her. "But I majored in history, which is pretty much useless. I wanted to do grad school to become a librarian, but—" She grimaced. "I told myself I'd still do it, but…later."

Cupcake's father had come along, Alec guessed. He was developing quite a dislike for Cupcake's father.

"You got married?"

She looked at him in surprise. "No. Oh, no. I was stupid, but not quite that stupid. We're not married, thank goodness. Just…" She indicated her belly.

"Do you know for sure that he's after you?"

"No-o." Memories pinched her face. "But he said I couldn't leave him. That he'd find me, and I'd be sorry if I ever tried."

"Bullies like that don't always follow through."

"No." Again she sounded doubtful. "But I'd rather make it impossible for him to find me."

Alec didn't like seeing that expression on her face. He smiled at her. "Well, there's the silver lining to your current predicament. I can guarantee you that Cupcake's father can't get to you right now."

Some of the tension left her. "That's true, isn't it? And I was so lucky that you came along. I told myself I could do this alone, but…I was scared."

"You weren't just lucky," he told her firmly. "You were smart, too. You got yourself from your car to a house, then into the attic. If you hadn't hung that white sheet out the window, I might not have come close. I knew this house was abandoned."

"Why was it?"

"Old guy lived here. Josiah Maynard. His wife died quite a while ago. He let the place go after that, from what I heard. Almost two years ago he had to move to a nursing home."

"He's still alive, then?"

"Far as I know."

She gave a little nod. "Then I'll go visit him once I can. I should thank him for…for leaving some clothes behind, and wood and even matches. And tell him I'm sorry I had to break a window to get in."

Alec laughed. "With water halfway to the ceiling downstairs, I think the house is history. One broken window doesn't make any difference."

"You mean, it won't be rebuilt—" She groaned, her grip on his hand tightened, and they were off again.

After a quick glance at his watch, he counted with her. He hadn't checked the time with the last one, but he thought contractions were still spaced about five minutes apart. Probably no surprise, not if it had taken her nearly two days to get to this point. Still, he'd feel better if they were getting closer together, even though he wasn't looking forward to the denouement.

"Are you hungry? Or thirsty?" he asked, when she was resting again.

Wren shook her head. "No. I'm okay."

"Warm enough?"

She seemed to do an internal check, then answered with faint surprise, "Yes."

"Let me get the window completely closed." He left her to pry the grappling iron out of the wood. The sodden white sheet dropped into the water below and was whipped away. He stood looking out for a minute, having one of those moments of disbelief, then shook his head and shoved the swollen casement window down.

The attic was not noticeably warmer.

"I really am sorry. I mean, that you got stuck here with me."

He turned to face her. "I didn't *get* stuck. I made a decision. You couldn't climb out the window and get down to the boat while you were in labor. If the outboard motor had failed on the way back, we'd have been up a creek, if you'll pardon the pun. It's better to hunker down here with you. It would be nice if we had a working woodstove, maybe a kettle and some cocoa—"

"Marshmallows."

He laughed. "Yeah, why not? But this isn't so bad, is it? You gathered enough bedding and clothes to keep us from freezing. The water has risen as high as it's going to get. We're safe. You've got me to help Cupcake be born. Somebody will come looking for me eventually, or we'll wait until the water goes down." He shrugged. "We're fine, Wren. You have nothing to be sorry for."

She thought that over, then said, "But now you can't rescue anyone else."

He shook his head. "We were winding down. This was one of the last places I was going to check."

Forehead still crinkled, she asked, "But don't you have family? People you're worried about?"

"A sister and her kids, but she has a husband." Useless, in Alec's opinion, but his sister hadn't asked for it. "I'm hoping their house is high enough to be dry, but they may have gone to a shelter. I wasn't working that part of the county."

"And you couldn't call them."

"I tried my sister's cell, but it was off. She tends to let the battery die down."

"*Are* you worried?" She scrutinized him carefully.

With a stir of amusement, he thought, *She's persistent. A bird after a worm.*

"If I'd been really worried, I would have taken a break to go look for them. I wasn't."

After a minute, she said, "Okay."

"You?" he asked. "Anyone you wish you could call?"

Her eyes widened. "You mean…*him?*"

"No." His voice was rough. "I didn't mean him."

"Oh. Um…no. Except Molly. I mentioned her, didn't I? She's my best friend. We were college roommates."

"No family?"

"Nobody who'll worry about me."

What did that mean? He didn't ask, because she was having another contraction.

The world outside ceased to exist in any meaningful way. She had contractions. They talked. Alec suggested she walk around a few times. He poked in boxes to see if he could find anything useful to add to their meager stash, but found mostly the kind of useless crap people shoved in their attics: picture frames with the glass long broken, plastic food containers and lids, none of which seemed to fit with each other, Christmas ornaments and carefully folded bits of wrapping paper, saved from long-ago holidays, canning supplies… He paused at that one, and removed a couple of jars. He could piss out the window, but Wren might not feel comfortable doing that.

Mostly they didn't talk about anything important, but it occurred to him as every hour melted into another hour, then another, that he couldn't remember ever sharing quite so much with another woman—or anyone at all, come to that—as he was with her. She told him her favorite books, but in sharing that much offered memories, too. He heard a wistful story about her dreams of being a ballerina. Her mother had eventually put her into lessons, but then the shy girl Wren was had learned she would have to perform in front of an audience at the recitals and had refused.

"I kept dancing," she said, "but only for myself. Dreaming, yet knowing I'd never go anywhere with it."

Bothered by his impression of a lonely childhood, he talked, too.

He told her about fishing with his dad, of triumphs on the football field, of the first Thanksgiving after his father died, and then of how responsible he'd felt for his younger sister, Sally. Trying to disguise how much he'd admitted to, he ended on a light note. Smiling, he said, "My favorite part was scaring the crap out of any boy who looked at her twice."

Too bad he hadn't been around when Sally met Randy. Ancient regrets played on a spool that should have been long since worn-out. What if he'd moved to rural Arkansas from St. Louis ten years ago, when his mother and sister came here to live with Aunt Pearl, instead of waiting until a year and a half ago when Mom was already dying of cancer? If Alec had been around from the beginning, would Sally have made better decisions? Would Mom still be alive?

Great timing to ask himself unanswerable questions.

Unsettled, he realized if Wren was really listening, he'd given away too much. He grunted. If? He knew damn well she'd heard everything he said, and everything he didn't. Just as he'd heard her.

Contractions were four and a half minutes apart, then four. She walked some more, grumbled, "Cupcake isn't in any hurry, is she?" and groaned through yet more pain.

"I hope you weren't looking forward to that epidural too much," Alec commented.

She rolled her eyes and sang, off-key, from the Rolling Stones' song "You Can't Always Get What You Want."

As expected, he laughed. It occurred to him, as morning became afternoon, that he'd laughed more today than he had in a couple of years.

She did finally confess that she needed the canning jar, and he turned his back when she used it. He pretended he couldn't hear the tinkling sound that ensued. Finally, a small voice said, "Do I dump it out the window?"

He turned around. "I can do it."

Expression defiant, she held the jar behind her. "Not a chance."

Alec grinned. "We're going to get to know each other even better, you know."

Wren scrunched up her face. "I don't want to think about that. And I don't want you carrying a jar of my pee around, either."

"All right. I'll open the window for you."

He muscled it up, then, smiling, looked away while she did the deed. Only when she gave her permission did he turn back and tug the window down again. Cheeks flushed, she set the wet jar—which he guessed she'd rinsed out with rain—some distance away and then retired to her pallet.

Three and a half minutes.

Three.

The contractions were growing in intensity, seizing her and shaking her in great, vicious jaws. Alec would have given one hell of a lot to be able to do something, anything, besides hold her hand, count for her and smooth hair from her damp forehead.

She kept shifting on the pallet as if she was increasingly uncomfortable.

"Shall I find something to make that softer?"

"I don't know if it would make much difference. My back hurts."

"Ah." She'd said that earlier, hadn't she? He wished he'd remembered sooner. "Roll over," he said, disengaging his hand from hers and helping her heave onto her side to face away from him.

Grateful for something useful to do, he gently worked the flannel shirt up, careful to keep the blanket covering her hips—although her body would hold no secrets from him by the time they were done. Then, starting tentatively, he spread his hands over her back and began to knead taut muscles.

Wren moaned, and he stopped. "Did I hurt you?"

"No. Oh, no! It felt so good."

He relaxed. "Okay."

It was the first time he'd touched her much, beyond holding her hand. She was a dainty woman, her vertebrae delicate, her shoulder blades sharp-edged, her neck so small his hand would engulf it. In fact, he could splay the fingers of one hand and cover her entire lower back. That's where the pain seemed to be centered, although she sighed with pleasure no matter where he squeezed. He dug his thumbs in at the small of her back, and she arched as if in ecstasy. When he gentled his touch, she made a funny little noise in her throat that sounded for all the world like a purr.

Alec was dismayed to realize he was getting

aroused. Crap. He couldn't let her roll toward him and notice.

Think about something else, he ordered himself. Anything but fragile bones and taut muscles and throaty sounds of feminine pleasure. *Think about…* Yes, there it came, another contraction rolling over her body, changing the sounds that emerged from her.

He counted as he smoothed the flannel shirt down, his hands more reluctant than he wanted to admit.

"I'll give you another massage in a bit," he said, as he helped her turn over again.

Hair clung in sweaty clumps to her forehead and cheeks. "How far apart are they now?"

"Two and a half minutes." Without even thinking about it, he stroked the hair from her face, trying not to react to the unconscious way she nuzzled his hand when he was done. Hoarsely, he said, "We're getting there."

He'd become—almost—accustomed to the intense way she fastened those big brown eyes on him.

"It doesn't feel like it," she whispered. "It's…surreal. Like it's been going on forever, and will keep going."

"I know," he said. "I know." The strange part was his contentment. He tended to be restless. He'd always gotten bored easily. Law enforcement, with physical and mental challenges intertwined, had kept him engaged. He'd known he couldn't bear straight office work. Carlene hadn't understood that. Or maybe she had, and didn't care. Marriage to a cop wasn't easy.

"I didn't know what I was signing on for," she'd kept saying.

Alec still didn't know if he'd let her down, or she'd let him down. In the end, it didn't much matter.

Except…it did, because she'd taken his two little

girls with her when she left. In the end, she'd taken them so far away, he had lost them.

Not a good time to think about his daughters.

He didn't really even want to think about Cupcake. Wren, yes. He liked thinking about Wren. With her, everything felt good. Better than it should, considering they were strangers.

"Ohhh." She grabbed for his hand.

"That was quick," he murmured. "Breathe. That's it, honey. One, two, three, four…"

Alec had the odd thought that he knew her face better than he'd known Carlene's. He'd counted the scattering of freckles across Wren's small nose. Studied the whorls of her ears and the minute flecks of gold and green in her eyes.

The contraction past, he found himself reassuring her with a gentle massage of her shoulders and neck that worked its way up to her sweaty head. He pressed circular patterns into her temples, used his fingertips to smooth her forehead. It was all he could do not to run his thumb over her chapped lips.

Not a stranger. Not anymore.

Jarred, he had the thought that, eventually, she'd get taken to the hospital, and he'd go to work. If they kept her long, he might stop by to visit once.

Her eyes were closed. She was breathing softly, for this moment utterly relaxed. She wouldn't see the way he was frowning, or the inner quake that probably showed on his face as he imagined a future when he'd never know what had happened to Wren.

CHAPTER THREE

WREN KNEW SHE OUGHT TO BE really, really scared. She had never in a million years imagined having her baby on the floor of an old attic in a house being swallowed by a flood. She hadn't even wanted to go the at-home-with-a-midwife route. She'd planned on a hospital, a fetal monitor strapped across her belly, a surgical suite down the hall if necessary. She'd had every intention of being surrounded by all the technology possible—not to mention obstetricians and nurses.

Yet here she was, and although fear did tiptoe through her consciousness now and again, mostly she was okay. The surprising sense of security was entirely thanks to Alec, who had, without hesitation and with considerable risk to himself, climbed into the attic and stranded himself along with her. All because she needed him.

She remembered that terrifying moment when his hands had slipped and she'd been sure he was going to fall. All in a flash, she'd *seen* it in Technicolor—the splash, then the sight of his head bobbing as he was swept away until he disappeared in the eternal rain, leaving her utterly alone again. More alone, because he'd briefly given her hope that she wouldn't be.

Somehow, with superhuman strength, he'd hauled himself upward and made it through the window. If she could have chosen anyone in the world—well, except

for an obstetrician, maybe—it would have been him.
He'd had enough training to give her confidence, and
he'd actually delivered a baby before. He was calm, and
so kind. After hours and hours of either kneeling or sitting on the floor beside her, his back probably ached
as much as hers did, and the way she'd been squeezing
his hand, it had probably gone numb. She hoped it had
gone numb so it didn't hurt.

He encouraged her to talk, and he listened. Really
listened, she could tell, unlike James, who had only pretended. Alec had talked to her, too, as if they were best
friends. There were parts of himself he didn't offer, of
course. Flashing yellow caution lights clearly marked
those areas, but that was okay. There were things she
didn't talk about, too. People.

She was glad he didn't ask any more about James.
She didn't want him here even in spirit when her baby
was born. He hadn't wanted Cupcake, and now she was
glad. Glad!

Wren couldn't help having the sneaking wish that
Detective Alec Harper was Cupcake's biological father
instead. It was wrong of her to even think that, sort of
like having a sudden and inappropriate crush on your
obstetrician. Women probably fell for their doctors
often; after all, they projected a calm air of confidence
and knowledge that no rattled husband could possibly
match. But Wren bet Alec would project it, even if it
was his baby being born. And he'd never know she was
wishing, would he? So what did it hurt to dream a little?

Deciding she'd squelch all these surprising emotions
later, she let herself enjoy his care, and even feel entitled to it. Except when he rolled her over so that he
could give her the best back rub she'd ever had, Wren
hardly looked away from him. She probably wouldn't

have anyway, because he'd become her lodestar. And the truth was she liked looking at him.

She often felt dwarfed by men, but Alec's size along with everything else about him made her feel safe instead of small and insignificant. Probably a woman in labor shouldn't notice things such as the way his jeans pulled taut over the hard muscles in his thighs. Or the thickness of his wrists, and the dusting of hair on powerful forearms, but she did. Usually she didn't like the unshaved look on men, but dark stubble emphasized the hollows beneath his cheekbones and enhanced the air he had of being pure *male*.

He had a habit of shoving a hand through dark, unruly hair. And his wonderful mouth seemed to be made for smiling, even though he'd looked surprised the first few times he did smile and laugh. Maybe that was just because of everything he'd seen these past two days. He'd told her about some of it: the dead animals floating past, the scared children, the despairing adults sitting in emergency shelters knowing everything they owned was gone. People had died, too. He was one of the rescue workers who had pulled two people out of a submerged car, and known even as they worked that they were too late. Wren had seen the dark flash of emotion on Alec's face.

She had a feeling, though, that he didn't do much smiling these days. At least, not heartfelt smiles or real belly laughs. He was so very guarded, she knew there had to be a reason.

Once she asked if he was married, and his response was a terse, "No. Divorced." She hadn't dared ask more.

As appealing and sexy as he was, his eyes were what drew her most. As dark as his hair was, his eyes should have been brown like hers, but they weren't. They were a pure, rich blue, much deeper than the summer-sky blue that blonds often had. The color alone made his eyes riveting, but beyond that they expressed an intensity that she guessed was just him. And even when his face stayed impassive, his eyes betrayed emotions Wren wished she could better read. His clear irises were often darkened by shadows. But his eyes smiled, too, sometimes even when his mouth didn't. She loved the glints of humor and, yes, the kindness.

The contractions were closer together now, barely giving her any rest between. They came like ocean waves, rolling over her, ebbing slowly even as the next built. The whole "pant, pant, blow" thing *had* helped, but it wasn't so much anymore. She kept losing track, crying out, her entire body arching in agony. She quit noticing how sexy Alec was, and cared only that he was *here*.

Finally, one of those waves was stronger than the others, and she crushed his big hand. "I need to push."

"Not yet." He bent close over her, compelling her by sheer force of personality. *"Breathe."*

She groaned as the wave receded. "Why can't I?"

He pried his hand from hers. "I think it's time I take a look, Wren. I want to make sure you're completely dilated."

She didn't ask how he'd know, because she preferred to believe completely in his ability to deliver her baby.

An hour ago she would have been self-conscious when he lifted the blankets, pushed up the flannel shirt and gently spread her knees. Now, with another wave lifting her, cresting, she couldn't afford any emotion so petty.

"Breathe."

She tried. Oh, God, she tried, but she'd never felt

anything like this, a compulsion so powerful it gripped every cell of her body. Strange, guttural sounds came from her and her hips rose.

The contraction eased and she sagged back down, although already she felt the next gathering force. "Please," she whispered.

Alec's hands squeezed her thighs and he said, "Okay. I think we're ready."

He moved away from her briefly, and she felt him lifting her, putting some of the clothes she'd dragged up under her hips. Because this would be messy, Wren realized, in a corner of her brain not quite overridden by pain.

Then he knelt again between her thighs. "This time push."

She couldn't have done anything but. Her mind blanked of everything but this huge, overwhelming need—and the sight of Alec's face, his rumbles of encouragement.

"I see Cupcake's head. That's it. I know you're tired, but…you're amazing." He flashed her a huge grin. "I've got her head, honey. A little more."

There was a brief pause, just enough for Wren to gather strength, and then she heard herself screaming as she pushed with everything she had. She felt her baby slip from her. Satisfaction roared in her ears, but already she was levering herself to her elbows.

"Is she all right? Why isn't she crying?"

He was utterly preoccupied, there between her knees. "Give her a second. I'm wiping her face."

Then it came, a thin wail, and he laughed, exultation in those blue, blue eyes as they met hers.

"Let me wrap her up." And finally he lifted a flannel bundle and laid it on Wren's stomach. She could see his delight. "Meet Cupcake."

Wren looked disbelievingly at the small, scrunched face of her daughter. She didn't look anything like television-commercial babies. She was beet-red, and her eyes were squeezed shut as if she was absolutely refusing to see this cold, scary world. She was smeared with blood and slimy stuff, but all the same Wren had never seen anything so beautiful.

"Oh, sweetheart," she whispered, and smoothed a hand over a head damply fuzzed with a shade of brown the same as her own hair. And she was filled with joy, because at first glance there was nothing whatsoever of James in her baby.

"I need to cut the cord," Alec said.

Wren lifted her gaze from Cupcake. "I didn't even think of that. What can you… Oh! I brought a knife up from the kitchen."

He laughed. "I have scissors from the first-aid kit, thankfully sterile." He brandished them as he ripped off the packaging. "And I found some twine I think will work."

That *hadn't* come from the first-aid kit, which made Wren realize it must have been one of the things he'd been looking for earlier, when he'd been opening boxes. She remembered once hearing a grunt of satisfaction.

She watched anxiously as he tied the still pulsing umbilical cord. Then the scissors flashed, and without hesitation he cut the cord.

"She's her own person now," he murmured, and Wren realized her face was wet with tears.

She looked and touched and marveled, hardly aware that she had more contractions and that Alec was still occupied. Eventually he said, "I'm going to clean you up as well as I can without water, and then we'd better figure out something for a pad."

A pad? *Oh.*

"Um…" She turned her head. "There are some pajama bottoms here somewhere. I couldn't have gotten them on before, but maybe now…"

"All right. Why don't you try putting her to your breast? Even if you weren't planning to breast-feed, you have to for now."

"I was." She undid a couple of buttons and lifted Cupcake—who needed a real name now. As she did, her daughter opened her eyes and, in the gray light through the window, Wren saw that they were a murky blue, which likely meant they were going to turn brown like hers. She felt another moment of fierce delight. Her own mother might have been disappointed when she'd first seen Wren, tiny and wizened and not very pretty at all as babies went, but Wren was glad Cupcake had gotten nothing from her father.

It took some doing to figure out what angle worked best, and to coax the baby to begin nuzzling for her breast. But finally she latched on and began to suckle as though she knew exactly what to do.

"Like a pro," Alec murmured, and their eyes met over Wren's knees.

"Isn't she amazing?"

"So are you." He was stuffing her into those pajamas as he spoke, although he laughed and paused to roll the hems up. And up. Then, sounding awkward for the first time, he said, "I've, er, folded a T-shirt in there to be a menstrual pad. It's not ideal, but as long as you're not moving around a lot, it ought to do."

His momentary discomfiture made *her* feel embarrassed for the first time, too. She couldn't believe she hadn't given a second thought to letting a man who was a virtual stranger do such intimate things for her.

"Thank you," she said stiffly.

He nodded. "Is the baby asleep?"

Filled with tenderness, Wren glanced down to see that Cupcake's mouth had slipped from her tingling breast. "Yes."

"You need to have something to eat and drink now."

She thought about it, and realized she was hungry. And her mouth felt...gritty. "Do we have anything?"

"Bottled water and energy bars. Not very exciting."

"You're *apologizing?*" She stared incredulously at him. "What, because you didn't bring big juicy hamburgers and fries with you?"

There was that grin she already loved. "No, I'm apologizing because we're going to have to ration what we do have. We could be stuck here for another day or more, you know."

That momentarily dimmed her delight. "Is it going to get cold once night falls?"

"Afraid so." He set a big plastic water bottle beside her, watching as she eased the soundly sleeping baby onto the pallet. Then he slid an arm around behind Wren and helped her to a sitting position.

She winced. Her stomach muscles seemed to be shot, and she was definitely sore. Instead of sitting cross-legged as she would normally have done, she tucked both feet to one side of her and reached for the water.

"Is this all we have?"

"Yes, but we can catch some rainwater. Drink what you need."

She guzzled enthusiastically. It was probably plain tap water, but it tasted like ambrosia. So did the peanut butter-flavored bar he peeled open for her.

"Want another one?"

"How many do we have?"

He counted. "Ten. You haven't eaten since…?"

Wren had to think back. "It's been…two days. And I was feeling unsettled then. My back was starting to hurt, and my stomach felt weird. So I ate only half the BLT I bought at a restaurant."

"Then you're definitely having another one." He pulled an array of them out of the zippered bag he'd thrown through the window. "You have a choice of more peanut butter, apple and cinnamon or…" He squinted at one. "Chocolate."

She sat up straighter. "Chocolate?"

"We have a winner." Looking amused, he handed one to her. "Do all women love chocolate?"

Wren gaped at him. "Don't you?"

"Not particularly. I don't much care about candy."

"Chocolate isn't candy," she assured him. "It's a basic food."

"Dairy, grains, fruits and vegetables, meats…and chocolate."

She grinned. "Right."

"I'll remember that."

Wren ate this bar more slowly, drawing out the pleasure. A cramping in her stomach made her really, really wish she had something with more substance to eat. Or maybe more comforting. Thick, steaming split-pea soup with bits of salty ham. Or a stew filled with chunks of potato and carrots and tender meat.

Her sigh was unconscious. She only became aware of it when she saw Alec raise his eyebrows.

"Oh…I was planning a menu for after we get out of here."

"Ah."

Wren frowned. "You haven't eaten anything."

"Unlike you, I've been getting regular meals. And I didn't go through labor. I'll wait until later."

That gave her pause. He really was afraid they might be trapped here for days. If she didn't get enough to eat, would her body fail to produce the milk her baby needed?

Again, he seemed to read her mind. Maybe it was easy, given the scared look she flashed at Cupcake.

"She's going to be fine." He gave a rueful grin. "Our biggest challenge may be finding enough cloth to keep her in some sort of diaper. Doing laundry isn't exactly an option."

"No. I didn't think of that." Wren studied the sleeping baby again. For the first time, she noticed that Alec had bundled her oddly, with a sleeve of the flannel shirt doubled over between her legs, while the other sleeve wrapped around holding the whole arrangement in place. He'd been remarkably clever.

Cupcake scrunched up her face, made a grunting sound, then gradually relaxed again. She had a surprising amount of hair, which clustered in stiff tufts. Wren wished she had one of those small knitted caps that babies always seemed to wear in hospital nurseries.

"I'm most worried about keeping her warm," Alec said quietly, as if once again he was reading her mind. "I think that when night falls we'll need to keep her between us. I don't want to scare you, but I'm going to lie down next to you."

Wren shivered, but she wasn't cold. It was... She didn't know. She was suffering from nerves, she guessed. And something that felt oddly like excitement. She *liked* the idea of lying stretched out beside him. Which, she supposed, shouldn't be such a surprise, given how attracted to him she'd been from the minute he'd shoved back the hood of his rain slicker and looked up at her window, like the prince there to rescue Rapunzel.

The ridiculousness of that would have made her laugh under other circumstances.

Wow. Call me shallow.

Apparently her body was on board with the whole concept of offering herself to any guy who rescued her. She'd escaped from James only four days ago, and here she was eyeing another man.

Yes, but she hadn't had sex in something like six months. No, more than that. James had been repulsed by her body once Cupcake's presence showed in a slight thickening around Wren's waist and then a bump below her belly button.

He had been furious from the moment she told him she was pregnant. In those first weeks, she'd still been delusional enough to imagine that he'd come around. That soon he would rejoice, too, in the life quickening inside her.

Instead, as the depths of his need to have her belong to him and him alone had become apparent, she'd finally seen how dumb she'd been. How blind.

The thought was enough to make her shudder.

Alec's sharp eyes saw that, too. "You're getting cold."

"No, I'm okay. Just…feeling a little scared," she admitted. "Not of what's going to happen, but of what *could* have happened." She tried to smile, but her lips trembled. "I haven't said thank you yet, but… Thank you. From the bottom of my heart."

"You're very welcome," he told her, with equal formality. "I should probably thank you. I'll think of this at Christmas. If only we had a manger for a cradle and a heap of straw to keep Cupcake cozy."

Blinking, Wren had to admit that their current conditions were every bit as primitive as that long-ago stable. Well, except for the energy bars and the scissors Alec had triumphantly torn from their sterile packaging.

Cupcake would have died if anything had gone wrong. Terror poured through Wren as she gazed at her daughter and let herself acknowledge a truth she'd managed to block out all day. She and Cupcake—mother and child—were incredibly lucky.

Blessed.

She very gently cupped her daughter's head and waited for the fear to ebb, as the labor pains had. She closed her eyes and thought...*thank you*. God or whoever was listening, thank you.

A lump of emotion seemed to be caught in her throat. What was it Alec had said to set her off? *I'll think of this at Christmas.* Where would he be at Christmas? With his sister and her family?

On another tremor of uncertainty that wasn't so different from the earlier fear, Wren wondered where *she* would be at Christmas. Would she have found Molly by then? Or...or perhaps a motel room? Except, she didn't have a cent. This was one time she would have to ask her mother for help. After that, if Wren couldn't find Molly, maybe she could rent a room, if there were such things as boarding houses anymore. She would have to look for a job, too, of course. Finding one where she was allowed to bring a baby wasn't going to be easy. Day care. There must be day-care centers around. Or maybe she could be a night janitor. No one would be around to be bothered when Cupcake got hungry or un-happy because her diaper was wet and cried.

The terror was surging again, building in power, be-cause now she didn't have to worry only about herself, but about another entire person. And she knew she was woefully unprepared to take care of her daughter. Es-pecially knowing James would try to find them. She wished Alec was right and James wouldn't bother, but Wren didn't believe it. He hadn't let her go the first time she'd tried to leave him, a month ago. If anything, he'd gotten more obsessed since then. She couldn't imagine that he would be able to shrug and decide to let her go. And…she'd seen his violent side.

Don't think about it, she decided. *Not now. Not yet.*

Here and now, she and Cupcake were safe. They might get chilly, and hungry, but they weren't alone, and they were safe. She'd never in her life trusted anyone completely, but there was always a first, and this was it. Alec wouldn't let anything bad happen to her or her baby, as long as they were with him.

"I think I need that applesauce jar again."

With a low, deep chuckle, he rose to his feet and held out his hands to help her up. "Is that what it was for?"

"Well, some kind of preserves. In the old days, they canned green beans and things like that, too. The jar's too big for jam."

He hoisted her up, frowning when her face changed. "What is it?"

"I wonder if, um, I need to replace the T-shirt. Or refold it or something."

"Ah."

She loved the way he said that. Acknowledgement, understanding, no need to comment. He bent and pro-duced another item of clothing from the shrinking stack. Boxer shorts? Oh, heavens, had she grabbed the former resident's *underwear?*

"We might have to do some washing. I mean, between me and Cupcake. Maybe we could rinse things out in the rain...."

Alec shook his dark head. "I don't think they'd dry."

Worrying over the problem, she retired to the end of the attic, aware that Alec had politely turned his back again. Flushing with embarrassment, she used the jar, dumped the contents out the window he'd already opened and let the rain rinse it. Then, before she could struggle to close the window, he reached around her and did it. She felt the heat of his body behind her, the strength of the arms that momentarily caged her, and her stomach did a dip and roll.

Stepping back, he said in a curiously gentle voice, "All right?"

She bobbed her head and, without looking at him, retreated to her pallet. Her throat had formed another of those impossible-to-swallow lumps. Cupcake was so tiny, and Wren realized suddenly that she was exhausted. It had to be hormones that were causing her mood swings. Joy to fear to gratitude to lust and back to fear again in mere minutes. Realizing that she wasn't altogether sure she could lower herself to a sitting position gracefully and without pain was enough to make her eyes burn. Had she torn? Alec hadn't said, and why would he when he couldn't do anything about it?

Before she could begin any kind of undignified maneuvering, Alec lifted her up and laid her down. She squeaked, and he smiled.

"You were giving the problem more thought than it deserved."

"My body is holding a major protest."

He crouched over the first-aid kit. "It hadn't occurred to me, but—" He made a pleased sound. "Here we go. Aspirin or ibuprofen?"

"Really?" Wren struggled up to her elbow, careful not to shift Cupcake, who she'd snuggled against her.

"Yeah, I thought about it earlier, when you were in labor, but I wasn't sure what was safe for you to take." He grimaced. "Or how much good either would do. Sorry that I'm only now remembering it's here."

"I haven't hurt that bad. But I won't say no to some ibuprofen." She took the two capsules, popped them in her mouth, then swallowed them with a sip of water. "Thank you," she murmured, settling back down.

"Hey, these dressings should work as menstrual pads for at least a few changes." He sounded pleased. "I should have thought of it."

Paper rustled as he laid out a small pile of sterile dressings then closed the velcro fasteners on the case, and stood. "I'm sorry, but I need to…" He gestured toward the window.

"Feel free." Wren curled more comfortably around Cupcake and tugged the blankets higher over them. One of them was particularly scratchy wool, but it was warm. She tried not to listen to the sound of Alec lowering his zipper and then, a moment later, pulling it up again, and was grateful she *couldn't* hear what he did in between.

The window grated as he shoved it down, and then his footsteps neared.

"The sun is going down, isn't it?" Wren whispered.

"Yeah."

She'd hardly noticed the deepening of the gray light. "Is it still raining?"

"Yeah," he said again.

"If we're going to be biblical, it's poor Noah we ought to be identifying with. And his wife. Doesn't it figure that nobody can remember *her* name? She probably took care of all the animals and still put dinner on the table every night for him, and all anyone remembers is her husband because he built the boat."

Alec knelt beside her. "I suspect he's remembered because the vision was his." Amusement roughened his voice.

"Who says? Maybe it was *her* idea. Wouldn't it figure he took the credit?"

He sat and untied his boots. "As it happens, I know her name. Emzara." He tugged off the first boot and set it aside. "Don't ask me why that stuck from Sunday school." In the act of pulling off the second boot, he paused. "Come to think of it, I know why. It was Mom. She said something pretty similar to what you did."

"Smart woman." Wren was beginning to feel drowsy, even though she wished there was a whole lot more padding between her and the floor.

Jeez. Talk about ungrateful.

Alec dropped the second boot, then in a quick move lifted the blanket and stretched out beside Wren, sandwiching Cupcake between their chests.

"She won't smother under there, will she?"

"No. These blankets feel like wool. Wool breathes. And warm air would be better for her."

"Okay." She couldn't help being disconcerted by how close his face was to hers.

"I'm using the first-aid kit for a pillow," he said unnecessarily. "Why don't I stretch my arm out, and you can pillow your head on it?"

She noticed the careful way he spoke. Just as politely, she said, "Oh, but it'll go numb."

"I'll retrieve it if it does." She couldn't tell if that was amusement again in his voice, or something else.

But she lifted her head as he slid his arm beneath it. After a few wriggles, she settled far more comfortably onto his bicep. As if doing so was entirely natural, he curled his arm around her and she felt his big hand clasp her shoulder.

"Let me know if you get cold," he said. "I've got on a heavier shirt than you do. I can give you the vest. Or we can find some other things for you to wear."

Although she had no intention of taking his down vest, she said, "Okay."

He squeezed her shoulder. "Go to sleep, Wren. I'll watch out for Cupcake."

She snuggled into him and let her eyes drift closed. She could smell male sweat overlying soap and a hint of forest. She liked how he smelled. "Okay," she heard herself murmur again, drowsily.

Falling asleep hadn't been so easy in a long, long time.

CHAPTER FOUR

ALEC SLEPT IN SNATCHES, an hour here and there. He was uncomfortable, but unwilling to disturb Wren or the baby by moving. The floor seemed to get harder as the night wore on, the cushioning beneath him thinner and more inadequate. He felt as if he was pillowing his head on a square rock. Tomorrow night—if they were still here—he'd find something else. His arm did go numb under Wren's head, and sharp pains stabbed his right shoulder, the one he'd landed on when he fell through the window.

How long had it been since he'd slept cuddling a woman? Two years, maybe? No, longer than that— closer to three. Oh, who was he kidding? He and Carlene hadn't been that friendly in bed for a while before their divorce. And his few sexual encounters since hadn't included sleep—or much in the way of cuddling, either.

Early on, Wren had snuggled onto her side and shifted her head to his shoulder. He had a suspicion she would have been nestled against him if not for the small lump that was Cupcake between them. Wren, he thought, *was* a cuddler.

She was also a quiet sleeper, or maybe simply exhausted to the point where her body had decided to suspend all but essential operations. Once she settled in, she went boneless. He couldn't even hear her breathe.

Every so often, to reassure himself, he tilted his face so that he could feel a soft stir of warm air on his cheek when she exhaled.

He'd never slept in bed with a baby, although he'd been known to snooze on the sofa with one of his daughters on his chest, their knees tucked up and thumb in mouth. Remembering the sweet weight of a baby gave him a piercing pain beneath the breastbone that was sharper than the one in his shoulder. That memory led to others, even less welcome.

Maybe he hadn't been the best father in the world, not given his working hours. The last straw for Carlene had been when he'd missed India's fourth birthday party.

"You'll be here when I blow out the candles, won't you, Daddy?" India had begged him, her blue eyes wide. "You will, right?"

"I'll do my best," he'd promised, giving her a big hug and kiss on the nose before he went out the door.

But there had been a shooting, not an especially ugly one—he didn't even remember the specifics, except that Benson was out because his mother was dying and Molina had come down with the flu, so Alec and his partner had gotten the call even though they shouldn't have been top of the rotation yet. It was his job. Somebody had died. A kid's birthday party didn't cut it as an excuse.

India hadn't been that upset. Her Grandma Olson had been there, and half a dozen friends from preschool with their parents chiming in the birthday song. She'd gotten lots of presents, and when he did finally make it home had taken great pleasure in showing them to him one at a time, putting each carefully away before presenting the next. That was India, congenitally organized.

It was Carlene, predictably, who was furious, certain that Alec was teaching his daughters that they couldn't depend on him. The words she'd said that night still gnawed at him when he let his guard down. It was only a few weeks later that she'd packed one day while he was at work and announced when he got home that she and the girls were going to her mom's.

He swore under his breath and tried surreptitiously to flex muscles that ached.

Cupcake was considerably more restless than her mommy. Having her under there was unsettling, like sleeping with a cat that had burrowed beneath the covers. She snuffled and wriggled and periodically woke crying. The first couple of times, Wren barely regained consciousness, and only after Alec shook her awake. He had to unbutton the front of her shirt and help the baby find a nipple. The whole experience was weird and so intimate he tried not to think about the fact that he was groping in the dark for this woman's breasts and moving her body around so that the strange small creature between them could suckle on her.

He tried to keep the blankets pulled high to maintain the baby's body temperature. The air outside the cocoon they'd created was winter cold. During one of his periods of wakefulness Alec realized that he couldn't hear the rain. Incredulous, he lay listening to the silence. Had it finally stopped? *Forty days and forty nights.* No, it hadn't actually been that long. He remembered Wren saying that the day felt surreal, as if it had gone on forever and only *now* mattered. He felt that way about the storm. After the days of gray, slanting rain, bobbing on floodwaters, hauling soaked, scared people until their faces were interchangeable and his tiredness grinding, this attic was an oasis.

He should have slept like a baby, he thought, then smiled as he gently settled Cupcake on her back and pulled blankets higher over her mother, who was already burrowing onto his shoulder. Okay, maybe not. If he had made it home to his own bed, he might have slept like a log. *Not* a baby.

Probably he should have checked if Cupcake was wet, but he was damned if he was going to bare her butt or try to figure out an alternative he could wrap her in.

With a groan, he did slide his hand under her to make sure she wasn't soaking the comforter, but so far it was dry, thank God. He seemed to remember that a woman's breasts didn't produce much actual milk the first day or so. The trickle of colostrum apparently wasn't overwhelming Cupcake's bladder.

The next time he opened his eyes, it was to the gray light of day and to the contented sound of a baby nursing. What the hell...? Alec blinked gritty eyes a couple of times and oriented himself. Attic. Childbirth. Brown-feathered Wren and her wrinkly, red-faced baby.

No weight on his shoulder. He turned his head and saw Wren curled on her side supporting Cupcake's head. She smiled at him, her face so close he could see the lighter flecks in her brown eyes.

He stretched and discovered that pretty much every muscle in his body ached and he was hungry.

"Damn," he muttered. "What I'd give for a heaping plate of scrambled eggs, crispy bacon and country-fried potatoes."

"*After* a hot shower." Longing suffused her voice.

"Yeah. Definitely after a shower."

WHO NEEDED TELEVISION or a morning newspaper when you had a new baby and a gorgeous man around?

Since waking, Wren had spent most of the time—well, half the time—minutely studying her daughter. Less exhausted this morning, she felt wonder bubbling in her like champagne shaken until it threatened to pop the cork. To think that *she* had created this beautiful, perfect, little person! Wren loved everything, from the tiny, fuzzy eyebrows to the pink lips that pursed and occasionally smacked, to the curve of cheeks and high forehead. When she nursed or bobbed against Wren's shoulder, Cupcake's head fit in the cup of her hand as if made for it. She weighed hardly anything, but as Alec had pointed out yesterday, she was doing well, so if she was a week or two early it obviously hadn't mattered. Wren could tell how relieved he was when he said that. She suspected he, too, had hidden a few shudders at the thought of how many things could have gone wrong.

Astonishingly enough, watching him sleep, and gradually wake, had been almost as engrossing as staring at her beautiful baby. Every so often she looked away from Cupcake to study Alec's hard face, only slightly relaxed in sleep. No open mouth or drooling; somehow he managed still to seem guarded. And yet there was something about his closed eyelids, the dark lashes fanned on his cheeks, that gave him an air of vulnerability. He was dreaming; his eyelids quivered, and a couple of times his nostrils flared and his mouth tightened. One hand lay on top of the covers, and she saw his fingers twitch, make a fist, then relax again.

At last his lashes fluttered and his eyes opened. For a moment he stared blankly at the empty rafters before his head turned sharply and his deep blue eyes pinned her in place.

She smiled as if it didn't feel even a tiny bit strange to wake next to him.

His first words told her their minds were in sync. A chocolate energy bar didn't sound nearly as good this morning as it had yesterday. She could almost smell the bacon.

Wren sighed. Hungry as she was, she'd give up breakfast for a hot shower.

"Oh, well, we don't even have soap."

Alec laughed, a low, husky sound. "What would you do with it if you had it? You can't tell me you want me to dip some floodwater up for you to bathe in."

Wren scrunched up her nose. "I suppose it's cold."

"Safe to say." The humor left his face. "Not very sanitary, either. The town septic system got overwhelmed, and God knows what's floating around out there." He rose to his feet as easily as if he hadn't spent the night on a hard floor the way she had. "It's not raining."

"No. I noticed it quit."

"Damn," he said softly. "I should have filled some jars with rainwater yesterday."

"Will we run out of water?"

He went to the window. "No." The tension in his voice had dissipated. "No, it's still drizzling. I'll start collecting water."

He figured out how to hang a jar out the window before coming back to discuss breakfast.

"I'll have apple and cinnamon," she decided.

"Not chocolate?"

"Who has chocolate for breakfast?"

He chose peanut butter. Suspicious, she asked if he was trying to leave the tastiest ones for her, but he insisted he didn't care. There were more peanut-butter bars than either of the other flavors, so that's what he'd eat.

Then, before Cupcake fell asleep, they took advantage of daylight to refold and smooth their bedding, pile the wet or bloody clothes in one place, sort through what was left for suitable diaper or menstrual pad material and continue searching boxes for anything that might be the tiniest bit useful.

"Hah!" Alec exclaimed when he unearthed a trunk of old quilts.

Taking them out, one by one, Wren breathed, "Ooh, look at these. They're handworked. This one is from the 1920s, I think. Look at these fabrics. And I'll bet this one's even older. Alec, the fabric is so fragile. I hate to use them."

"I don't." While she still kneeled in front of the trunk, he lifted out the entire pile and carried it to their pallet. "I don't know about you, but my whole body hurts. That floor was *hard.*"

She giggled a little at his indignation. "Didn't you ever camp?"

"You mean outside? Good God, no. I'm a city boy."

"You don't look like a city boy," she said thoughtfully.

He glanced at himself. His jeans were faded and fit as if molded for him. They were also dirty, the denim stiff from wetting and drying—probably repeatedly. The equally well-worn red chamois shirt stretched across broad shoulders. It had a long tear above one cuff. He was walking around in saggy wool socks. His dark hair stuck out in every direction. The dark stubble on his cheeks was going to be a beard in another day or two.

In fact, he'd confessed as he dug through boxes,

that he was wishing for a razor. Even an old-fashioned straight razor.

"Dull would be okay," he'd muttered.

"Remember? No soap."

"I just want to scrape it off." He cast a look of dislike toward the first-aid kit. "If the scissors would just open farther—"

"I have that knife."

"Did you look at it? It's worse than dull."

She shook her head, then smiled. "You look good in a beard."

He scowled. "I *itch*."

He found no razor. She'd noticed him scratching his cheeks and jaw unhappily every now and again.

By the time his watch told them it was midday, he'd filled several jars with rainwater. Finally, he hung a white sheet out the window again as a signal, the way she had...was it only yesterday?

While she nursed Cupcake again, Alec spread two of the three quilts atop their pallet.

"So, I think it's time I give Cupcake a real name. Before she starts kindergarten and the other kids make fun of her."

Alec grinned, as she'd expected he would. She loved his smiles, each and every one of them. The corners of those blue eyes crinkled, the creases in his lean cheeks deepened and the sense that smiles came rarely for him warmed something inside her.

"Might be a plan."

Cupcake's mouth slipped from her breast and Wren decided she had to change her diaper-slash-outfit. Alec saw what she was doing and picked out a man's white T-shirt which he deftly ripped so that they could pass one fold between the baby's legs and then tie it over her tummy. Wren had to laugh when she saw the final result. Cupcake gazed fuzzily at her as if bemused by the sound.

"The latest in baby wear."

"Yeah. Maybe we should go into business."

"Well...we could advertise in survivalists' magazines."

He gave a hearty laugh. "I could submit one of those housekeeping tips to them, too. Multiple uses for canning jars."

Wren laughed, too, feeling ridiculously happy. Hungry, yes, but still happy.

"I want to name her after you." Ignoring his stunned expression, she suggested, "Alexa? Only that's not quite right. Alisha? Why didn't you have one of those convenient names that's easily convertible to a female version? Like Robert to Roberta, or..."

"Edwin to Edwina? What a hideous thought."

She wrinkled her nose. "Definitely not Edwina. That sounds like my grandmother or something."

"I had a Great-Aunt Edwina. Also a Great-Aunt Pearl."

"Did you." Her forehead furrowed. "I don't think I had any great-aunts at all. At least...I don't know."

"No big extended family?"

"I don't actually know my father's family," she admitted. "I hardly remember *him*."

He stared at her, his eyes oddly intense. "Did you mind? I mean, when you were a kid? That he wasn't there?"

She gave an awkward shrug. "I imagined sometimes that he'd come storming back into my life." Trying to keep her voice light, as though to say, *how silly I was,* she continued, "Furious at my mother for lying and tell-

ing him I'd died. Or moving and not telling him where
she was going. Or something like that. And he'd snatch
me away to be his little princess. I never bothered to
give him a second wife or kids, because that would have
made me the outsider. Naturally he had amazing parents. Cozy and loving." Aware her attempt at a smile
was a complete flop, she bent her head to gaze at Cupcake. "You know. Homemade chocolate-chip cookies.
Piles and piles of Christmas presents. A room they kept
just for me. I decided it would have a four-poster bed
with a canopy. And lots of pink, of course."

"So it wasn't him so much you missed as family."
Alec's tone was odd.

"Well, him, too. Because he was the important part,
right?" She looked up to be sure he understood. "It
might not have mattered so much if my mother had
been, um, maternal. But she wasn't especially. Although I admire her, now that I'm an adult." She felt as
if she had to say that. And it was true. "She's a school
administrator. I sometimes think it's a little funny, because of course she started as a teacher. And, well…"

"She isn't maternal," he said drily. "Which would
suggest she isn't crazy about kids."

He handed her another apple-and-cinnamon energy
bar. Lunch. Oh, yum.

"No." Absentmindedly she tore open the wrapping.
"But Mom actually taught high-school math, so it's not
like she started out as a first-grade teacher. And admin-
istration is what she always intended to do. Mom's am-
bitious. She was a vice principal by the time I was old
enough to know what she did. She was principal when
I was a freshman at the high school, which really sucks,
by the way, because everyone knew whose kid I was.
Then she got promoted to assistant superintendent of

the whole district, and just this year to superintendent. She talks about waiting three to five years and then applying for a superintendent position in a bigger school district. New fields to conquer, and all that."

He nodded as if he understood more than she'd actually said. So, okay, she was proud of her mother, but Wren couldn't help also wishing… She ducked her head again to be sure he couldn't see her face. Wishing for the impossible.

She knew better.

"Um, back to Cupcake. I thought of bird names. Since I'm Wren, I mean. These days it's not so odd. People are naming their kids things like Sparrow or Hawk. But I've always hated my name. I've never met another Wren."

"There were plenty of Alecs." He opened his own lunch. "I was Alec H. in fourth grade." He frowned. "Sixth, too, I think. In fourth, though, there were three of us. Alec C., Alec M. and Alec H."

"Did anybody ever make fun of you for that?"

Around a bite, he shook his head.

"Then be glad you aren't Hawk." She sounded more tart than she'd intended, but to this day she *always* had to spell her name and explain it.

"No Sparrow, then?"

She shook her head.

"Why don't you pick something pretty?"

She frowned. "I like the idea of naming her after you. Hmm. What's your mother's name?"

"Past tense," he said gruffly. "Mom died a few months ago. Her name was Marian. Actually, Abigail Marian Harper. When she was little, she was embarrassed by the Abigail. That was *her* grandmother's name, so of course it was old-fashioned in her eyes.

Later, she admitted she always thought it was pretty, but by then she was Marian to everyone."

"Abigail." Wren's smile dawned. "That was actually on my list."

"Really?" There was something defenseless in his eyes.

"Really. I like it. Abigail Fraser." Wren smiled. "Abigail *Alexa* Fraser. That's a lovely name."

He groaned, but laughed, too. "Thank you. You didn't have to do that, but I'm honored."

"I'll tell Abigail about you. The man who leaped for the windowsill, abandoning his boat and marooning himself with me so he could help her be born. She'll know that's part of her history. A special part."

"I'm going to blush," he warned her, but a smile still played at the corners of his mouth.

"I won't be able to see it under...under..."

He rubbed a hand over his jaw, using the opportunity to do a little scratching. "The shrubbery? Hell. What do you want to bet I have a rash by the time I shave?"

"If that's the worst that either of us suffers, we'll be lucky."

His face went still. "We'll be okay. Someone will come along."

"I know. Starving to death takes ages, and we have plenty of water now, don't we?"

"Yeah, I think we do." He cast a glance of satisfaction at his row of jars, yawned, stretched and winced. "I'm hoping for a better night's sleep tonight."

"I'll find something else for a pillow."

His gaze returned to her face. "Cuddling keeps us warm."

She shouldn't still be able to blush—after all, the man had seen and groped every part of her body, hadn't he? And heard her tinkling into a jar, for goodness' sake. Her cheeks were heating anyway.

"Do you think we could make a cap of some kind for Cupcake? No," she corrected herself. "For Abigail...for Abby."

"Sure. That's a good idea."

In the end, he cut a sleeve off an ancient thermal knit shirt, tied the top into something like a pom-pom with a bit of the twine he'd used for Abby's cord and rolled the edges several times until it covered her to her eyebrows. Adjusting the fit, he said, "She has ears like yours."

Wren moaned. "You mean, they stick out."

"It's cute."

"On her, maybe," she muttered.

"On you, too." For a second, it seemed his eyes darkened, but he looked away.

Was it even remotely possible that *he...?* No, of course not. Imagining this truly gorgeous, sexy man being attracted to her was akin to the stories she'd made up about her father, a man who in reality didn't give a flying leap about the little girl he'd abandoned. Alec was only being nice, something he did very well.

"She's asleep," he commented, voice soft, and Wren looked down. Abby's eyes had closed and her sweetly shaped mouth had gone slack.

"She does that a lot."

He watched as she snuggled the baby on her back and pulled the blankets to her chin. When he suggested she nap, too, Wren gave in to the seductive notion and slipped under the blankets, her body curled around Abby's. Insisting he wasn't cold, Alec folded his down vest several times and tucked it under her head for a pillow. He moved away, then, to stand looking out the window. Watching for rescue? she wondered fuzzily, and slept.

Of course Cupcake—no, Abby now—inevitably got hungry. She'd slept for two hours, Alec told her, when Wren asked.

"I don't snore, do I?" She felt self-conscious at the idea of him watching her sleep, the way she had him.

"No, you were so quiet I kept wanting to check to be sure you were still with me." He sounded a little embarrassed at that.

"So you don't find yourself on your own with a newborn?"

Oh, lord—what would happen to Abby if I died? The last thing in the world Wren's mother would want was to raise another child. And James... No. Never.

The thought filled her with anxiety. Molly. She would find Molly, and ask her to become Abby's godmother and agree to raise her if something happened to Wren. That's what she'd do.

"Hungry?" Alec crouched beside her. The position emphasized his muscular thighs in a distracting way. And there was the rather significant bulge that his jeans clasped so lovingly.

She couldn't possibly stare. Instead she focused somewhere past him. "Yes, but I can wait. In case we're here for another day."

Or more, but she didn't want to say that.

His hand caught her chin so that she had to look at him. "If either of us goes hungry, it will be me. I told you, I've eaten more recently, and I'm bigger. I haven't gone through childbirth. For Abby's sake, you *have* to eat. Snack now, another bar for dinner later."

After a minute she nodded. "Okay."

"The water level is going down some. Did you look for food in the kitchen?"

"A little bit, but I wasn't all that hungry then." Considering she'd been in labor, that was no surprise. "There were some canned goods."

"We'll see how it goes. If no one comes by morning but the water has dropped enough, I might go downstairs and see what I can find."

He meant push his way through waist-deep, or higher, water. The way her stomach was chewing on itself, *she* would have been willing to go swimming for a can of baked beans, say. Surely they could figure out how to open it.

"So eat." He tore open a chocolate bar without asking and thrust it at her.

Grateful, Wren ate. It didn't begin to fill her up, but it did help.

Although she'd noticed books in some of the boxes she'd opened, the dim gray light that fell through the narrow window didn't encourage reading. Instead they spent the afternoon talking, told each other the paltry collection of jokes they remembered, played some word games and sang—Wren did, Alec insisted he couldn't carry a tune and had been shushed from age five on when he tried to belt out hymns in church.

The light deepened and darkness crept up on them. Wren sat cross-legged beside the sleeping baby, while Alec, apparently restless, paced and from time to time stood staring at the night outside the window.

There had been silence for a while when he said, in a tone she hadn't heard yet, "There's something we need to talk about."

She looked up in alarm. She knew—*knew*—what he

was going to say. He was a cop. Of course he couldn't let her hints go.

And she was right. Voice somehow implacable, he said, "It's time for you to tell me about Abby's father."

CHAPTER FIVE

WREN FELT HER EXPRESSION grow mulish as she stared at Alec's dark silhouette. Part of her knew it was useless to argue—he was being pushy because he thought it was necessary—but that didn't make her any happier. Her stomach tied itself in knots when she even *thought* about James.

"He can't find me here."

"True. But what if he's waiting in Saddler's Mill or Mountfort?"

Saddler's Mill she knew—even though she hadn't seen the town that was Molly's mailing address. But the other place she'd never even heard of. "Where?"

"Saddler's Mill is the closest town. Mountfort's the county seat. He could have traced you here."

"How? I didn't tell anyone where I was going. I didn't bring a cell phone because of the whole GPS thing, even though I don't understand it."

"Your friend. Does he know her? Of her?"

She shivered, but said, "I don't think so."

Alec didn't have to say anything, only wait.

"I had an address book, but a couple of months ago I hid it."

"Was he the kind of man who would have already copied the information in it?"

Wrapping her arms around her knees, Wren rocked slightly. "Maybe. If he thought…"

"You might run?"

She nodded, then remembered he couldn't see her any better than she could him. "Yes."

"You thought he'd come after you. Did he threaten to?"

"Yes. And also—" She swallowed. "I tried one other time." She hated having to remember. *Tell him fast so I don't have to relive it.* "I didn't even get out of the condo."

"What happened, Wren?" Suddenly he was speaking much closer to her, relentless. The quilts compressed and the air beside her stirred. He was sitting down.

"I told him I was leaving." She closed her eyes, as if that would help. Kept rocking. "He, um…"

When she faltered, Alec finished for her. "He hit you."

It was the astonishing gentleness in his deep voice that brought tears burning in her eyes. She didn't cry. She didn't.

"Yes," she whispered. "Over and over. He was enraged. When I fell down, he…he kicked my stomach. Because…he didn't want—"

"That son of a bitch." Even in the dark, Alec found her. He wrapped an arm around her shoulders and tugged her forward, until her forehead rested against his chest. "Did someone call the cops?"

"A neighbor."

"Didn't they offer to take you to a women's shelter?"

"Yes, but I couldn't believe—" She cleared her throat. "I was so stupid. The thing is, he'd never hit me before. That's why it was so shocking. And then he cried when he called me. And…I'm pregnant. That ties me to him. He swore he wanted Cupcake, that he didn't know why he went so crazy, that he'd get counseling."

A small laugh that was closer to a sob broke from her. "I wanted so much to believe him."

"How long ago was that?"

"A month." She shuddered. "I knew within days that I should have escaped when I could have. I thought at least this gave me the chance to plan. You know. To secretly pack and make sure I had some money."

"I hope I get a chance to meet this guy," Alec said grimly.

"No!" She straightened. "No, no! Don't even say that. All I want is to never see him again!"

He tugged her back, a big hand curved around her nape. "You're talking about living on the run. What if he doesn't lose interest right away, Wren? What are you going to do? Move every couple months? Never establish a bank account under your own name or take a job where you have to give a social security number? Never see your mother?"

"I guess you think I'm being dumb."

"No." Alec squeezed her neck. "Of course not. What I think is that you're not aware how easy it is to find someone nowadays. Anyone good with a computer and the phone can do what they'd have once had to hire a P.I. for. Running to your friend…"

She saw, dully, that he was right. "Was stupid. I thought—"

"You needed help. Someone who cared."

Wren nodded, burrowing her face, just a little, against his chest.

"Well, right now, you have me."

That made her heart squeeze, but the *right now* also rang clear. He cared because it was his job. And maybe because they'd shared a lot this past few days. He'd been the first person to hold Abby; he'd cut her cord.

That had to mean something. So he wanted to be sure she and Wren were okay, because he was that kind of man. Just so they both understood that his caring was temporary.

"Thank you."

"You don't have to thank me. You named your kid after me." Suddenly there was a smile in his voice.

She stiffened. "I wasn't trying to bribe you."

"I know." He bent down and…well, she was pretty sure he'd kissed the top of her head. "Never crossed my mind."

"So, um, what *do* I do now?"

"Now? You get a good night's sleep."

She made a noise. "You know what I mean."

"First, you tell me his name. I check around the minute we get back and make sure he isn't here in the county somewhere. I call… Where are you from?"

"Seattle. That's where he lives."

"I call the Seattle P.D. and ask them to verify if he's there. That gives us a starting point. We consider getting a protection order." His voice was a comforting rumble in the dark, but…

"You mean, from the court?"

"Yes."

"But doesn't that give him one more way to find me?"

"Only if he's figured out you're in Arkansas and thinks to scan court orders."

"Everything I've read said those don't do any good. If the guy is crazy enough to stalk a woman who's left him, something like that won't stop him."

"If he's sane at all, it sends the message that this isn't okay. That when you said no, you meant it. It also gives law-enforcement officers the power to take action if the man even comes near the woman. You."

"I still want to find Molly."

"We'll do that, too."

She wished she could see Alec's face. She wished she was still leaning against him, but she'd eased away when he brought up the order..

"James Miner." Wren didn't like the wobble in the middle of his last name, but she'd gotten it out. She took a deep breath. "James Vincent Miner. He didn't like the Vincent part. Vincent is his dad's name."

"Did he not like his father?"

"He's dead." She frowned, thinking about it. "James didn't say much, but I'm pretty sure he was angry at his dad."

"His mother?"

"I never met her. She lives in Oregon somewhere. I heard him talking to her on the phone, though, and sometimes he sounded so *scathing.*" Even in the early days, when she thought she was in love, that had worried her. Whether he liked his mother or not, did he have to talk to her that way, his voice sharp with contempt? It was as if he thought everything she did was stupid. Wren had wondered why she even called.

"If his father abused him and his mother failed to protect him, that might have left him angry," Alec said matter-of-factly. "Worse, if the dad also abused the mom, James would have seen her as weak. He wouldn't want to identify with her."

"You mean, he might deliberately copy his father's behavior?"

"Not necessarily, but our subconscious does funny things. Hey." His voice had changed. "I'm reading a whole lot into your impressions. Maybe he had great parents. Maybe he's simply an—" He swallowed whatever he'd been going to call James. "A domineering SOB."

"Well, he is that."

"When we get back, you can give me his address, phone number, place of employment. Anything you can think of."

Resigned, she said, "Okay."

Abby snuffled, sounding like a dog rooting around in the shrubbery for delicious scents. Both adults went still, waiting. A thin wail followed.

"Mommy's here," Wren murmured, unbuttoning her flannel shirt. At least in the dark she didn't have to worry about modesty. Silly as *that* was, she couldn't seem to help herself.

Alec laughed. "I swear she hasn't slept more than two hours at a stretch. That doesn't bode well."

"Babies are supposed to keep Mom and Dad awake, haven't you heard?"

He was silent. In the act of settling Abby to her breast, Wren didn't notice for a moment. Then she said, a little uncertainly, "You don't have kids, do you? You said you only have your sister and her family."

He didn't answer for a minute. She quailed a little inside, thinking she'd been nosy and that he didn't like it. If he'd wanted to tell her more about himself, he would have. It wasn't as if it was any of her business.

Finally Alec said, "I have two daughters. I'm divorced. They don't live with me."

"You said you'd delivered a baby once, but you didn't say—"

"Carlene was one of those women who thought she had a little heartburn and an hour later gave birth. Not normal."

Wren made a face even though he wouldn't see it. "You mean, not fair."

"No." Amusement had momentarily relaxed his voice. "My oldest daughter, Autumn, was born within an hour of our arriving at the hospital. I missed India's birth entirely. I was working. It came fast."

"How awful."

He grunted. "Carlene wasn't happy."

"I meant for you. Well, her, too, of course. You must have been sad you weren't there."

"I was."

That was all. Two words, clipped. He was *not* encouraging her to ask more.

Even so, after a minute, during which Wren was switching Abby to her other breast, she asked one anyway. "How old are they?"

"Six and eight." He rose abruptly and floorboards creaked as he walked away.

Escaping her as best he could, she realized unhappily. She should have kept her mouth shut.

Of course, *she'd* told him all kinds of really personal things. But Wren's stirring of resentment didn't last long. He'd asked because he needed to know so that he could help her, not out of idle curiosity. This wasn't a date, where an even trade was required. If your house was broken into, you didn't start asking the investigating officer personal details about his life, even if he did now know your bra size because he'd seen the one hanging on the towel rack.

"I'm sorry," Wren whispered, so softly she wasn't at all sure he heard her.

If he had, he didn't say anything. He stayed away, doing whatever he was doing—staring out the window at the impenetrable darkness was her best guess. Wren burped Abby, settled her under the covers again, then herself. She didn't even say good-night.

MUTTERING CURSES under his breath, Alec pushed his way through the waist-deep water that flooded the first story of the house. He'd stripped to his boxer shorts, and he was shivering but had no desire to dive in and acclimate himself the way he might have during a summer swim at the lake. He watched warily for the sinuous movement of a snake. From his boat, he'd seen both harmless northern banded water snakes and dangerous water moccasins. One could easily have washed into the house through a broken window.

Wren had told him she'd poked through lower kitchen cabinets, but not all the upper ones. He could see why as he reached the kitchen. As with most older homes, this one had ten-foot ceilings, and a petite woman like her would have needed a step stool to reach into those cabinets even if she hadn't been hugely pregnant. Unusually for a house of this era, there was no pantry. He started opening doors and in the first couple of cupboards found only dishes, sturdy workday stoneware. Mixing bowls with chipped rims, an ancient handheld blender. Cookbooks, now saturated, with frayed spines.

In the third cabinet, he hit pay dirt. Canned goods. Around a dozen cans of soup, creamed corn, pinto beans and tomatoes. He was so damned hungry it all looked good. Without being obvious about it, he'd skipped having an energy bar that morning; they were too close to being out of them. Wren looked peaked enough without having to quit eating altogether. The baby needed her milk.

He'd brought down a gunnysack he'd found in the

attic, and now loaded up his trove, waded through the house and climbed the creaking steps to the attic. He was glad to be out of the water. Alec really hated snakes.

"Did you find— Oh, Alec!" Wren had obviously been hovering around the opening. Her big brown eyes longingly fastened on the sack.

"Lunch," he said, handing it to her.

In turn, she offered a pair of well-worn denim overalls to use as a towel. Not ideal, but they might need the flannel and knits for other purposes.

"Turn your back," he suggested, and when she did, he stripped off the wet boxers, roughly dried himself and pulled on his jeans. Once he'd scrubbed his hair and tossed aside the overalls, he walked over to where Wren sat cross-legged, savoring the sight of each can as she pulled it from the sack. She crowed when she found the spoons in the bottom.

"I'm starved!"

"Me, too." He put on his flannel shirt and buttoned it, then dropped beside her. Affecting a French accent, he said, "Now that *madame* has had a chance to examine ze menu, what would be her pleasure?"

She gave a little bounce. "Soup. Or...no. Creamed corn. I *love* creamed corn. Well, I love it warm, but who cares?"

Unfortunately, like her, he hadn't found a can opener. The baby slept, though, right through the racket of him hammering the knife through the lid repeatedly until he could pry it up. With a flourish, he presented it to Wren, who was waiting with spoon in hand.

"Not sure those are clean..."

"Don't care." She shoveled a bite in then closed her

eyes in bliss. A moment later, she thrust the can toward him. "Your turn."

"I'm opening my own," he said, suiting action to words.

Both of them ate their way to the bottom and all but licked the insides. Then Wren fastened her gaze on the unopened cans.

"Do we need to conserve?"

"I don't think so. The water's dropping. I can't imagine we won't be out of here by tomorrow, no matter what."

He hammered open a can of tomato-rice soup for her and cream of mushroom for him. Neither of them was even slightly deterred by the gelatinous texture of the concentrated soups. When she finished hers, Wren gave a small burp, which made him laugh.

"I hope that wasn't too much for you, when it's been days since you've had a decent meal."

"Oh, but it was so good!" Her face all but shone. "Thank you. You didn't see any snakes, did you?"

"Not a one, thank God."

"I didn't even think about that when I got out of my car." She shuddered. "We don't have poisonous snakes in western Washington."

He knew vaguely that rattlesnakes liked dry country. Seattle was famous for coffee, not for being dry.

Wren made her excuses and retreated to a corner of the attic to use a jar, dumped the contents out the window then lay down next to her baby. He guessed it was natural that she was tired, but she was also more reserved this morning and Alec knew it was his fault. He'd been a jerk last night, so unwilling to feel the pain talking about his daughters brought, he'd shut down Wren without even a pretense of civility. He couldn't say that she was sulking today—that didn't seem to be in her nature—but she wasn't as chatty as she'd been yesterday, either. When he started a conversation, she participated, but the first real enthusiasm he'd seen had been for the creamed corn.

He didn't even know why it bothered him. They weren't in a relationship. He wasn't hoping to get her into bed. She'd soon be tucked under the wing of her friend Molly, although Alec intended to take what measures he could to make sure Wren and her baby stayed safe.

He kept an eye on her now, but with her back to him he couldn't tell if she was actually sleeping. He was getting more restless by the hour. Cabin fever, his mother would have called it. Although by that she would have meant boredom, and he couldn't say he was bored. Not when Wren was awake and talking to him, anyway. Or singing softly to her baby.

He'd catch himself watching in amazement. How did women know instinctively to hold babies to their shoulders and pat their backs? Her body would curve around the baby, and she'd rock in place and talk in the quietest singsong voice that he would have sworn Abby recognized. Well, he guessed she did; she'd been hearing it for a while, hadn't she?

Carlene had changed when Autumn was born. He'd experienced the same amazement then. He felt so clumsy handling their tiny daughter, while for Carlene it seemed to come naturally. There had been moments when he'd been bothered by how utterly her focus had shifted from him to their baby, as if he barely registered on her radar. He'd told himself that was natural, too, and that he wasn't the only new father who discovered his sex life had gone down the tubes. Carlene hadn't gotten excited about sex again until she decided she was ready for a second baby. They had a few passionate months ended by morning sickness that wasn't confined to morning. Looking back, Alec realized he should have seen that his marriage was in trouble long before he did.

And that was why he was restless—because being around Wren and her baby couldn't help but stir unwelcome memories. He'd be glad to be on the job again. Home. Even if he could hardly stand to sleep in the house, it was so damned empty.

He paced to the window for the thousandth time. The floodwaters had dropped noticeably since this morning—landmarks were reappearing. Walking out of here still wasn't going to be an option in the immediate future. He held on to the belief someone would come looking sooner rather than later.

He'd cracked the window this morning so that he'd hear an outboard motor if one neared, although if it didn't come close, a shout wouldn't do any good. He wished he'd been carrying his handgun. To keep it from getting wet, he'd locked it in a waterproof container in the prow of the boat.

Had anyone found his boat? Were they looking specifically for him? Unlikely—Alec could only imagine how many people were listed as missing. Most, of course, weren't actually; it would take a while for members of families to find each other, with so many scattered across the county in shelters. Others would be holed up the way he and Wren were. No one was really keeping track of the rescue personnel like him.

How many deaths would be attributed to the storm? He'd seen too many of the bloated carcasses of animals floating by. It would be by the grace of God if some waterlogged human corpses weren't found as well, to join the bodies already in the morgue at the hospital in Mountfort. Momentarily he saw the faces of the two men he'd help pull from the submerged van, then managed to suppress the memory. He'd worked homicide long enough to be good at that.

Wren eventually woke from her nap, seemingly in a better mood although without having lost that indefinable air of reserve. She seemed happy enough to talk about anything impersonal, but the only real questions she asked were about local mores, food, flora and fauna. She listened carefully when he talked about how central church was in the lives of most of the county residents.

"I told you I'm a city boy. Most of the people I arrested in east St. Louis didn't worry about what their pastor would think."

She chuckled at that, as he'd thought she would, but she didn't ask why he'd made such a life-altering move. Just as well, he told himself.

They were hungry enough to enjoy the tomatoes and pinto beans they shared for dinner. Neither even mentioned the energy bars. As far as Alec was concerned, they'd once again become a food of last resort. He guessed Wren felt the same.

As he had last night, he used the down vest for a pillow and Wren used him. During one of his wakeful periods, Alec acknowledged then dismissed his many aches and pains. It was disconcerting to realize how much he enjoyed holding a woman. He could have done without having her baby squeezed between them, but Wren... Yeah, he liked having her in his arms, her head nestled on his shoulder, her hair tickling his chin. He thought about it long enough to get an erection, but the feeling wasn't entirely sexual. Wasn't even mostly sexual, not at the moment. It was…

Hell. He liked her. He'd missed a lot about being married, including this: having someone to hold.

Yeah, well, don't get too used to it. Another day, two days, Wren and the baby would be going to the hospital to be checked out, he would locate her friend, make sure James Vincent Miner was where he was supposed to be, and that would be that.

This uncomfortable stirring in his chest was for the memories, for what he'd once thought he had. Not for what he'd never have again.

Wren awakened in the morning, unhappily used the jar while pretending Alec wasn't there and considered which of the decreasingly interesting remaining food options would be most bearable for breakfast.

Lord, what she'd give for a toothbrush! *Forget the hot shower and shampoo, just give me a toothbrush,* she thought whimsically, then made a hasty add-on. *And toothpaste.*

Alec had already assumed his now familiar stance beside the window, one shoulder resting against the frame as he stared out. She allowed herself a moment of resentment at how good he looked. His breath probably wasn't any sweeter than hers, but his hair wasn't long enough to become lanky and greasy, the way hers felt when she ran her fingers through it. *He* at least was wearing his own clothes, which formed to lean muscles.

Wren wrinkled her nose at the sight of the saggy flannel shirt that made a knee-length dress on her over the men's pajama bottoms with the legs rolled up. The baggy socks were a cute touch, too.

She glanced at Alec to find him watching her with amusement in his eyes.

"Don't laugh at me," she warned.

His teeth flashed in a grin, as if he couldn't help himself. "You can't feel any scruffier than I do. These jeans creak when I move. I swear they feel like they got soaked in starch. And then there's this." He yanked at the dark growth of his beard.

Wren sighed. "Abby loves me anyway. She doesn't care what I look like."

"Kids don't." He resumed staring out the window.

"Watched pots don't boil."

With reawakened amusement, he looked at her. "Yeah, they do. Eventually."

"I don't suppose you'd consider opening a can for me?"

"Sure." He straightened from his relaxed slouch. "What'll it be?"

"Soup, I guess."

It was back to tomato rice. Whoever had stocked the kitchen hadn't gone for variety.

Picky, picky. They would be going hungry by now if someone had cleaned the canned goods out of the kitchen.

Bang. He drove the not-so-pointed tip of the knife into the lid of a second can. *Bang.*

"Wait!" Wren lifted her head.

His head came up, too. He looked first at Abby, his sharp gaze returning to Wren's face only when he saw that her baby hadn't stirred. "What?"

"I think I hear…"

Alec went straight to the window, Wren right behind him. She couldn't see a thing when she peered past his broad back, but she could definitely hear the distant sound of some kind of motor.

Alec wrenched open the window and leaned out.

"Can you see anything?"

"No." He cupped his hands and bellowed, "Help!"

Behind them, Abby let out a startled cry.

"Oh, no." For the first time feeling torn, Wren finally went to her daughter, who was working herself up to a serious tantrum.

"Maybe we should stick her out the window," Alec muttered, and she turned in outrage to find he was again leaning out and yelling.

Abby's scream reached a crescendo she hadn't even tried for yet in her short life. Groaning, Wren picked her up and rocked her.

"You're not hungry, are you, sweetie? You can't be yet."

Abby was inconsolable. Wren had no choice but to sit down to feed her. Her daughter latched on with something that felt like desperation. She was going for comfort, Wren realized.

Unless... Oh, dear Lord, what if she wasn't producing enough milk? What if Abby *was* starving? Horrified, Wren thought, *Would I know?*

For the tiniest of moments, she had the childish wish for her mother, which was absurd. Her mother hadn't even breast-fed. She had stayed home from work for only two weeks after Wren was born, so she'd started her on formula right away.

Suddenly Alec let off shouting and brought his head and shoulders inside to say, "They've seen me!"

Her heart jumped, mostly with excitement. Apprehension... No, she told herself firmly. That could wait until she'd had that hot shower and a doctor had told her that Abby was fine.

The roar of the outboard motor grew in volume. Wren took a chance and lifted Abby from her breast to her shoulder. She patted until her baby burped then slipped the buttons through the holes. She climbed to her feet and joined Alec at the window.

He gave her a huge smile and wrapped an arm around her shoulder. They stood side by side, watching as a metal boat that looked not much different than the one he'd used drew near, finally bumping against the wall below them. There were two men in it, both wearing yellow rain pants and suspenders over flannel shirts.

The sound of the motor lowered to a throaty idle. One man stayed seated at the rear with a hand on the throttle. The other, with graying blond hair and a half-grown beard as disreputable as Alec's, stood with his head back so he could grin at them.

"Well, well, if it isn't Detective Harper. We got to wondering where you'd gone off to. There's people gonna be real glad to see you."

Alec only laughed. "You offering a lift?"

CHAPTER SIX

PAPER CRACKLING UNDER HER as she moved, Wren carefully got down from the exam table. She was reaching for the tie behind her neck to remove the hospital gown when there was a quick rap on the door. After she'd agreed that she was decent, the smiling nurse popped in and handed her an unopened package of pads.

"We keep them on hand here. I gather it'll be a bit before you can replace your credit cards or money, and you can't do without these."

Can't? Thanking her, Wren had an inappropriate desire to laugh when she thought of the substitutes she'd used the past few days. Once the nurse closed the door behind her, Wren hurriedly dressed in the scrubs they'd supplied. It felt fabulous to be clean. Someone had even scrounged up a disposable razor so she could take care of her underarms and legs. And a toothbrush and toothpaste!

She looked at herself in the small mirror. Her hair was wet, slicked to her head, and her ears poked out in a way that might have gotten her cast as an extra in *Lord of the Rings* if she'd been hanging around in New Zealand at the right time. So—she didn't look great. She made a face at herself. It wasn't as though she ever looked great. She just wished...

Forget about it, she told herself firmly. The man had delivered her baby. Rescued her. Full stop.

And she had a lot more to be grateful for. People had been so nice. Nobody had even asked her yet if she had health insurance. Instead, once Alec dropped her at Emergency, she'd been enveloped in coos of delight at how darling Abby was, sympathy for her plight and offers of help. She might not have a penny, but she now had a toothbrush and toothpaste, a hairbrush, a set of slightly faded blue scrubs, rubber flip-flops and her very own entire package of pads. Plus, while Abby was being weighed and examined, a different nurse was rushing home to grab a bag of clothes and receiving blankets that her baby no longer needed.

"She's my third," she'd said, waving off Wren's stammered protestations. "Third and last." A freckled redhead, she had grinned. "I grabbed my husband by the collar in the middle of a contraction and told him I quit. Love every one of my kids, don't want to do it again."

Now that she was dressed, Wren hesitantly stepped out into the hall and immediately heard Abby's cry. Breasts tingling, Wren hurried to the next room, where her tiny daughter lay in the cup of a baby scale, which was metal and probably cold.

The nurse was already lifting an indignant Abby when Wren arrived in a rush.

"Six pounds, three ounces. A darned good weight, considering she might have been a week or two premature and you're such a little thing yourself. And it's normal for her to have lost some since she was born, you know." The nurse wrapped the unhappy baby in a soft blanket and escorted them back to the room.

A pediatrician, a woman with steel-gray hair and a friendly smile, came to examine Abby and pronounced her in good health.

"How confident are you of the due date?" she asked. "Her lungs seem mature, her muscle tone excellent. From what you've said, she's had no problem nursing. Did you have an ultrasound?"

Wren shook her head. "The obstetrician guessed."

"Well, my suspicion is that she's close to full-term, if not right on the money." Her gaze, steady now and not amused, met Wren's. "You do know that you were extraordinarily lucky."

"Yes."

"Traveling in the last few weeks is not recommended."

Ashamed, Wren knew her cheeks were burning. "I... really didn't have a choice."

Frowning slightly, the doctor studied her. "I'd say all is well. There's no reason for us to keep you. I'm going to give you a handout with recommendations for well-baby visits and vaccines. Will you be staying in the area?"

A lump in her throat, Wren admitted, "I don't know."

"If so, make an appointment for that first visit. And call if you have any concerns."

She talked more; gave the number for a nurse practitioner who was available to answer questions about problems with breast-feeding, sleep patterns or anything else that might plague new parents. Finally, she gently stroked Abby's cheek and left.

The lump in Wren's throat had slithered to her chest, where it seemed to have swollen until it was closer to boulder-size. She'd wanted to know that Abby was okay, but a cowardly part of her had been hoping that the doctor would want to admit them for the night. As it was, as soon as the kind nurse showed up with the bag of clothes, Wren had no more excuse not to walk out, Abby in one arm and her small cache of supplies in a plastic bag clutched in her free hand.

She'd been told there were shelters. She'd ask at the front desk; surely they'd be able to tell her where to go. That would give her some breathing space, food and a roof while she tried to find Molly. And she had to call the rental-car company. Thank goodness she'd paid for their insurance.

Despite her personal pep talk, she felt a rush of… *something*—relief, probably—when the first person she saw after she pushed through the door into the waiting area was Alec. He'd been sitting, but rose to his feet at her appearance.

Relief was swamped by completely inconvenient lust. If only he didn't look so good. Like her, he'd had a shower, but it must have been at home because his clean jeans and thermal henley shirt fit like they were his own. He wore slightly battered athletic shoes and clipped to his belt were a badge and a holstered handgun. His jaw was freshly shaved. He'd nicked his chin, Wren saw, which only made him look a little bit human instead of formidably handsome.

"Everything okay?" he asked.

She nodded. "The pediatrician thinks Abby might actually be full-term. She's not very big, barely over six pounds, but, well…"

His mouth twitched. "You're not very big, either."

"No. James is, I don't know, five foot ten maybe, but I guess she took after me." *Thank goodness.*

"Wren, I've made some inquiries about your friend."

She could tell from his expression that he didn't have good news. She only waited.

"Molly and her husband have moved. Over a year ago. The post office forwards mail for a year, so they should still have the address. Only there's been a screwup, and they don't. Nobody I've found yet remembers where they went." He paused. "When were you last in touch?"

Scared, really scared now, she could hardly breathe. Abby gave a little squeak, and Wren realized her arm had tightened around her.

"I—I guess it has been a year. Or maybe longer. I wrote, but I didn't hear back from her. And, well, there wasn't any reason for me to keep a cell phone, and James found a better deal so we shared an email account and I can't be sure Molly got my emails."

Alec was looking at her with pity, and she had a suspicion she deserved contempt instead. How could she have been so stupid? So *weak?* Why had it taken her so long to see what was happening, what James was doing to her? He didn't want her to have her own cell phone, her own car, her own bank account. Her own anything. Molly probably had responded and he'd deleted it. She might even have called, but he'd answered. Or written, and he'd thrown her letters away. *And* it meant he would have her address.

Her former address. Oh, God. And maybe her new one, too?

Voice shaking now, Wren said, "I tried to email her from a computer at the airport, but it bounced back. So that's no good. Can't I find her online? You said people are easy to find these days. I've read about it, how it's, like, impossible to disappear anymore."

Alec nodded, his face kind and still pitying, which she hated.

"We probably can find her, but it might take a while. It would have helped if they'd owned their house, but they only rented. I was lucky to find someone who knew that much. No idea yet who the landlord is, or whether he has any records that will help."

"Oh." She stood stock-still. "Well. Is there a library where I can use the computer?"

"The one here in Saddler's Mill is closed. There's some water damage. You can use my computer at home, but with dial-up it's torturously slow. We have high-speed at the police station and I'm told we're back online. You're welcome to try on your own, but I might get further. I promise I'll start some searches."

It was tempting to burst into tears. So tempting she had to battle herself for a minute before she could say, without any quaver at all, "Thank you, Alec. For everything you've done. Now looking for Molly, too, first thing, when you must be worried about your own family and friends and neighbors. I can't tell you how much I appreciate what you've done for me." She even managed a smile. "And Abigail Alexa."

He opened his mouth to say something, but the redheaded nurse pushed through the swinging doors with, of all things, a wheeled suitcase.

"Here's the clothes for your cutie, and we're loaded at home with luggage—way more than we need—so I thought this might make life easier for you. No, don't argue. I wish I could do more." She looked rueful. "Unfortunately, you and I aren't even close to the same size, so my clothes wouldn't do you a speck of good."

Wren had to laugh. The other woman had to be five foot ten and was statuesque. "No, I don't suppose they would." She thanked her again, and then the nurse was called away, leaving Wren standing there with Alec.

"Well," she said, feeling awkward, "I'd better get going."

He frowned. "Get going? Where did you have in mind?"

"I thought one of the shelters. I understand a few people have been able to go home, so there should be room."

"You shouldn't go to a shelter with a newborn. You can stay with me."

She stared at him. "What?"

There were still creases between his dark eyebrows, but she couldn't exactly call it a frown anymore. He looked more as if he was disconcerted. Because he'd blurted out an invitation he hadn't intended to make?

"I have plenty of room," he said slowly. "Too much—the house has four bedrooms."

She wasn't any genius at reading other people's thoughts—if she had been, James wouldn't have been able to fool her so easily. But right now, Wren could swear she knew what Alec was thinking. Feeling. He was uncomfortable at what he'd offered, but also determined. He didn't want her in his house, or maybe he didn't want the bother of having a baby who would wake crying at all hours. But he'd abandoned his boat and leaped for the attic windowsill because she needed him, and he thought she still did.

I do. It was a silent cry, one she would never let him hear. Because she knew she couldn't accept any more from him. He'd given so much already. Other people needed him, too. More. He hadn't said whether he'd found his sister and her family yet, and because of his job all the citizens in the county relied on him, too.

"That's so nice of you," she said. "But unnecessary. Gosh, have you found your sister yet? Surely her family will need to stay with you?"

"I found them. Their house is high and dry so they

don't need me. And you do. I want to know you're
safe until we locate James and you have a plan for the
future. You'll be on your own all day while I'm at work,
but even if he shows up he'd have no way to trace you
to my place."

No waffling allowed. He'd made up his mind, and
assumed he'd made up hers, too.

"Alec…lots of people are in need right now."

"We've been through something unusual together."
Looking right into her eyes, his voice low and husky,
he said, "Let me do this for you, Wren."

Her pride and determination to stand on her own collapsed. "Thank you. We would love to stay with you."

He reached for the handle of the suitcase. "Let's get
you settled, then."

She hurried after him as he strode away. "Wait!
Don't I have to talk about payment with them, or—"

"I already stopped by the business office. We can
handle it later. I picked up a car seat from them, too."
He glanced back as the automatic doors opened for
them. "Wait here, and I'll pick you up."

It was definitely an order. He was in cop mode. As
she snapped her mouth shut and dutifully waited instead of traipsing across the parking lot after him, Wren
struggled with uneasiness she didn't fully understand.
Shouldn't she be glad to know that his offer *hadn't* been
an impulse? Which it couldn't have been, not if he'd
gone to the trouble of getting a car seat already. So why
did she feel anxious instead of happy?

Dumb question. She had every reason in the world to
be worried about an alpha male deciding to take charge
of her. Only…Alec wasn't anything like James. All she
had to do was remember how gentle and kind he'd been
to know that. She should be grateful he'd thought of a

car seat rather than alarmed because he'd made such a huge assumption.

A black SUV pulled to a stop at the curb, and Alec got out. He'd already figured out how the car seat worked and now helped her strap Abby in, then opened the front passenger door for Wren. He even put a hand under her elbow to boost her in. When he went around to the driver's side and climbed behind the wheel, she saw him glance to be sure she'd buckled herself up. "It's not far," he said. "Ten minutes."

Wren nodded. She should be thinking of practicalities, but couldn't seem to wrap her mind around what she needed to do. Maybe she was suffering from some sort of shock. She wanted a meal—a real, honest to goodness meal—and clean sheets on a comfy mattress. Figuring out how to replace a driver's license from another state—that seemed to be beyond her.

They must have driven for five minutes in silence when Alec said, "I figure we can scrape up dinner, and I'll run to the grocery store afterward. Make sure you're okay for tomorrow."

A bubble of laughter escaped. "Pretty much anything that's actually heated on the stove would taste good."

A smile flickered on his mouth. "No kidding. I have to admit, I'd have run through McDonald's earlier and grabbed a Big Mac if they'd been open."

"Flooded?"

"Yeah. No major damage, but the building got its feet wet."

She was surprised, looking around as he drove, that there was a McDonald's here. Saddler's Mill wasn't big, and there didn't seem to be much new construction. It was picturesque, especially the oldest parts that probably dated from the nineteenth century. The core of

the town had been built on a bluff high enough above
the river to save it from the worst of the flood. The
businesses on the main street looked as if they'd been
passed from father to son for several generations. She
didn't see any chain stores. But the town had expanded,
probably in later years, onto lower lying land that had
been enveloped by the rising river. She could see whole
streets below where only the upper stories of houses
and telephone poles showed above water. The sight was
horrifying and weirdly awe-inspiring.

"People must have lost everything," she murmured.

Alec was silent for a minute. "Yeah," he said finally.
"I picked up people who didn't have time to grab a
family photo album or their purses or wallets. You're
not the only one who doesn't even have ID. And Saddler's Mill isn't in as bad shape as Mountfort, the
county seat. I plucked people off rooftops there. The
water rose so damn fast."

She remembered. Trudging up the rutted lane that
was been no more than muddy, then waking a couple
of hours later, if that, to water already knee-deep in the
house.

He pulled into a driveway that led into a single-car
detached garage beside an aging two-story house. The
house was neatly if unimaginatively painted white, had
a deep porch that spanned the entire front and small-
paned windows covered by what she thought might be
storm windows. She'd never seen any before. Roses,
neatly pruned, lined a front walk.

"Are you a gardener?" she asked.

"No." His voice was unusually clipped. "This was
my mother's house. I'm just trying to take care of it."

It bothered her to picture him out here joylessly
weeding and pruning and mowing out of a sense of

duty and not even pride of ownership. Though plenty of people considered yard upkeep to be a necessary evil and not fun, didn't they?

Abby had fallen asleep, and Alec took the whole car seat out with her in it. Pulling her red suitcase, Wren followed him to the porch and waited while he unlocked.

The entry held a spiral-legged side table and an old oak coatrack. Stairs opened ahead. To one side was a formal dining room, to the other a parlor. Well, really a living room, but Wren didn't see a TV or a recliner or anything that wasn't old-ladyish. There were crocheted doilies on the arms of the sofa and chairs, for goodness sakes. Alec didn't say anything, and, hovering behind him, Wren thought how empty the house felt, as if no one had lived in it for a while. Except Alec did.

"I haven't changed much," he said, sounding a little uncomfortable, as if he was seeing it through her eyes. "And I guess Mom didn't, either. She inherited the house from her aunt."

Trying to imagine him sprawled on that sofa, Wren said, "Edwina?"

He gave a rough laugh. "I forgot we talked about my great-aunts. Actually, it was Pearl. They were sisters, but Great-Aunt Pearl never married. Edwina did and had children, too. Her husband took her away to Georgia. I've only met those cousins a couple of times."

"The house, um, looks like someone named Pearl should live here."

"Yeah." He was looking ruefully at the living room. "It does, doesn't it? I don't so much as set foot in there. I have someone who comes around every couple of weeks to vacuum and dust." His shoulders moved. "You know."

All those porcelain figurines would have to be dusted, wouldn't they? It occurred to her to wonder if his daughters stayed with him. Nothing she could see looked remotely kid-proof.

Oh, dear. What would his ex-wife think of him having Wren living here?

She didn't ask. She'd already discovered how he shut her down when she poked into his personal business.

He suggested leaving Abby in the kitchen while they took the suitcase upstairs and he showed Wren where she'd be sleeping. Then he started work on dinner after insisting she sit and watch.

The kitchen was old-fashioned, too, but cheerful with yellow-painted cabinets and yellow-and-white gingham curtains at the window over the deep double sink. A microwave sat on the counter. An obviously brand-new refrigerator was reassuringly shiny and white, but the range with gas burners showed its age.

"At least you have electricity," she realized.

"I'm told it came on only this morning. I'm going to have to throw out a whole lot of food. And we're lucky. A good part of the county doesn't have it and won't for who knows how long."

Wren kept looking around while Alec opened a can of what appeared to be baked beans. He mostly lived in here. The room was spacious enough to hold a farm table with chairs, and an upholstered rocking chair that faced the TV resting on one end of the counter. Sitting in that chair now, Wren gave an experimental push and her feet immediately left the floor as it reeled back. The chair was sized for him, not her. After a little thought, she tucked her feet under her and let it slow to a stop. She smiled at Abby, whose car seat was on the table. She slept with the intense concentration only a baby could achieve, her rosebud mouth open and her forehead wrinkled as if in deep thought. So, okay, her ears did stick out, but Alec was right—it was cute on her. Maybe with a little luck her hair would grow in curly like James's, and could disguise the ears when she got to those awful teenage years. It would be nice if James's genes had something useful to offer.

"Are you sure I can't help?" Wren asked.

"This isn't going to be fancy. Baked beans, canned peas, cornbread muffins that were frozen and still look okay. Heavy on the starch." He grinned at her over his shoulder. "Sorry. No creamed corn. I can pick up some if you crave it."

She chuckled. "I can probably live without it."

"After dinner, we can make a grocery list."

Wren watched him stir the beans. "I don't know if I can pay you back. I had cash instead of travelers' checks. It never occurred to me…"

He shook his head. "It wasn't like you were heading abroad. And I know you don't have any way of replacing that money, Wren. You need help right now, and I can give it. Okay?"

It wasn't easy to echo his *okay,* but she did. The only time in her life she hadn't held a job was this past year when James insisted there was no reason for her to work some crap job when he made plenty.

"Not when you know you'll be going to grad school eventually," he'd said. When she told him she still thought she ought to work, he got mad because she didn't trust him to take care of her, and he accused her of wanting to be out there so she could meet other guys. And by then she was…not scared of him, exactly, but anxious not to upset him because it wasn't worth it.

And, wow, how dim could she have been?

Dinner smelled amazingly good, considering, and the growl of her stomach roused her from her brooding. Alec set the table with a tub of margarine and a basket filled with the cornbread muffins that he'd heated in the microwave and plates.

"It'll have to be pop," he said apologetically. "There was some orange juice in the freezer, but it's oozing out of the can. And the milk…" He shrugged.

"This looks fabulous," she said with one hundred percent genuine enthusiasm, and he laughed.

"You're right. It does. It's going to be a while before I can be picky again."

"Maybe never," she agreed, and dug in.

Of course Abby woke up before Wren had finished eating, but she was content with being jiggled on one arm while Wren unashamedly gobbled.

After she was done, Alec said, "Tomorrow I can check with my sister if she has a bassinet or crib up in her attic that we can borrow. In the meantime, I thought maybe an empty drawer padded with something soft."

"That's a good idea. I think there are some receiving blankets in that suitcase."

Abby was beginning to whimper, so Wren laid her down on the cushioned seat of the rocker and peeled off her soggy diaper. When she pulled a replacement from her bag of supplies, Alec said, "Oh, man. I didn't even think about you needing those."

"At the hospital, they gave me half a dozen, but we'll need more. I always intended to use cloth ones, but until I'm really settled that's probably not very practical."

He didn't say anything. She sat in the rocker and, doing her best to be discreet, lifted the scrub top enough for Abby to latch on. Looking at her daughter's fuzzy head, she felt a renewed pang of fear. How and when would she and Abby actually *be* settled? Right now, she was totally dependent on charity.

"I'll have to call my mom." She hadn't even known she'd made the decision until she said it out loud. Wren looked up to find him watching her.

"Did she know you were heading out here?"

Feeling her cheeks heat, she ducked her head. "She doesn't even know I was pregnant. At first, I thought I'd wait to tell her until James and I got married, and then… I knew I should leave him, and I was ashamed that I hadn't. Mom would never understand. We didn't talk all that often, so it was easy not to say anything."

"She's not in Seattle?"

Wren shook her head. "California. The Bay area. That's where I grew up."

"Would she take you in?"

She tried to picture herself and a baby in her mother's small condo. "If she had to, I guess. She doesn't really have room, though. It would have to be temporary. And…" She bit her lip. "That's where I met James. In San Rafael. So he knows where Mom lives."

"What are you going to tell her, then?"

She shrugged and made a face. "Everything. I know she'll send me money, at least. Then I can pay you back."

Exasperation flashed on his face. "What, for a few groceries? Don't be so prickly."

She tensed. "I'm sorry."

He shoved back his chair and rose. At the abrupt motion and the sudden awareness of him looming over her, she instinctively curled around Abby.

"You're afraid of me." Alec sounded incredulous.

Wren closed her eyes and made herself breathe. In, out. Finally she lifted her gaze to him. "I'm sorry." She winced at the expression on his face. She shouldn't have said that again. "I couldn't help it," she whispered. "I know you wouldn't hurt me. I do."

"That son of a bitch," he growled, and turned away. "You can finish nursing in peace. I'll go get a bed ready for Abby."

Wren was mad at herself even before he left the room. She hadn't once felt scared of him, not until now. Wary when he got bossy, but that was different. She didn't know why something about the way he moved this time had reminded her, for one painful moment, of James, of the time he hurt her, but it had. She hated knowing she'd probably hurt Alec's feelings.

One thing for sure, he wouldn't welcome any more apologies. There had to be some other way to let him know that she did trust him. Like *not* cringing the next time he got too close. Wren sighed, and gently lifted Abby from her breast to burp her.

CHAPTER SEVEN

ALEC LEANED BACK in his desk chair, feet up on his desk and phone to his ear. He hated being on hold. Like most cops, he spent an irritating amount of time on hold, waiting for someone, somewhere, to look up information he needed. He rubbed his forehead, waiting for the ibuprofen to kick in. If he didn't start sleeping better…

"Detective Lontz," a gruff voice in his ear said. "What can I do for you?"

Alec introduced himself and explained Wren's situation. "The boyfriend lives in Seattle. I'm hoping you can send someone to find out whether the guy is where he ought to be. That would give her some breathing room."

"Arkansas," the Seattle cop said thoughtfully. "I've been reading about the floods. Your county had trouble?"

Alec laughed, although the sound was grim. "Yeah. I spent most of the last week in a twelve-foot aluminum boat plucking people off rooftops. In fact, the lady I called about got stuck in it. Her rental car is still underwater, all her belongings are gone, and she gave birth in the attic of an abandoned farmhouse."

"I'll see what I can do. You got a name?"

"James Vincent Miner." He gave the address, phone number and name of employer that he'd extracted from Wren. "Any history on him would be good, too."

"You're taking this seriously."

"He stopped her from running once before. Hurt her pretty bad, kicked her belly presumably to try to kill the baby. You should have a domestic call on that one." He paused, knowing he hadn't really answered the unspoken question. With the best will in the world, cops couldn't devote a lot of attention to threats from stalker ex-boyfriends and husbands. There were enough crimes happening *now*, resources tended to be stretched to their limit without wasting them on future maybe/maybe not assaults.

"I delivered her baby," he said, reluctantly.

"You're taking this personally."

"I guess I am." He braced himself.

"I can spare time to run a check on this guy. What's the best number to reach you?"

Alec gave his cell phone number and thanked him.

He was frowning into space when he realized someone was standing in front of his desk. His sergeant, a wiry little guy with thinning red hair and the personality of a blow fly—loud, persistent and capable of hurting you.

"Nice to know you've got time to put your feet up."

Alec only raised his eyebrows. Never let 'em know you're afraid. "I'm thinking. That's what you pay me to do."

"Right now what I'm paying you to do is head down to Carter's Computers and Cameras. Everybody else is tied up. We've got a report of looters."

Alec grunted and swung his feet to the floor. Nothing like general misery to bring the termites crawling out of the woodwork. "Do I need a boat?"

Sergeant Pruitt shrugged. "Probably not. Hipwaders, maybe."

In other words, he would be getting wet again.
Damn, but he wanted his corner of the world to dry
out again. Heading for the door, he had a wistful image
of spring with the dogwoods and hawthorn blooming
and the yellow honeysuckles that grew along creeks
releasing their sweet scent. Leaves coming out on the
oak trees, the smallmouth bass spawning in creeks and
rivers burbling gently within their banks. Alec didn't
look forward to the sweltering heat of summer, but
spring… That was something else.

Two hours later, he was booking the one looter he'd
gotten his hands on—a seventeen-year-old kid who
kept claiming he was just looking around even though
there were three high-end digital cameras in his back-
pack. Despite the rubber boots Alec had worn, his jeans
were soaked to his thighs—he'd had to go into the
restroom to dump the water out of his boots and wring
his socks out—and he was pissed. He knew the kid's
family, which made it worse; they were decent people.

That was how the day went. Bodies were found, most
probably drowning victims, but the coroner would have
to make that determination. One had a bullet hole in
his back. He might have drowned, too, but he'd had a
little help on the way. Unfortunately, he had no ID on
him and the body had been in the water for two days
or more. Alec couldn't help wondering if he'd been a
looter trying to run for it. People didn't take kindly to
someone taking advantage of the misfortune Mother
Nature had already visited on them. Until the body was
identified, there wasn't a damn thing he could do.

He shouldn't have had a minute to think about Wren,
but that's not how it worked. She seemed to be simmering in the back of his mind most of the time, waiting to
pop out front and center when he was incautious.

He worried that she'd get it into her head that she ought to leave. Maybe think she shouldn't be accepting help from him. He figured her for more sensible than that, but he couldn't be sure. He also couldn't afford the time to check on her. Last night he'd loaded up on groceries, grateful that the store's generator had kept the freezer cases frozen and the milk cold. The shelves were stripped of bottled water, flashlight batteries and a host of other practicalities, and produce was skimpy since new deliveries weren't making it into town yet. But he'd been able to buy enough diapers for a week or more, milk because he had a vague feeling a nursing mother ought to be drinking it, meat and eggs and cereal and even some staples like flour, because Wren said she would like to do some baking what with all the time she had on her hands.

At odd moments he wondered what she *was* doing with her time. He pictured her kneading bread dough, her small hands working it, flour dusting her arms and a sprinkling of white joining the freckles on her cheeks. Or holding that baby of hers, smiling with so much love shining out of her it shut down something inside him. Feet curled under her as she sat in his rocker, nursing Abby.

That was the hardest thing of all for him to picture.

It seemed as though with every day that passed, he was seeing her increasingly in a sexual light. That first day, at the Maynard house, he'd been okay. She was nothing but a tiny dab of a thing with that enormous belly being squeezed with vicious power. He'd heard the agonized moans and seen the sweat, astonishing determination and resilience. She was giving birth in terrifying circumstances. She'd needed him.

She still needed him, but now it was different. Now

he was having to avert his face when she lifted her shirt to expose her breast, because he wanted too much to look. She had possibly the world's prettiest breasts, crowned with dainty nipples and aureoles more pink than brown. He groaned at the thought of touching them, then stole a look around to make sure nobody had noticed. Given the general chaos of the police station, he'd have to do a lot more than give a low groan to get attention. A good, heartfelt obscenity didn't do it, either. Some major bloodshed, maybe.

With a sigh, he pushed back his chair. He would drive a few blocks that had suffered some looting, make sure everything was quiet, then go by the hospital to see whether Doc Bailey had yet looked at the stiff with the bullet hole. That would get his mind off of Wren.

He was creeping down Chestnut, craning his neck to see in storefronts, when his attention was caught by a group clustered in front of Slater's Guns & Ammunition. His foot tapped the brake and he eased to the curb, though he recognized two of the five men.

Unfortunately, one of them was his brother-in-law, Randy Young.

Tension tied some new knots in Alec's neck and shoulders. This was where he would expect Randy to be, beer in hand, laughing with some buddies at the gun shop. Randy was real fond of hunting and fishing.

Because he'd already stopped, Alec rolled down the passenger window to exchange abbreviated greetings with the men. The first to appear in his window was Dan Slater, who'd taken over the business after his father had suffered his second heart attack.

"Much damage?" Alec asked, although he knew most of the street had gotten off lightly, maybe a foot of water making it inside the businesses fronting it.

Slater propped a forearm on the door. "More than you'd think. I'm going to have to take all the cases out and tear up the floor. It's a mess in there."

Alec nodded. Water alone would have been bad enough, but the flood had deposited muck and debris everywhere it had gone.

"Don't carry flood insurance," Dan added with a grimace. "I thought we were high enough."

"Lots of folks in the same boat."

"Bet you're keeping busy, too." After Alec had agreed that he was, Slater nodded and stepped back.

Randy took his place. "Sally's been bitching because you haven't been to see her yet."

Alec worked hard to keep his expression blank. "I talked to her. She says you stayed dry."

"Water came up to the top porch step. Yard's a god-damn mess, and she's fussing about her garden." He shrugged. "We got off easy, though."

"She says she took the kids to a shelter." Without her husband.

"Yeah, I was trying to help some others out," Randy said, winking. "Hear you've been tied up yourself."

"You could say that."

"Darcy at the hospital says you've got a pretty lady at your place."

Anger flared in Alec. "I'd appreciate it if word didn't get out about that."

Randy gave one of those big, loopy grins that had rubbed Alec the wrong way from the beginning. "Maybe in St. Louis folks don't talk about an unmar-ried man and woman living together, but it's different here."

Between gritted teeth, Alec said, "She has a three-

day-old baby, lost everything in the flood and has nowhere to go. I'm giving her refuge for a few days."

"I'm surprised Sally hasn't already been over there,
looking her over."

Oh, hell. He hadn't thought of that.

Alec looked hard at his brother-in-law. "I mean it. I
don't want people talking. This girl's got some trouble.
It would help if nobody remembers seeing her and has
no idea where she went if they did."

Randy raised his eyebrows. "Best you talk to Darcy,
then. She brought us a six-pack earlier and told everyone about how you brought them this woman wearing
nothing but a man's wool socks and an old flannel shirt
to her knees. Cute baby girl, too, she said. And she says
you didn't just bring her, you took her away again."

Alec cursed. "I'll talk to her. I'm on my way to the
hospital now." He frowned. "I suppose the mill's shut
down."

"Yep. Got myself a vacation." Randy didn't sound
too bothered, although Alec couldn't imagine the mill
would be able to pay workers for the time off and Sally
sure couldn't work, raising three kids as she was.

For his sister's sake he bit off what he wanted to say,
only lifted a hand, rolled up the window and pulled
away. In the rearview mirror he could see his brother-
in-law rejoin his buddies. One of them opened a cooler
and tossed Randy another beer, which he caught one-
handed. He'd been a catcher in high school, spent a year
in the minors before they let him go, so there was one,
useless thing he was good at.

At the hospital, Alec did corner Darcy, who handled
admissions at the front desk. He tried to make his tone
friendly when he said, "I should have asked you yes-

terday to keep quiet about that woman with the baby I brought in."

She smirked. "Looked like you knew her well."

"Not until I delivered her baby," he said grimly. "She's got a man stalking her. I was hoping to slip her in and out of here quietly. If anyone comes looking, nobody's ever heard of her. Okay?"

Her face got serious. "You mean, like an ex-husband or something?"

He left her assumption intact. As Randy had intimated, this part of the country was still conservative. There were people who wouldn't approve of her having a baby out of wedlock. And no, those same people wouldn't approve of her staying with him, except nobody would raise any eyebrows right now with so many people homeless and her in obvious need with a newborn.

"Yeah. Not a nice guy."

"Oh," she said, eyes wide. "Well, I'll make sure everyone here knows."

"Thank you."

He went to the basement, where Dr. Elijah Bailey was leaving the autopsy room. Even though he'd already stripped off gown and gloves, the odor wafted out after him. Alec had stood through plenty of autopsies, but he never had gotten used to that smell. His stomach did an unhappy roll, but he didn't let the weakness show.

"Detective, I was just going to call you."

Bailey had dug a .44 bullet out of the body. A .44 Magnum cartridge was common locally, used in rifles for hunting as well as handguns. It would have passed right through if it hadn't slammed up against the breastbone. "He was dead before he hit the water," he concluded. "Hardly any in his lungs. You can't blame drowning."

Alec nodded. They talked about trajectories and Alec accepted the bullet in an evidence bag. He'd send it to the state lab, for what it was worth.

Bailey couldn't tell him much about the guy that Alec didn't already know. Caucasian, best guess twenty-five to thirty-five years of age, a few fillings but no major dental work, a scar in one knee—he'd had some cartilage damage, typical of a sports injury—and nothing especially distinctive about him. Dark blond to brown hair, hazel eyes, average height. Fingerprints had gone off for ID, but who knew when any results would come back?

"All right," Alec said. "With luck someone'll call looking for him, although it may be weeks before we determine who's actually missing. Or we might get lucky and find a car and no driver to go with it. Or stuff left in a hotel room."

They talked about two other unidentified bodies, both also male and Caucasian. One, forty-five to fifty-five years old, had suffered a blow to his head that Dr. Bailey thought preceded his drowning death. The other, approximately the same age as the shooting victim, had simply drowned, although the body had gotten battered in the ensuing day or two in the water. He, too, had had arthroscopic knee surgery at some point.

"High-school sports," Dr. Bailey said with a disapproving shake of the head. Come to think of it, Alec had never seen him *approve* of anything.

The doctor further expressed the hope that they wouldn't have to wait on fingerprints to put names to all three corpses, as they were filling three drawers in his small morgue.

When they parted, Alec didn't offer to shake hands; call him squeamish.

It was nearly six o'clock now. He would drop off the bullet at the station, then go home. He was disconcerted by how much anticipation he felt. It had been a long time since he'd looked forward to anything. And in this case, he had no right. He wasn't returning to a woman of his own. Although a dinner he hadn't put together himself, that was something to appreciate—assuming she'd cooked. Any more hopes than that, he was just setting himself up for a fall.

He turned the key in his department-issued Chevy Tahoe. He didn't *want* anything from Wren. He was too mixed up to be thinking about a relationship, even assuming she would be interested, which he couldn't imagine she was. Running from an abusive man, with a newborn baby and a less than solid childhood…none of that sounded like a woman who would be wanting a man for anything but protection.

Having a woman in such close proximity was all that had set him to wishing a little. Remembering what he'd lost.

He didn't ever want to hurt that way again. Bad enough lusting after his brown-feathered Wren. She came as a package, though, and he didn't want anything to do with that little girl.

He would help Wren get on her feet. It was an act of kindness. Perhaps a form of redemption. There had been so much he couldn't fix, but maybe he could fix part of what was wrong with Wren's life. Then, before he knew it, she'd be gone, and he wouldn't have to find ways of not noticing her smile or the delicacy of her bones or her small but perfectly shaped, pink-tipped breasts.

His stomach growled as he put the Tahoe in gear. It had been years since he'd walked in the door to the smell of fresh bread from the oven. That would be better even than home-cooked dinner on the table.

WHY IT HAD FELT SO NATURAL sharing the cramped space in the attic with Alec, and so different sharing a house with him, Wren didn't fully understand. But it *was* different.

Maybe it was because this was so weirdly normal, except for the fact that they hadn't known each other a week ago and were still, in many ways, strangers. In that attic, nothing was normal, so it was okay to be sleeping with the kind stranger's arms around her, his heartbeat comforting her.

He'd been so pleased with the homemade bread and pot roast last night, she slipped downstairs before him this morning to start breakfast, and soon heard the shower running upstairs. Coffee was ready to pour and bacon was sizzling in the cast-iron frying pan when she heard footsteps on the stairs.

"You didn't have to get up," he said.

She turned from the stove with a smile that probably belonged on the face of a Stepford wife, bright and sunny as though she cooked for him every morning. "I was already up. Didn't you hear Abby?"

"I heard her during the night." He sounded wry.

Out of the corner of her eye, Wren saw him stroll toward her and take two mugs from the cupboard. The gun and badge he wore on his belt disconcerted her anew, making him somehow more intimidating. One more thing to remind her how broad and solid and muscular he was; how male.

"She made it almost three hours last night," she said,

putting the bacon on a plate and soaking up grease with a paper towel.

He only nodded. "You ready for coffee?"

"Thanks." She held an egg over the pan. "Fried okay?"

"Sure." But his assessing gaze was critical. "You shouldn't be up. You can't take care of Abby if you don't rest when you can."

She *was* tired, and maybe that's what made her snappish. "Don't you think I can decide that?"

His eyebrows rose.

"Anyway, cooking is the least I can do."

"I don't expect payback." He sounded exasperated.

Wren cracked another egg. She couldn't bring herself to look at him. "That doesn't mean I can't try to do something good for you while I'm here." What did he think, she was going to lounge around watching soap operas all day? Yes, her whole body hurt, she was cramping and she felt like crap, but she hadn't felt any better in bed than she did up and about. *He's being nice,* she reminded herself. She was unbelievably lucky that he'd insisted on bringing her and Abby home with him. The last thing he deserved was her to be grouchy. Deliberately easing her tone, she said, "Although we can't have eggs every day, it's not good for your cholesterol."

He relaxed enough to laugh, that low, gritty sound she loved, and pushed a mug toward her. "So what's it going to be tomorrow morning?"

"Waffles, I think. I found a waffle iron yesterday. That is—" she stole a peek at him "—if you like them."

"Oh, yeah." He leaned a hip against the counter and stole a slice of bacon. "My mom used to make them every Sunday."

"Well, then, that's what I'll make."

"As long as you promise me you won't get up only to cook breakfast. I don't want you going short of sleep."

"I promise," she lied, and slipped the first pair of eggs, sunny-side-up, onto a plate and handed it to him. "Toast should be done."

Once she'd sat and reached for her fork, Alec asked, "Did you reach your mother last night?"

He sounded barely curious, not as if he was hoping her mother would take Wren and Abby off his hands. Even so, Wren's cheeks flushed with guilt.

"Um, I looked at the calendar and realized it was the third Thursday of the month, which means she'd have had a school board meeting." She concentrated on buttering her toast. If she met his eyes, he would be able to tell she was lying. Again. The truth was, she'd plain chickened out and wasn't proud of it.

"I don't suppose you're eager to talk to her," he said mildly, and she could tell he'd guessed.

Wonderful.

"I'll call her tonight. I promise."

"Doesn't matter to me. You're safer here anyway."

The promise inherent in his words made her feel squishy inside. It also sharpened the apprehension that she'd lived with since she and Alec were rescued from the attic. Returning to civilization meant she was vulnerable again, and she hated that.

Seeing that Alec had risen to put his dishes in the sink, she said hesitantly, "You will let me know if you hear anything about James?"

He looked at her, his blue eyes sharp enough to see more than she wanted him to. "I'll call the minute I know anything. I was surprised not to hear back from Lontz yesterday."

"I don't suppose I'm a very high priority for them."

Gaze still on her face, he said, "It depends what gets in the way."

She nodded. He knew she was scared.

"I really believe you are safe here," he said slowly. "If I didn't, I wouldn't leave you alone. There are people who know you're here, but if some stranger comes asking, they're likely to be closemouthed."

She looked at him in alarm. "Who knows I'm here?"

A muscle flickered in his jaw. "People saw you leaving the hospital with me."

"Oh."

"I've talked to a couple of them and asked them to keep quiet." When she nodded, he added, "All the same, don't answer the door unless you know who's knocking." He hesitated. "I hate to say this, but it wouldn't surprise me if my sister shows up. I ran into my brother-in-law yesterday. Sally knows you're here, and she's always been nosy. Won't bother me if you don't want to let her in. But if it's a woman leaning on the doorbell, that'll be Sally."

He left the room, then stuck his head back in. "I meant to say last night that you could poke around in the closets and dressers upstairs. I still haven't gotten rid of Mom's clothes and I'm not sure she did anything about Aunt Pearl's, either." He appraised her in the now wrinkled scrubs with a grease spot over the left breast. "Mom was taller than you, but Aunt Pearl was a little thing. Probably nothing they had is what you're used to wearing, but feel free if you can find something. I'll call later today and check. Otherwise, let me know your sizes and I'll stop by a couple of stores."

"Are they open?" she said in surprise. "This is such a small town. *Are* there any clothing boutiques?"

"One dress shop and a general store that sells some

basics. Underwear, jeans, that kind of thing. One of them might be open." He shrugged. "Even if they're not, most of the storekeepers are there cleaning up and won't mind doing some business."

"Oh. Okay. Um, thanks."

He nodded and left. The house was awfully quiet once the front door shut behind him. Wren hesitated, thinking she should clean the kitchen, but on the other hand wouldn't it be a good idea to take advantage of the fact that Abby was still asleep and do as Alec had suggested? She'd really, really like to have something else to wear.

She hesitated in the doorway of the bedroom where she knew he slept, but after a minute went in anyway and pushed open the closet. Sure enough, while a small portion of it was taken up with clothes that must be his, women's garments were pushed toward the back. Some cardboard boxes sitting on the floor held clothes, too, she discovered.

It felt like the worst kind of intrusion, digging through a dead woman's possessions, but Wren was desperate and Alec had given his permission. She hadn't detected even a flicker of sentimentality when he suggested she raid the closets, so she'd take him at his word.

The hardest part, maybe, was ignoring his clothes and the shoes scattered carelessly on the floor. At the end, encased in plastic from the dry cleaner, was a dark suit. She couldn't help imagining him in that, with a crisp white shirt setting off his dark hair and tan. There were at least a couple of more casual suits and a row of pants and dress shirts that made her guess he didn't always wear jeans on the job. Well, obviously not when he had to appear in court. She cringed to think how much he would hate knowing she was looking at his clothes and speculating about him. He'd made it plain enough that he didn't welcome her curiosity.

With an effort, she focused on his mother's garments, which she could see were too big for her. Even so, she set aside a few things she thought she could use. She could roll up sleeves, and it didn't matter if the hem reached midthigh. A soft flannel nightgown looked hardly worn, and socks...well, socks were socks.

Pearl's clothes in another bedroom were about Wren's size, but she grimaced at the thought of wearing the dresses or old-lady shoes. Pearl had apparently gone with the times, though, and Wren triumphantly found a couple of pairs of denim pants and practical shirts that the woman might have worn for gardening. There was even a pair of rubber clogs that, to her delight, fit perfectly.

Happy with her stash though she still lacked a replacement for her single pair of panties and bra, Wren changed just in time for Abby to wake up.

She gave the baby a bath in the big kitchen sink, patted her dry and dressed her in a cute red sleeper, then nursed her. Abby didn't immediately fall asleep afterward, so Wren decided to do a bit of exploring with the baby cuddled to her shoulder.

She talked cheerfully while she went.

She tried out the sofa and one of the wingback chairs in the parlor and determined that they were hideously uncomfortable. She quickly moved on to the framed photographs on the mantel and wall.

What she was really doing, she was embarrassed to realize, was looking for clues to the man who had taken her in and vowed to protect her, while guarding his own history and emotions so zealously. His great-aunt had lived here, then his mother, and now it was his house. Why *hadn't* he changed anything? Was there something about the room or what it represented that made him so uncomfortable he was unprepared to deal with it? Why would he stay in a house at all that he could barely stand to live in?

He won't know I'm wondering, she told herself. Looking at photos that were on open display wasn't the same as peering at his clothes in the closet, was it? How could she *not* wonder?

Central on the mantel was a silver-framed photograph of two women and a man gazing sternly at the camera. From the clothes, she thought it might have been taken in the thirties or forties. All three were dark-haired and clearly siblings, although one of the women was noticeably prettier than the other. Probably Edwina and poor Pearl, she decided.

The brother must be Alec's grandfather. On his mother's side, presumably, since Pearl had left the house to her. Wren was sure she could see a little of Alec in the shape of his face and the thick, dark hair. She moved on to pictures of the prettier sister with her husband and later with her children, and then reached a photo of Alec's grandfather when he was a few years older with a woman who must be his wife, holding a baby girl in her arms. Alec's mother?

The phone rang, making her jump. Abby's head bobbled, and Wren steadied it as she hurried to the kitchen to snatch up the receiver. "Hello?"

"It's Alec. You okay?"

She must have sounded breathless. "Sorry, I rushed for the phone. I did find some clothes to borrow, if that's why you're calling. I felt a little funny looking through their things, but—"

"Don't worry about it." He clearly didn't care. "Wren…"

Her heart thumped. Very carefully, she laid Abby in the car seat that still sat on the kitchen counter. "Yes?"

"The detective in Seattle got back to me. He can't find James."

"You mean he's not home?" That initial uncomfortable bump in her chest had turned into a rhythmic hammering. "I told you where he works. And…and he just might not be home…."

"Wren," Alec said again, his voice gentle, "he hasn't shown up for work since the morning after you left. The super let the detective into the apartment and Lontz says it looks like he hasn't been there since. Dishes were growing mold in the sink. Appears he left in a hurry."

"Oh, God," she whispered. "He did come after me."

"Yeah. I think we have to assume he did." He paused. "I'm sorry, honey."

"Me, too." She barely managed to squeeze the words out.

CHAPTER EIGHT

WREN CAREFULLY SET THE PHONE in its cradle, Alec's reminders and cautions ringing in her ears. Her desperate gaze fixed on her baby, so small and vulnerable, and she was suddenly breathless, reminded that nothing was the same. Love swelled in her chest until it hurt. Protecting Abby was all that mattered. And in that moment, the panic swirled and took on a new shape.

She would *not* let James hurt her baby. She'd kill him if she had to before she let him lay a hand on Abby. In some peripheral part of her mind Wren realized she was shaking, and not with fear this time. She was mad. So much outrage filled her, she couldn't contain it.

What right did he have to terrorize her? To threaten his own child? What kind of man was he?

"Scum, that's what he is." She paced the kitchen, wanting to kick something. Throw something. Hurt him the way he'd hurt her.

That so wasn't like her, but she let herself revel in images of herself committing violence. Right this second she would have given anything to take him on. He would be so sure she was still scared, that she'd cower and let him beat on her, but he was in for a big surprise. A gigantic surprise. It wasn't going to be that way anymore.

Was he here in Saddler's Mill? Had he already been to Molly's old house, or had floodwaters made it inaccessible? Alec would hear if James was asking questions about her locally, wouldn't he?

But wait—they'd figured out that there was a good chance James already knew where Molly had moved to, which meant he might have gone straight there. Wren's thoughts bumped to a stop. Except—he was so controlling, it would be like him to be confident he'd kept her from learning the new address. Which meant he'd be sure she had come here instead.

Probably. Oh, she wished she could warn Molly to watch out for him.

And she should have called her mom last night. That wasn't only cowardly, it was dumb. James might show up on her doorstep. He'd always been charming with Mom, but who knew now? What if he threatened her?

Agitated, she swung around and stalked the length of the kitchen again. *Tonight.*

Right now what she wanted to do was…

Was…

Wren found herself face-to-face with the refrigerator, which held a variety of take-out menus and some indecipherable scrawled notes with phone numbers in what she presumed was Alec's handwriting.

Stop, she told herself. Rewind.

Right now… Oh, Lord, her mind seemed to be a big blank. Which meant… There wasn't a single thing she could do.

Lots of adrenaline, and no way to burn it.

Bake, that's what she could do. She seized on the idea, because she absolutely had to do *something*. She couldn't sit and fret. She could nap later, when her fear and anger quit simmering. Take some ibuprofen now for the cramps. And then…

Cinnamon rolls. If she could find any cinnamon. She

bet Alec would like them. Cookies, although she hadn't noticed raisins or chocolate chips yesterday when she went through the cupboards. Maybe shortbread. Or... hadn't she seen a bottle of molasses?

Abby had fallen asleep sometime while Wren brooded and paced. As she stood looking at her, filled with that same, helpless love, Abby briefly scrunched her small nose as though something had tickled it, then relaxed again.

Wren almost carried her upstairs, then decided to keep her right here, where she could see her.

Wren started by preparing a meat loaf to go in the oven later, then washed her hands and began assembling ingredients for the cinnamon rolls. The selection of spices wasn't broad—she guessed Alec's mother wasn't an enthusiastic cook—but the basics were here.

The doorbell rang as she finished measuring white flour into the big, ceramic mixing bowl. Wren froze.

The door was locked.

He could break a window and be in faster than I can grab Abby and run.

A weapon. She needed a weapon.

Wren whirled and grabbed the marble rolling pin. Then, heart thudding, she slipped into the living room and edged up to the lace-covered window. Very carefully, she eased aside the lace and peeked out.

She couldn't quite see.... No, there. The person stepped back, and she was sure it was a woman.

A gasp of relief escaped her. Wryly she thought, *Didn't I decide I* wanted *to confront James?* She sighed. No, what she *wanted* was never to see him again. She looked down at the rolling pin in her hand.

I would have hurt him. If I had to.

She was at the door and undoing the dead bolt before

she'd thought through whether she actually wanted to meet Alec's sister. Which must mean she did.

When she swung the door open, she knew immediately that this was her. Sally? Wasn't that her name? She was four or five inches taller than Wren and had the same bright blue eyes and dark hair as her brother. The hair was bundled on top of her head, and she wore a bright pink sweater over a turtleneck and blue jeans. Permanent smile lines crinkled beside her eyes.

At her feet was a huge, cardboard box, and beside that was a white wicker bassinet on wheels.

"Hi," she said, her voice friendly, "I'm Sally Young."

"Alec's sister."

"None other." She looked past Wren. "I don't suppose my big brother's home."

It wasn't a question, which told Wren she already knew the answer.

"No, but you're welcome to come in. Can I offer you a cup of coffee?"

She beamed. "I'd love a cup. And, as you can see, I come bearing gifts."

"This is so nice of you." Wren wheeled the bassinet in while Sally scooted the box over the threshold. Her gaze turned quizzical when Wren closed the door behind them and carefully set both locks.

"I can tell you're not from around here."

"Alec made me promise."

"Oh, Alec." Sally rolled her eyes. "He sees the worst in everything."

"He spent half the day dealing with looters yesterday. So I guess he does see the worst."

His sister made a face. "Randy—he's my husband—did say looting was going on. So maybe Alec has a point."

Once they reached the kitchen, she oohed and aahed quietly over Abby while Wren made coffee.

"You're baking?"

"I have to do something," she explained. "And I thought it was one way of paying back Alec for being so nice and letting me stay here for a few days."

Sally grinned at her. "I'm dying of curiosity. I heard he had a woman staying here."

"It's not like that," she said awkwardly. "He really is just being nice. Did he tell you…?"

"Yes, but I wasn't sure I believed him. I mean, he spent days rescuing people, and he didn't bring any of them home."

Wren poured the coffee and carried the cups to the table. "I guess I was a little different. Because he delivered Abby, you know."

Sally's face softened with sympathy. "That must have been really scary."

"It was." Wren found herself telling the other woman about it, and hearing tales of Sally's own childbirth experiences.

"Three children," she said, in answer to Wren's question. "Randy was determined to have a boy. Thank goodness number three wasn't a girl, too, or I'd probably be pregnant again."

She said it laughingly, not as if she would have minded that much, and talked about how much she loved being a mother. Apparently Randy worked at the mill and money was often tight, but Sally didn't mind.

"Alec worries more than we do," she said with a shrug. "I don't know what he thinks Randy is supposed to do. Turn around and go to law school when he's thirty-five and already has a family? He does his best, and it's good enough for me. I'll get a job, too, when

Evan's old enough so we can start putting some money away for college if any of the kids want to go."

Wren cocked her head. "You're so different from him. I suppose being in law enforcement changed him."

Sally set down her cup, her face suddenly sober. "Oh, it's more than that. I was always happier, Alec the serious one. I think Daddy expected more of him, for one thing. And then he died when Alec was only fifteen. It was different for me. He missed Dad more, and he thought he had to take care of Mom and me. He did so much he shouldn't have had to do." There was something in her voice now that said maybe he hadn't always succeeded. But then she shook her head and laughed. "This house feels like a funeral parlor. Maybe it's got him feeling like an undertaker."

Wren couldn't help laughing. "It is sort of frozen in time. I wondered why he hasn't made the house more his."

"Alec's not so good at letting people go," his sister said, somewhat cryptically.

Wren was horribly tempted to ask about Alec's marriage and the two daughters who apparently didn't visit, but she knew she shouldn't. It wasn't any of her business.

It was probably just as well that Abby stirred then. Sally said with delight, "Oh, your cutie's waking up. Can I have a quick cuddle? Evan's about to turn two and ever since he learned to walk he's go, go, go. I miss having a baby."

She did hold Abby gently and tell her how pretty she was while insisting Wren go through the baby paraphernalia she'd brought. Wren was especially delighted with the denim sling designed for the mother to carry her baby close to her body while having her arms free, and the bright-colored mobile that would clip onto the hood of the bassinet.

As the nurse at the hospital had, Sally cut Wren's stuttered protests and thanks short. "I don't need any of it. I'll give it away to somebody, and it might as well be you. Alec said you had some clothes for her, but let me know if you need more."

Wren felt absurdly weepy by the time Sally made her excuses and left. Everybody was being so nice. Was it because this was a small town?

Between nursing and changing Abby's diaper and cuddling and talking to her, it was close to an hour before Wren was able to get back to her baking. She barely got the cinnamon rolls out of the oven before it was time to put the meat loaf in.

Alec looked tired when he came in the door, although Wren, who had come out of the kitchen at the sound of the key in the lock, saw him relax subtly at the sight of her. Or maybe it was at the smell of dinner cooking.

He inhaled. "I could get used to this." Following her into the kitchen, he glanced at Abby, who was sleeping in the bassinet, but his gaze barely touched her before zeroing in on the sink, where the cups sat unwashed. "Sally stopped by," he said with seeming resignation.

"Yes, and she brought lots of nice things for Abby. Not just the bassinet. I tried to tell her she didn't have to, but she wouldn't listen."

He snorted. "She's a busybody. The bassinet was her ticket in the door."

"She's your sister!"

He only grinned. "Yeah. Unfortunately."

Over dinner, Wren asked if he thought most people would rebuild.

She could see the worry on his face. "I don't know. No. Not everyone. There'll be some FEMA trailers for people to stay in for the immediate future, but… Hell. Some of the older folks are giving up. They lost too much. And what are people supposed to do who didn't carry flood insurance?"

"Won't the government offer low interest loans?" she asked tentatively.

"Sure." He sighed. "But what if you're already got a mortgage? Can you afford another loan? Most of the jobs here don't pay that well. I had to take a hell of a cut when I moved."

"Why did you? Because your sister's here?" She almost held her breath, waiting to see if he would answer.

For the longest time, he didn't. He took a bite of meat loaf and chased it with a swallow of orange juice. Finally, when she was about to give up and fill the silence with chatter to show she didn't care if he didn't want to share anything about himself, he said, "No. Mom was still alive. I moved in to help take care of her."

"I'm sorry," she said softly.

He looked at the bite of baked potato on his fork as if he didn't know what it was. "She had breast cancer. By the time they found it, it was too late."

"Oh, no." Wren touched his arm, then quickly drew her hand back. "No wonder…"

His eyes met hers. "No wonder?"

"Well…that you don't seem very happy in this house."

His mouth twisted. "That obvious, huh?"

She managed a smile, if a shaky one. "It sort of looks like you're camping out here."

"Yeah." He took the morsel from his fork, chewed

and swallowed. "It doesn't feel like anyplace I'd live. Mom hadn't changed much in the house—I guess you can tell that."

"Yes."

"Funny, too, because she'd been living here for—" he calculated "—most of ten years. Sally was still in high school when they came to live with Aunt Pearl. Her health was going downhill, and she needed someone. Mom was the closest to her of the nieces and nephews."

"I saw the picture on the mantel. Is that Pearl and her sister and your grandfather?" She waited anxiously to see whether he'd be annoyed at her interest. But they had to talk about something, didn't they?

He didn't seem to mind. "The one in the middle? Yeah. I never knew my grandfather. He was a policeman killed in the line of duty. My grandmother talked about him a lot. She never remarried. I suppose it was her stories that got me interested."

"Edwina was prettier than Pearl, wasn't she?"

"You noticed? *Grandad* was prettier than Pearl."

Wren giggled.

"She was a feisty old lady, though. We used to stay with her when I was a kid. Scared the daylights out of me. I was afraid if I so much as twitched I'd break something." He was smiling, remembering. "I'd sit in that parlor with my elbows squeezed to my sides so I didn't bump some ugly porcelain thing off a table, and then I'd start to drum my heels and Aunt Pearl would say, 'Doesn't that boy ever stay still?'"

The laughter felt good. So did having him open up this way, even if it wasn't about the hurtful parts of his life.

But then she noticed how far away his gaze seemed

and that his mood visibly changed. "If Mom had stayed in St. Louis, she might have gotten better medical care."

"You blame doctors here?"

"It's somebody's fault she didn't get regular check-ups." His voice held dark, deep, long-held anger. "Maybe if I'd been here sooner…"

"Your sister was here."

His gaze, bright and fierce, pinned hers. "She was busy raising her own family."

Weren't you? Wren wanted to say, but didn't dare. Because…where was his family? Why didn't he talk about his daughters?

Horror touched her. Oh, dear God. Had they *died?* Was that why he carried such sadness? Why they didn't visit and he couldn't stand to talk about them?

No, no. It couldn't be. That would be too awful. She couldn't bear to think of Alec having to survive anything like that. He'd taken his mother's death hard enough.

"Was it slow?" she heard herself ask. "Your mother, I mean?"

His eyes focused again. "She wasn't too bad until the last six weeks or so. That was hard." He shook himself. "We shouldn't be talking about things like that. Your dinner's too good to spoil."

Understanding that he'd told her all he wanted to, Wren said, "I made cinnamon rolls for dessert. I hope you like them."

"That's what I smelled." His smile was warm and barely shadowed at all. "Man, you're spoiling me."

"I'd go crazy with boredom if I couldn't find something to do." Although, it wasn't just boredom she was combating, was it? He'd told her he didn't expect pay-back, but she had to offer what she could. James had stolen enough of her pride; now she had to cling to what she had left.

"You're a reader, aren't you?" Alec asked. "I usually have some books out from the library, but I guess I don't have much right now."

He'd already said that the library was closed, but he promised to pick up some paperbacks and magazines for her tomorrow at the grocery store. He apologized for whatever selection he made, but said he wanted to keep her out of sight for now.

"Oh, by the way…" He'd set a bag on the table earlier, but now he grabbed it and held it out to her. "For you."

She peeked inside and was astonished to find a package of cotton bikini underwear and a simple white bra.

She was blushing. She knew she was. This wasn't the world's sexiest lingerie, but every time she put it on she'd remember Alec had picked it out. "Um… How did you know what size to buy?"

He cleared his throat. "I looked when your bra was hanging in the bathroom to dry. The underwear…" He shrugged. "I guessed. I, uh, saw some bras designed for nursing, but I couldn't find one in your size. I'm sorry."

"The bra is front-closing. It'll be perfect." Her smile wobbled. "Thank you. This is really great."

Abby woke and Wren took her upstairs to nurse, seizing the chance to stow her stash of new underwear in her bedroom. She felt self-conscious nursing in front of Alec. He had offered to carry the bassinet up, but she refused.

"I think I'd rather keep it down here so she's close during the day. I don't want to have to haul it around the house."

"Up to you."

He must have turned on the TV, because she heard the local news start up as she climbed the stairs. He was probably breathing a sigh of relief at having a few minutes to himself.

When Wren came down again, it was to find him still sitting at the table, the television off. She paused, unnoticed, in the doorway, wondering what he was thinking about and whether she should steal upstairs and leave him alone. All he was doing was sitting there, staring in front of him at something she couldn't see. While she watched, he made a rough sound and scrubbed a hand over his face.

That decided her, and she strolled into the kitchen as if she hadn't been hovering. "Headache?"

"What?" He immediately controlled his expression. "No. I thought I might have a cup of coffee and another one of your cinnamon rolls."

He insisted on getting his own, especially once she admitted that she didn't want any.

"I thought too much caffeine might not be good for Abby."

Alec nodded in that way he had of acknowledging whatever she'd said without expressing an opinion. It occurred to her that he never responded by saying, *Good idea to be careful. Carlene had a dinner that was too spicy, and...* Not when the subject was Abby.

"I, um, need to call my mom. But I was thinking." She paused. "I know you haven't done anything to the house, but... Well, is that because it upsets you to get rid of things, or have you just not gotten around to it?"

His eyes narrowed slightly. Was she getting too personal for him? But he said, "Strictly inertia. Why?"

She didn't totally believe him, but she wasn't suggesting a major remodeling project and he was the one to suggest she raid his mother's clothes. So she forged on.

"Unless you want to keep your mom's and your aunt Pearl's clothes and shoes and stuff, there must be an awful lot of people in the same boat as me. I mean, having nothing. And somebody could use those clothes."

"You're right. I can't believe I didn't think of it. I guess I've avoided going through Mom's stuff, but not because I wanted to keep her tennis shoes or her favorite sweatshirt. Of course I should take it all to one of the shelters."

"If you'd like, I could pack everything tomorrow," Wren offered, even though she was quailing in fear he'd think she was overstepping some invisible bounds. "Unless you think there might be something you'd want to keep."

Alec shook his head decisively. "No." He hesitated. "Wren, you just had a baby. You shouldn't be working."

"It's not work to fold clothes. I can mostly sit while I'm doing it."

He was still hesitating. She didn't move.

Then he let out a long breath. "Would you really do that?"

"I'd like to help. And I need to keep busy."

"Then thank you." His smile was warm. "I don't have any boxes around, but you can use garbage bags."

She nodded, thinking that if she'd been a puppy her tail would be whipping and she'd be piddling on the floor in relief and pleasure because he wanted her help, because he was smiling at her. And that made her mad at herself.

Mad at him, too, but none of this was his fault.

He was watching her, but she couldn't tell what he

was thinking. "Are you nervous about calling your mother?"

Oh, boy. She was all over the map emotionally. Letting go of one worry, Wren embraced another. She wrinkled her nose. "Dragging my feet. I feel like a kid going home to confess she threw a rock that shattered the neighbor's front window."

He had the world's best laugh. It made her tingle in places that she shouldn't, considering he didn't feel that way about her. And considering one of these days soon, she'd be leaving Saddler's Mill, and she'd never see Alec Harper again.

It was like teetering on the edge of an abyss. And knowing you were going into it.

The anxiety was enough to bring her to her feet. "I'm going to get it over with right now." She grabbed the phone without looking at him, but she could feel his gaze. Intense, caring, kind. That made her heart hurt.

Alec stood. "I need a shower. Unless you think it'll wake Abby?"

"Nothing wakes Abby except the growling of her own stomach."

With another of those laughs, he left the kitchen. She stood there, gripping the phone so hard she was surprised the plastic didn't crack.

Why had she been so stupid, getting involved with a man like James? Why hadn't she waited for someone like Alec?

Now, that really is stupid, a voice in her head said. *He wouldn't have looked at you twice.* This…this togetherness was all pretense. She couldn't forget that.

Wren suspected her mother had been surprised James was interested in her. Maybe that was one of the reasons she'd wasted so much time telling herself she was lucky, when she should have been heeding the huge, neon warning signs flashing in front of her eyes.

With a sigh, she sank onto one of the chairs and made herself dial.

Her mother answered right away.

"Hi, Mom. It's me."

"Wren, for heaven's sake. James called looking for you."

"That's because I left him, and I don't want him to find me."

"What?"

Wren told her…not everything, but near enough. Not about the ongoing humiliations and cruelty to which James had subjected her, but about the time he beat her until she was curled in a fetal position on the floor. About how he tried to kick her stomach.

"You never even told me you were pregnant."

"I should have. But things weren't very good with James and I hadn't decided what to do and…I guess I wanted to decide first."

"I have a granddaughter?"

"Yes. Abigail Alexa. She looks like me, not James." Wren heard the defiance in her voice. *No, she's not rosy pink with pretty blond hair, but I don't care.*

"He has some rights as a parent."

"He didn't want her. He wanted me to get an abortion."

"That might have been more sensible, under the circumstances." Her mother voiced the unforgivable.

Wren stiffened. "*I* wanted her. And I love her."

"Well…" There was an excrutiatingly long pause. "What's done is done." She took an audible breath. "So you're stranded in Arkansas, of all places?"

"I was looking for Molly," Wren explained again. "My college roommate, remember?"

"I thought I raised you to have more sense than to go off without even finding out whether she still lived there."

She *should* have had more sense, but Wren wouldn't have admitted it out loud under torture.

"I'm assuming you need money," Mom said briskly. "Of course I'll send you some. Are you desperate enough that I need to find out where to wire it? Or will the mail do?"

She wanted so much to say, *I don't need your money.* But she did, of course. Alec was already doing enough. So much for clinging to pride. Closing her eyes, she mumbled, "The mail will be fine. Thank you, Mom."

"Will a thousand do for now?"

A thousand dollars. Enough for Wren to buy an airline ticket if she needed to and still have enough left to get by for a while.

Wren would have traded it in a heartbeat for her mother to say, *Oh, sweetheart, I'm sorry. I love you.* But that wasn't Mom, and it never would be. Wren had given up hoping.

"Thank you," she said. "I'll pay you back when I can."

"Don't be silly. You know I can afford to help." That was closer to *I love you,* enough to bring a lump to Wren's throat.

"Mom… Please don't tell James where I am if he calls again. I'm scared of him. Please."

"All right," her mother said after a moment. "The decision is certainly yours."

Mom *had* raised her to be independent, to make her own decisions, which was something.

No, it was a whole lot. Just…not enough.

"He hasn't phoned again," Mom said.

"Do you remember when he called?"

"It's been a week. When did you leave him?"

They decided he'd contacted her the same evening Wren left. She would have been at the cheap motel by the airport in St. Louis by then. She passed along Alec's address then asked about her mother's work. Finally, she thanked her again and hung up the phone. Her mind immediately turned to what her mother had said, and, maybe even more importantly, her own reactions.

She felt light-headed. *That's why I stayed with him.* The realization had the force of an epiphany. *Not because I was too dumb to notice what was happening, but because I didn't believe in myself enough to know I deserved better.*

"You okay?"

With a start, she swung to see that Alec had entered without her noticing. He was so big and strong, she wanted desperately to lean against him and hang on.

But, of course, she was already doing too much leaning.

"Fine," she said brightly, without meaning it. "Mom's sending some money."

"Did she want you to come home?"

She doubted that had even crossed her mother's mind. "No." She cleared her throat. "She didn't suggest it." Her life must seem so pathetic to him.

He was frowning slightly. "Good. I was afraid she'd try to talk you into it."

"No. She did say James called looking for me the day I left. She hasn't heard from him since."

"So he hasn't come knocking on her door."

"I think he's here," Wren said, in a small, tight voice.

"Yeah. I do, too."

He stepped toward her, but on a flare of anguish she stepped back.

"I think I'll go to bed. I've got to sleep while Abby does, you know."

There was a brief pause. "Go on," he said, sounding gentle in that way he had. Tender, even, although that was probably her own wishful thinking. "Sleep tight."

She stood very still for a moment, wondering if he'd intended to take her into his arms. Hold her tight, comfort her. Part of her wanted that, yearned for it. The more sensible part—and, mostly, she *was* sensible, because she'd been raised to be that, too—knew it was better if she didn't let Alec hold her, because that would only make leaving harder.

"Good night," she said, and left him. Alone, as he'd been before she came, and would be again after she was gone.

CHAPTER NINE

"YOU DEFINITELY SPOKE to your brother?"

"Yes." The young woman's face was flushed with relief. She'd been lying curled on her side staring into space when Alec reached her cot in the shelter. "I was so scared. But it turned out he'd driven all the way to Beebe and couldn't get back after the flood. Neither Mama nor I have a cell phone, but he finally reached a neighbor."

Alec smiled. "Good. I'll cross him off our list of potentially missing persons."

He moved on to the next cot and asked the same questions. He checked the names of individuals here in the shelter as well as the names of family members against the list of missing persons. He asked about neighbors and close friends, as well. By the time he had made his way through the shelter set up in the community room of the First Baptist Church, he'd drawn a decisive line through four names on the list.

Unfortunately, he'd added two more names with question marks.

The lists were slowly shrinking. Each night volunteers correlated them. People were popping up all over the county, or, as with Ginny Griffith's brother Judd, had been out of the reach of the flood entirely.

Alec had yet to identify any of the three bodies in the morgue, however. He wasn't looking forward to having to bring family members to view the remains in hopes of identifying them.

Alec could see his breath when he walked out of the church. The clearing weather had brought a cold snap that was increasing the misery of people who were still inadequately housed. He turned up the heat in his Tahoe and sat waiting for the engine to warm up. Dogged all day by a headache, he wasn't in the best of moods.

He swore Abby had woken every hour and a half all night long. He wasn't even the one who had to get up with her, but his eyes would snap open and he'd lie there tense until the soft sounds across the hall told him Wren was lifting her unhappy daughter from the well-padded drawer that was serving as makeshift crib and talking to her. Then he'd start wondering if she was nursing, and if so whether she simply bared her breasts when she was alone in the night. Was she rocking Abby in the walnut rocker that had been in Great-Aunt Pearl's room as long as he could remember? Or did she take the baby into bed with her, and lie on her side smiling sleepily at her suckling daughter?

The worst part for him was wishing he was in that bed with them, helping position Abby and guide her mouth to her mommy's nipple the way he had in the attic. Staring into the dark, he'd remember the mixture of tenderness and lust he had felt then until his body hardened and sleep retreated beyond hope of him achieving it.

Oh, he'd slept eventually—for half an hour, an hour, when the baby's cries had startled him awake again to start the cycle.

He didn't think he'd ever been so tired in his life, and that was saying a lot, given the grueling week he'd lived through. Frequently interrupted sleep was more torturous than no sleep at all, as far as he was concerned.

When he'd asked Wren this morning if she thought Abby was getting sick, she'd shaken her head. She looked exhausted herself.

"She's not warm, and she settled fine every time I picked her up. I don't know why she was so restless. If she gets feverish or anything today, though, I have the number of the pediatrician who saw her at the hospital."

"You shouldn't have gotten up for me," he told her, but she ignored him and flipped the pancakes.

She'd been quiet this morning. Actually, it had started after she spoke to her mother. Wren liked to talk, but he hadn't been able to get anything more from her beyond the basics. Her mother hadn't suggested she come home. James had called. She was sending money.

He couldn't tell if Wren was disappointed, hurt, indifferent. He knew she hadn't raised her voice when she was on the phone—he would have heard that—so they must not have argued. All he knew was that Wren had retreated inside herself. Not so obviously that he could press her for answers, but the blank way she looked at him reminded him of how she'd been when he cut her off so sharply because she was asking questions about his girls he hadn't wanted to answer.

He guessed her mother had hurt her.

None of his business. Wren had already made it clear that she and her mother didn't have a close relationship. She was an adult who must have mostly come to terms with it. Maybe it had gotten to her last night because of her circumstances. Most of the flood victims he was seeing had family they could turn to. Despite having a mother, Wren was as alone as anyone he'd ever met. Alone except for a newborn, utterly dependent on her.

And him.

Panic moved in his chest at the thought. He'd shut down these past months, told himself he was done with the kind of involvement that meant someone depended on him long-term. He couldn't do it again. He simply couldn't.

Find her friend Molly.

Yeah, in his spare time.

His cell phone rang and he reached for it instantly, his heartbeat quickening. What if Abby *was* sick? But the number was his sergeant's, not his own home phone.

"Harper," he said.

"Where are you?" Pruitt asked.

"Just leaving First Baptist. Why?"

"I've got Colt Burgoyne here. His father's been missing since day one."

Alec reached for his clipboard and saw the name immediately. Donald Burgoyne.

"They got word his pickup's been found. Empty. Colt says his father set out for the feed store. He was sure he could get there and back before any flooding."

"And he didn't make it."

"His father's fifty-six years old. Brown hair, some arthritis in his hands. He was wearing a camouflage jacket, carpenters pants, lace-up work boots."

"Oh, hell," Alec said softly. There wasn't much doubt that one of the bodies in the morgue was Donald Burgoyne. "Can you ask Colt to meet me at the hospital? He'll have to make a positive ID."

"I'll send him. Damn," his sergeant said. "I've known Donald most of my life. I was hoping—"

"I'm sorry."

Alec met the son at the hospital and remained present when Elijah Bailey pulled out the sliding steel drawer and folded back the sheet to expose the face.

The stocky farmer, about Alec's own age, recoiled, swallowed, swallowed again and said in a stifled voice, "That's him."

"You're certain?" Dr. Bailey asked. "Let me show you the mark on his shoulder—"

"It's a birthmark." Colt retreated a step. His unwilling gaze stayed on his father even as his Adam's apple bobbed a couple of more times.

Alec gripped his shoulder and led him away. "Let's go sit down."

Colt stumbled, his head turned to allow him to keep staring. Not until the drawer slid closed did he dash at his wet eyes and follow Alec from the room.

"If he wasn't so damn stubborn. We had enough feed to hold out, but he wouldn't listen. Never would."

Hell of an epitaph, Alec thought, letting Colt talk about his father. A good man, but rigid.

"My Kylie softened him some." Colt's eyes focused briefly on Alec, as if he'd remembered he had a listener. "Kylie's my wife. And we've got a little boy, too, Damien. Light of my father's life."

He wept some, then finally pulled himself together enough to sign the necessary papers and leave with the promise that he'd have the body transferred to the funeral home today if possible.

One down, two to go, Alec thought wearily.

He was still in the hospital basement when his phone rang again.

"Are you avoiding me?" his sister demanded the minute he answered.

"I'm a little busy."

"Too busy to stop by for five minutes?" Her voice

held a sting—anger and the potential for tears, neither of which he believed in, neither of which he could ignore. "We were scared to death when you went missing."

He knew exactly what she was trying to do and wouldn't have had any problem resisting if he hadn't had to watch Colt mourn his father. Alec sighed and looked at his watch.

"Wren will have dinner on. But I can come by now."

"Fine," Sally snapped, then hung up.

Swearing, Alec drove to his sister's place, which irked him every time he saw it. As much as he loved Sally and his two nieces and nephew, he didn't like to come here.

The house didn't have a foundation—it sat on concrete blocks. The couple of steps to the front door lacked a handrail. Paint peeled, a new roof was ten years overdue—or tearing down the whole place was ten years overdue, depending on your point of view. The yard had been nice—Sally was a gardener. The huge vegetable garden out back would have been fallow, so it would be less painful to look out, but the lawn and flower beds were under a thick sludge. Not much had been done to remove it. The handlebars and front tire of one of the girls' bikes showed above the crusted top of the mud.

Angry, he parked on the street and stomped up the walkway—which had been shoveled although more mud had oozed onto the cracked concrete—to the door.

Sally came to the door with Evan ensconced on her hip. His sister had been an exceptionally pretty woman with dark hair and blue eyes like his, white skin and a leggy, curvaceous body that had boys panting after her from fifth grade on. She was still good-looking, but three children had thickened her waist, her hands looked ten years older than she did, and he couldn't remember the last time he'd seen her wear makeup or do anything fancier than put her hair in a ponytail.

She met his glower with a grin. "Nice to see you, too."

"This place looks like hell."

"Not any different from the neighbors'."

Most of the houses on the street were run-down. Some were rentals, some were owned by young families scrabbling for economic survival.

He'd offered Sally and Randy Great-Aunt Pearl's house after Mom died. He still couldn't believe they'd said no.

"Una Alec." His two-year-old nephew beamed and stretched chubby arms to him.

"Hey, Ev." Alec reached for him and Sally let go. Evan wrapped his arms around Alec's neck and, carrying him, Alec followed his sister inside. He did his best to ignore the familiar stab of pain he felt at seeing his sister's kids. "Thanks for the baby stuff. It's been a big help."

"There was nothing I'll need again." Sally took Evan and set him on the floor. "Listen, Maribeth just put *The Little Mermaid* in. Do you want to watch it?"

He trundled off to join his sisters in the small living room. Alec might have followed to say hi to his nieces, except Sally planted her hands on her hips and said, "Okay, why do you have a stick up your butt today?"

"Where the hell is Randy?"

Her expression hardened. "Helping out friends who are worse off than we are. Which is exactly what he should be doing."

Thinking of that dumb-ass grin and the beer can

casually snatched out of the air, Alec unclenched his teeth. "Ever occur to him to put his own family first?"

"Have you heard me complain? Even once? Maybe we don't have the standard of living you think we should, but we own our own home, we have enough to eat and we've got three great kids. Randy holds a job and brings home a paycheck, he makes me laugh and he's good with his children." Her voice had been rising as she went. By the end she was yelling. "So you tell me. What's so wrong with him?"

"He's a loser, that's what!" Alec yelled back. "He's lazy and self-centered. Open your eyes, Sally."

"Mama?"

Both adults swung toward the kitchen doorway. Six-year-old Maribeth stood there, eyes alarmed.

"Why are you mad, Mama?"

Sally's gaze skewered Alec, then she smiled at her daughter and said, "For the same reason you get mad at Amanda and Evan. Because Uncle Alec is my brother and sometimes he's such a jerk I can't believe it."

The little girl's expression was still anxious, but her body language loosened. "Do you ever want to hit him, the way I wish I could hit 'Manda sometimes?"

"Frequently," her mother assured her. "But he's bigger than me, so I have to yell at him instead."

She was rewarded by a tiny giggle.

Alec went over, swooped up Maribeth and smacked a kiss on her cheek. "Ignore us, Maribeth Wonder. I'm a policeman, which means I have to be polite even to sleazebags. When I can't be nice even for another minute, I come see your mom."

She giggled some more, went for a reassuring hug from her mother, then returned to the living room and the movie. Sally and Alec were left staring at each other.

"You could have done better," Alec said flatly.

"Oh, get out of here. I don't even know why I wanted to see you."

He found a smile creeping onto his mouth despite everything. "Because you love me?" He took a step closer to her.

She snorted. "Yes, but why? That's the part I can't figure out."

"I'm a good guy."

Her eyes were softer, but her mouth twisted. "So is Randy."

He opened his mouth, but after a moment closed it.

"Smart," she murmured, when he only leaned forward to kiss her cheek.

"Of course I am." He managed a grin, and left.

"YOUR RENTAL CAR got towed into town today," Alec told Wren the next day. He called at least a couple of times every day. Sometimes he actually had news. Mostly, she thought he was checking up on her, which caused an uneasy mix of emotions in her.

She *liked* that he wanted to be sure she was okay. It was so Alec, a part of his protective nature. She really, really liked talking to him.

But Wren couldn't help remembering that James, too, had called her several times a day. At first she'd been flattered, thinking he missed her. Wasn't it sweet that he wanted to know what she was up to? Eventually she'd realized it wasn't sweet at all. He timed his calls randomly. If she didn't answer the phone and produce answers to his questions that pleased him, he'd get ominously quiet and later come home sullen. He didn't want her going out, doing anything she hadn't cleared in advance with him. That was part of what made escaping at the end so hard. What if he raced home because she hadn't answered the phone, and he caught her before she could get away?

Alec's calls were different. Wren knew they were. But then she wondered if he thought she was so incompetent, so incapable of taking care of herself and Abby, that he *had* to check constantly to make sure she was all right?

She gusted a sigh she hoped he didn't hear. He probably didn't think any such thing. *She* was one thinking it.

At least this was one of those calls when he actually did have some news.

"I don't suppose the rental company will be happy about the condition I'm returning it in."

"That's safe to say." There was a smile in his voice.

"Should I call to let them know the car has shown up?"

"Already done. The insurance adjuster will take a look. It'll be totaled."

She didn't like thinking about the car. About squeezing out the window and being pressed against the door by the powerful current. After a moment, she asked, "Nobody's found my suitcase or my purse?"

"God only knows where they ended up. Can't imagine either stayed intact. One good thump, and the suitcase would've popped open."

Wren cringed, picturing her underwear embedded in the sludge in someone's yard.

"Did you drop off the clothes I packed up?"

"Yes, and the shelter workers were thrilled. Thank you, Wren."

"My pleasure," she told him, and meant it. She'd been glad to spend part of yesterday going through his mother's and Pearl's things, placing them in black plastic bags. The part she'd liked best was how cleansing her efforts had felt. That was a good word, she decided. Alec's closet and bedroom looked like they might actually belong to him now. She'd spread out his suits and shirts on the rod a little, so they weren't squeezed at one end like a shy kid at a birthday party who knew no one wanted him there. It couldn't possibly have been healthy for him to have to see his mother's shoes and clothes every time he reached for his own. Even if he hadn't felt emotionally ready to sort through her possessions, she thought he would have at least packed them into boxes so he didn't have to look at them.

Face it: what she'd liked was feeling that she'd done something worthwhile for him.

She wondered what he'd say if she suggested he think about tackling the living room the same way. He couldn't possibly *like* Pearl's porcelain dust-collectors. Wren thought some of the figurines might be worth selling on eBay, if Alec wanted to go to that much trouble. Or he could donate them to a nonprofit and let them do the work while he took a tax write-off.

She itched to rearrange the furniture in there, too. Maybe move the TV out of the kitchen. The fireplace in the living room was nice. It could be a comfortable room with a little work.

But she'd kept her mouth shut and would keep on doing so. She was a very temporary guest here, and how Alec lived was none of her business.

Even if she wished that wasn't true.

"I've got a pot roast in," she told him brightly.

"Damn it, Wren," he snapped. A moment of silence

followed, and when he continued she could tell he'd made an effort to soften his voice. "Take a day off if you feel like it. I'm not used to being taken care of."

As if he'd punched her, she couldn't breathe. He didn't want her cooking for him?

She strove for dignity. "If you'd rather not come home for dinner, you don't have to. I have to cook for myself anyway."

"I didn't mean it that way." He sounded gruff. Impatient, or something else? She couldn't tell. "I don't like you feeling you have to try so hard."

She hurt. Really hurt. She'd been so glad she could do something to make him happy. It wasn't hard to see that emotion came as a surprise to him, just as smiles had seemed to the first days they spent together. Now to find that she hadn't been making him happy at all...

"I was trying to contribute. Maybe I need you, Alec, but I'm not useless." Wren didn't wait for a response. She hung up the phone, shaking all over at her temerity.

Was something wrong with her, that she tried so hard to please the men in her life? Was she reenacting the whole James thing?

Okay, yes, she'd had dinner ready when he walked in the door from work, too, but she liked cooking. And, yes, of course she'd been trying to please him in those days. She'd convinced herself she was in love with him.

That was where she'd gone wrong. Hugely wrong. She'd missed a million clues that should have warned her how controlling he was.

This was different, what she felt for Alec. It was normal and human to like to do nice things for someone. Especially if you happened to be falling in love with that someone else.

Even if that someone was doing his level best to help her so that she could depart from his life as speedily as possible.

Her shoulders sagged. That was what she had to accept: Alec had insisted she come home with him out of a feeling of obligation. And what had she done but insist on playing wifey? The last thing he wanted from her. Look at her, leaping out of bed in the morning to cook him breakfast. Dumb, dumb, dumb.

The phone rang, and she ignored it. Who else would it be but Alec, and she didn't want to talk to him again. Not right now.

Shame burned through her, but anger rose in its wake. Okay, she was falling in love with him, but even if she hadn't been, she would have tried to be helpful. To make his life easier while she was here. Because he was helping her, and it was only fair that she did what she could in return.

Bristling, she decided that if he didn't like it, that was his problem, not hers. He didn't have to eat the meals she put on the table.

The phone quit ringing, but before she could quite get a grip on her turbulent emotions, the doorbell rang. Wren jumped six inches and looked for the rolling pin, spotting it on the counter. But she didn't feel the same panic she had the other day. It was mildly astonishing to find she wasn't scared of James in quite the same way. Maybe a person could only feel so much at one time. Leaving Abby sleeping in the bassinet, she went to the living room window and twitched the lace curtain to one side to see who stood on the doorstep.

It was Alec's sister, only this time she had three kids with her, the smallest anchored on her hip.

Somehow Wren summoned a smile by the time she

opened the door. "Sally. Oh, my. This must be… Let's see. Maribeth, Amanda and Evan."

The tallest, a solemn-faced girl with her mother's and uncle's blue eyes and dark hair, stared at her. "How'd you know who we are?"

"Because your uncle Alec talks about you. Your mom did, too." She stepped back. "Come in."

The middle child, chubbier and with brown hair tinted with red, veered immediately toward the living room.

"No, no, no." Her mother snatched for her hand. "You know you're not allowed in there."

"It's definitely not childproofed," Wren agreed.

"It isn't even grown-up-proofed," Sally muttered.

Wren giggled, glad to discover she felt better. Her indignation at Alec still burned bright, but the shame he'd made her feel had subsided.

"That's what Alec said. He remembers sitting in there with his elbows pressed to his sides, terrified he'd break something."

Sally laughed, too. "Great-Aunt Pearl would glower at us. *She* was sure we'd break something. Of course, it never occurred to her to put the fragile stuff away while we were staying with her. I'm pretty sure she flat-out didn't like kids."

"If you don't have any yourself, they probably start seeming like an alien species."

"Maybe." Sally smiled at her. "I hope you don't mind us dropping in. I thought you might like company, and with it so chilly I suspected you wouldn't want to take Abby out."

"No." Obviously Alec hadn't told her the real story.

With all the hubbub, Abby woke up. The other kids were briefly fascinated by her, and she stared at them, her gaze already sharper than it had been a few days ago. She seemed to find Evan, a redhead, especially entrancing.

Sally produced a video—*The Little Mermaid,* to which Maribeth was currently addicted. With rolled eyes, Sally said, "She watches it every day. I wake up in the middle of the night thinking I hear the music, and realize I was dreaming. Randy's taken to singing it to me just to be mean."

It felt so good to have something to laugh about. Feeling cheerful, Wren produced the cookies she'd baked that morning—of course she had, little Miss Susie Homemaker—and poured all three children glasses of milk. Sally had brought Evan's spill-proof plastic glass.

I'll hide the cookies, she decided. *To heck with Alec. He doesn't even have to know I baked them.*

Then she and Sally retired to the living room, where Wren nursed Abby while they talked.

"Alec wanted Randy and me to take this house after Mom died." Sally was looking around her incredulously. "Can you imagine?"

"Don't you already own a house?"

"Yes, but it's smaller than this. One story, though— I hated the idea of the stairs. Besides..." She hesitated. "It was a macho thing. Alec doesn't think Randy takes good enough care of us."

"He hasn't said anything. Not that he would to me." Wren hesitated. "I don't get the feeling he actually likes this house, though. Maybe he really didn't want it."

"Well, then why doesn't he sell it?" Sally asked in exasperation.

"I don't know." Wren couldn't exactly ask about the provisions of their mother's will. Surely the woman hadn't left her entire estate to Alec and cut Sally out. No—if his mother had done that, Wren knew Alec would have sold the house in a heartbeat so he could split the money with Sally.

"He's really mixed up about Mom." Frowning, Sally seemed to be focused on the parade of framed photographs on the mantel. "He blames himself that she died, you know."

"Himself?" Wren shifted Abby to her other breast. "How can he possibly? He said it was cancer."

"Yes, but he seems to think that if he'd moved here from St. Louis sooner, he would have made sure Mom got more regular checkups." Sally snorted. "She'd have blown her top if he'd tried organizing her that way."

"Then why—"

"I don't totally know." She sighed. "You probably don't care about our family problems. I shouldn't have gotten started, except... I worry about Alec. And there's something in the way he talks about you."

"I think you're imagining that." Wren lifted Abby to her shoulder and patted her back. "He really is only being nice." *He wants me gone.*

"He's different since you came."

"What he is, is sleep-deprived. Abby wouldn't stay asleep last night no matter what I did."

Sally accepted the diversion and they chatted about babies. Wren was grateful for the advice on diaper rash, teething and more. It was the kind of information that, in another family, a mother would pass on to her daughter.

Mom, Wren thought with an inward sigh, *will be full of advice on how I can make sure Abby gets the best teachers once she starts school.* Her mother had taken pride in selecting Wren's teachers. No random assignments for her daughter.

Parental love of a sort, Wren supposed.

Sally eventually gathered her children and departed. Maribeth was still complaining as they walked down the driveway. "But Mom, we weren't done with the movie."

The last thing Wren heard was Sally saying, "It's not like you don't know how it ends."

Laughing, Wren locked the door.

CHAPTER TEN

ALEC FELT CAUTIOUS when he let himself in the door and walked into the kitchen. Wren was there, but didn't even turn at the sound of his footstep.

"That smells good," he said.

He'd been a jackass earlier. He knew he had. The truth was, he loved coming home to dinner cooking. To Wren. He loved starting the day and ending it with her. And that scared the crap out of him.

Today he'd been glad to have an excuse to call her. So glad, he'd felt unsettled. Then when she said the pot roast was already cooking... He didn't know what had happened.

He was lucky she hadn't dumped it in the garbage and left him to prepare a frozen dinner.

Any other woman would at least have given him an icy look. Wren only sounded a little stiff as she said, "If you'd rather eat out with a friend or make yourself something else, my feelings won't be hurt."

"No." He laid the newspaper on the counter, aware that she hadn't met his eyes. "I was a jerk today. What I was trying to say was that I don't want you feeling obligated to wait on me hand and foot."

She cast him a look of near dislike. "What am I sup-posed to do all day, Alec? Take Abby in the stroller for long walks and wave at the neighbors while I'm out?

Lounge on Pearl's rock-hard sofa and eat bonbons?"
Sotto voce, she added, "Whatever bonbons are."

That was his Wren, finding humor even when she
had good reason to be grouchy.

"No," he said meekly. "I know you have to fill your
day somehow. You must be feeling trapped."

She sighed. "No, mostly I'm fine. But—" her gaze
slid sidelong to him "—I guess I'm making you feel
trapped, and I didn't mean to. Having us here has probably totally changed your life. I'm sorry."

"No," Alec said again, then grimaced. Why not be
honest? "Or maybe I should say yes. For the better. I
came home every day and made myself dinner, usually
in the microwave. I watched the news, I read, I went to
bed. You haven't gotten in the way of anything." Except
sleep, he thought, and belatedly cast a suspicious eye on
Abby, contentedly asleep in her bassinet. "Please tell
me you didn't let her sleep all day."

He was embarrassingly grateful for Wren's sudden
grin. "No, I tortured her into staying awake as much
as I could. But I thought it would be nice if we had a
peaceful meal."

"Yeah." He sighed. "Anything I can do?"

"Nope."

She sounded natural enough now that he guessed
he'd been forgiven. Another thing about Wren was that
she didn't hold grudges. She seemed to have a gift for
shaking off all the crappy things that had happened to
her and moving on with an optimism that might be un-
realistic, but which he couldn't help admiring.

Alec hid his amusement at her getup—a pair of
pants that must have been Great-Aunt Pearl's and a
baggy sweatshirt with a cute kitten cavorting in some
daisies on the front. He doubted Wren had worn any-

thing like that since she was about five years old. Her
feet were bare.

After a second, he quit noticing the clothes and
began picturing Wren without them. He was doing
that entirely too often, but couldn't seem to stop himself. She was so fine-boned, and he loved the way she
moved, like the dancer she'd once dreamed of becoming. She was long-legged for her height. He knew how
shapely those legs were, although he hadn't been con-
sciously noticing at the time. Funny how accurate his
memory was anyway. He remembered the slender line
of her back, too, and the feel of it under his hands, her
moans of pleasure when he found vulnerable spots and
kneaded them.

He suppressed a groan and, when she turned toward
the table carrying a serving dish, he sat quickly to hide
his all-too obvious reaction to thoughts he should have
shut down sooner.

Once she had the food on the table, she sat, too,
and they began to eat. "Your sister brought her kids by
today," she said.

Glad to be distracted from his increasingly erotic
thoughts, he raised his eyebrows. "Did she?" Now why
hadn't Sally mentioned that to him?

Wren apparently caught something in his tone, because she looked wary. "Would you rather she didn't?"

"I don't trust her," he muttered.

"Um…in a scary way, or a she's-going-to-reveal-all-
your-deepest-darkest-secrets way?"

"Deepest, darkest secrets," he admitted. "So why'd
she come?"

"To be friendly." Wren appeared to think about it. "I
think."

"Was she nosy?"

"No." Her forehead crinkled and she poked her lower lip out. "Mostly we talked about babies."

"Babies?"

"Yeah. Diaper rash, sleep patterns, teething. That kind of stuff."

"Sounds riveting."

"Sleep patterns are a subject of enormous interest to me right now, I have to tell you," she said, with dignity.

He gave a short laugh. "Okay, you've got a point."

"She said you offered this house to her and Randy after your mom died."

Now, why in hell would Sally talk about something like that to a woman she'd barely met? He didn't like knowing he'd been the topic of their conversation.

He sounded short to his own ears when he said, "I did."

But Wren apparently didn't notice. "Weren't you already living here? I mean, with your mother?"

"Yeah."

"When I was packing up her clothes, I was wondering why you were in her bedroom and not one of the others."

That, thank God, was an innocuous enough question. "By the time I came, Mom was sleeping down here, in what used to be Aunt Pearl's sewing room." Wren nodded; presumably she'd noticed the small, currently unused room. "We had to rent a hospital bed. I slept in Mom's room because—" He hesitated. "I don't know. Sleeping in Aunt Pearl's bed felt too weird."

He loved Wren's smile. She always seemed to understand whatever he tried to explain, however clumsily he did it. Maybe that's why he kept telling her things he hadn't meant to.

Wanting to keep her smiling, he said, "I don't know

if you've checked out the other two bedrooms. One of them was Sally's, believe it or not. I don't know how she stood it. The mattresses in both rooms have to date from the 1920s. Don't laugh," he said severely. "Try one."

Still giggling, she said, "I'll do that."

As he took a bite, Alec had the brooding realization of exactly how much he was going to miss Wren. Her giggles and her smiles warmed him deep inside, where he'd been cold for a long time.

He frowned. What an idiotic thing to think.

"It's a big house," he said after a minute. "Bigger than I need. Sally and her brood live in a rambler about one step up from being a shack. It seemed to make sense."

He could hear the angry edge in his voice. Wren watched him, her brown eyes grave.

"Sally's husband works at the mill. It's on again, off again. It never seems to occur to him to pick up any other work."

"*Is* there other work around here?"

"Not much," he had to admit.

"What does he do? Just sit around?"

"No." Being fair almost killed him, but Alec wasn't going to lie. "He's handy. Seems like every spare minute he's helping out some friend or other. Rebuilding an engine, adding another bedroom, caulking a boat. God forbid he add on a bedroom to *his* house. Or paint it. Or do a damn thing to make Sally's life easier."

"She seems to love him."

It bothered Alec that Wren sounded tentative, as if she was unsure how he'd react if she argued with him. He didn't like thinking he reminded her in any way of Abby's son-of-a-bitch father.

Disturbed by the awareness that how she saw him mattered, he pulled his mind to his sister and her husband. "I guess she does."

"Have you spent much time with him?"

"I've tried not to."

She opened her mouth, hesitated, then closed it.

"What were you going to say?" Alec asked. Whether he wanted to hear it or not, Wren shouldn't feel she had to stifle her opinions around him.

"Um…maybe you should spend time with him. And I know it isn't any of my business," she added hastily. "But it might help if you got to know him better."

He was silent. Sally had said the same. Alec's mother had said it, too. Implied he wasn't being fair. And maybe he wasn't, loath though he was to admit it. He'd been in a holding pattern these past eight months, since burying his mother. He'd done his best not to relate to anybody except on the most superficial levels. Even Sally. He didn't want to feel more than he could help.

"I suppose eventually I'll sell the place," he heard himself saying. "Hell, this might be a good time to do it. There'll be people who want to stay in town but would rather not rebuild, especially if this isn't the first time they've been flooded."

"But…where would you go?"

"I don't know." The idea bothered him, which might be why he hadn't started prepping the house to put on the market. "Something smaller, I guess."

"Yes, but…" Her forehead puckered again. "This house represents your family history, doesn't it?"

"I can't say most of the memories I have of it are all that good."

"I suppose not. Don't your kids come stay?"

He tried not to react. He didn't want to talk about

India and Autumn, but there wasn't any reason to shut down Wren the way he had the other time she asked about them. He'd shared plenty about himself with her, but this was different. You didn't tell a woman about your marriage, your children, unless you were becoming intimate in a way he'd sworn he never would again. Yet he had to answer her.

"They live too far away."

He knew right away he'd been too terse. Her expression closed.

"Oh, dear," she said, sounding, despite the words, relieved that Abby was waking up.

His cue to rise and take his plate to the sink. Just as well the baby had interrupted before he'd felt compelled to keep talking. Carlene had always accused him of being closemouthed, but he found it all too easy to spill his guts to Wren.

One more danger sign.

ONCE HE HAD IT in his head, Alec couldn't quit mulling over whether he ought to sell the damn house. What he couldn't understand was why he even hesitated.

Maybe it *was* the family history thing that stopped him. Alec's grandfather, as well as great-aunts Pearl and Edwina, had been born in this house. Had grown up here in Saddler's Mill. Pearl had spent her entire life here, sleeping virtually every night of it in that room upstairs where Wren now stayed. Alec found himself wondering whether his mother and Great-Aunt Pearl had ever talked about the future. Obviously, Mom hadn't considered selling, perhaps in part because Sally and her kids were here. Then, in her will, she'd left him the house. He still struggled with that. She'd left investments she considered to be equal in value to Sally, but the house to him. It sometimes felt more like a burden than a gift. What sense did it make to leave a four-bedroom house to a divorced man who didn't even see his kids every other weekend? What did he need with a house this size? It felt like a mockery to him, living in it.

Of course, Great-Aunt Pearl had rattled around in this house all by herself for thirty or forty years, after her parents had passed on. He wondered if *she'd* ever thought about moving, whether living in a house designed for a family felt wrong to her, too.

Prowling the internet at his desk the next day, he found his mind split, like a computer screen with two programs running. One was conducting the continuing search for Molly or Samuel Rothenberg. He made notes on the Rothenbergs that popped up, even as he kept thinking about Great-Aunt Pearl. His childish self had felt so uncomfortable in her house, so hemmed in by her fussy collectibles and lace doilies, he wasn't sure he had ever relaxed enough to see her as a human being.

From this distance, it was easier to realize that she must have had dreams and regrets like everyone did. Maybe seeing other people's children had given her a bitter taste, considering she'd never had the chance to have her own. If so, he and Pearl had something in common, didn't they? It was a nice irony that he was now living in her house, a hermit as sour as she could ever have been. He'd had the family, and lost it. She'd never had one at all. But they had both suffered from the same cause: they were alone.

He thought maybe she'd tried to be nice sometimes. She'd baked awfully good chocolate-chip cookies when Alec and Sally were staying with her. And made lemonade from real lemons, instead of concentrate, a novel concept to them. Maybe she'd made those cookies especially for her great-niece and great-nephew. If so, he hoped she'd known how much he liked them.

His attention abruptly focused on the computer monitor, where Samuel Joseph Rothenberg, resident of Gainesville, Florida, had popped up. It appeared he was a State Farm Insurance agent. A few minutes later, Florida State DMV records confirmed that a Molly Elizabeth Rothenberg held a driver's license and was listed at the same address.

Bingo.

Wren was going to be thrilled. Alec sat unmoving for a long moment, still staring at the monitor.

Damn it. Why wasn't he happy to have good news for her?

Why did he feel something more like panic?

Finally he took careful note of the contact information and turned off his computer. It was a little early, but he was going home, he decided. The county owed him a few hours. He and Wren had to talk, really talk, before she went off half-cocked and bought an airline ticket without thinking through her best choice.

The minute he let himself in the door, he could see the alarm on Wren's face. She was waiting in the hall with a rolling pin in her hand. Maybe she was planning to bake a pie, but her hands and the rolling pin were free of any dusting of flour.

"Alec?"

Belatedly he realized that he'd scared her. Her few freckles stood out against her pallor.

"I'm sorry," he said. "I should have called to let you know I was coming home early."

If anything, her eyes got bigger and darker and the

rest of her smaller, as though she was drawing in on herself. He'd seen her do that before and didn't like it.

"Is...is something wrong?" she asked.

"No." He pulled a smile from somewhere, because this *was* good news for her. "Something's right. I found your friend Molly."

She stared. Then joy suffused her, coming from the inside out, and she went from being as plain as the bird she'd been named for to being so pretty she made his heart ache. "Molly? You found her?"

"Pretty sure." Okay, now he was happy, even though underneath a part of him regretted knowing that she would never need *him* quite so much again. And...he'd liked being needed. At least, he'd liked being needed by her. He cleared his throat. "You'll need to call, but I found a Molly Elizabeth married to a Samuel Joseph Rothenberg."

"Where do they live?"

"Florida," he told her. "Upstate, not on the ocean."

She stood very still, as if drinking in his news, and then suddenly flew at him. So quick it was more like a hummingbird than a wren, she hugged him and kissed his cheek, then danced away. "Do you suppose she'd be home right now? Oh—maybe not if she works. Except—wait. Are they an hour ahead of us? I can try, can't I? You do have a phone number."

"I have a phone number."

Happiness had her lit up, something like when she looked at Abby but different, too. He hoped like hell her friend wasn't going to let her down. It was obvious Wren hadn't been able to count on very many people in her life.

"Can we talk before you call her?"

She whirled to face him. "What do you mean?"

"What if she invites you to come right away?"

Looking bewildered, she said, "I got Mom's check yesterday. I told you that, didn't I? If you'll cash it for me, I'll have plenty to get there."

"Wren," he said gently, "maybe it's not what you want to hear, but I'd like you to stay here until we locate James. Your friend's husband is an insurance agent. How can he protect you? Or Abby?" Tacking on her daughter was a cheap shot, but necessary if he was going to stop her from doing something stupid.

Her teeth closed on her lower lip for a moment as her eyes searched his. He couldn't tell what she was thinking.

"It's not fair that you have to take on all my problems just because you climbed in that attic window."

He wanted to take on all her problems. Stunned, he realized how much he wanted that.

"To some extent, your problems are my job." It was weak logic, but the best he could come up with in the moment.

"But I'm living in your house."

Still shocked at his own conviction that he was ready now and forever more to take care of this woman, Alec struggled to find the right tone.

An easy grin—yeah, he could do that. A voice that held an undercurrent of humor. He could do that, too. "Yep, and you're feeding me better than I've eaten since I can't remember."

Her face relaxed and she smiled at him. "I am feeding you well."

"Why don't you call your friend now?" he suggested. "If James hasn't shown up on her doorstep yet, tell her to be cautious. I'd feel better if you stayed here for now. Will you do that?"

Her smile became tremulous. "Yes. Thank you, Alec."

"Good. Then make your call."

WREN STARTED CRYING the minute she heard Molly's voice. "Oh, Molly. It's Wren. I've been looking for you, and… It's really you!"

Within seconds, Molly was blubbering, too. They talked over each other, and it didn't matter. The two years since they'd seen each other were erased. It wasn't until they became coherent again that Wren tried to explain how and why she'd lost touch.

"It's not like James was watching me 24/7. I could have emailed or called. But I didn't want to upset him, and if I used our computer or phone, he would have seen. But I'd have felt awful sneaking out to use a computer at the library or something." Tears pricked the backs of her eyes. "I don't even think it was James, though. Really, I was ashamed of myself. I didn't want to admit to you what my life was like. How could I have let myself be so *weak?*"

"You never had very much confidence in yourself where guys were concerned. You didn't even notice when some guy was hitting on you. Remember that soccer player? Garret, or something like that?"

"He didn't—" Wren heard herself say automatically, and then she flushed with the realization that *this* was her inner voice.

"He did," Molly said firmly. "Only you never gave any I'm-interested signals. I couldn't figure it out. I mean, you're sure of yourself in some ways. Like that time Professor Austin was being a racist jerk, and you were the only student in the class who was brave enough to stand up and say you weren't going to listen. He got in so much trouble when you reported him."

Wren drew her knees to her chest, which meant putting her feet on the sofa. Aunt Pearl was probably rolling over in her grave.

"I guess it has to do with Mom," Wren admitted. "Well, and my father, too. Knowing your own father never wanted you is kind of hard on the self-esteem."

Molly made sympathetic noises.

Wren explained the understanding she'd arrived at. "And at least I worked up the nerve to leave James."

Her friend was appropriately furious when Wren told her about the first time she'd tried to leave him, and how badly James had hurt her. Then Molly listened, aghast, to the tale of Wren's more recent escape— and to the news that James had apparently left Seattle within a day of Wren's disappearance.

"No, he hasn't called," Molly said. "And he might have been watching the house, but I don't know what he looks like."

"Alec thinks he's here. In Saddler's Mill, or maybe Mountfort."

"But if he's trying to track you down, wouldn't Alec have heard by now?"

"It's making Alec really unhappy that he hasn't gotten even a whisper about James. But there's so much chaos right now. If James thinks I'm in a shelter, he could be making the rounds. According to Alec, there are all kinds of out-of-town people here. FEMA workers, National Guard, adjusters from insurance companies, government people to assess environmental damage… James could pretend to be one of them."

"So maybe you'd be safer if you weren't in Saddler's

Mill. Why don't you come down to Gainesville and stay with Sam and me?"

"I was hoping eventually maybe I could for a little while," Wren said. "You probably guessed that, since I'm here because I came looking for you." She hesitated. "Would Sam mind?"

"Of course he wouldn't. I talk about you all the time. The only thing is— Oh, Wren, I'm having a baby, too."

They babbled some more. Molly knew from an ultrasound that she was having a boy. Her due date was only three weeks away. And she admitted that their spare bedroom was going to be the nursery. But she kept insisting that, after the baby was born, Wren could sleep on the pull-out couch in the living room.

"It would be so amazing if you could stay in Gainesville, Wren. I've missed you so much. And if you have to go to work, maybe I could take care of Abby for you. I'm going to stay home for at least the next year."

Wren had to swallow a couple of times before she could talk. Her voice came out husky. "I think I'd like that. I— Oh, Molly, I've missed you, too."

She had to explain why Alec thought it was safer for her and Abby to stay with him until James was located, though, and Molly finally admitted that made sense.

Eventually Wren heard Abby crying and had to hang up. Molly took Alec's phone number and address, and they promised to talk every few days.

Alec had gone upstairs, she presumed to reassure her that she had complete privacy to say anything she wanted to Molly. But over dinner she told him about the conversation and Molly's offer.

"Is that what you want?" he asked, his tone quiet.

She couldn't even let herself think about what she really wanted. "I don't know for sure," she said, "but I'd definitely like to see her. And it would be really great to have a friend nearby. Plus, I'd be a lot happier going to work knowing Abby was with Molly than having to put her in day care. You know?"

"What if you hate Florida?"

Surprised, she asked, "Do you think I will? Have you been to that part of the state? Is it awful?"

"Never been to Florida. I'm just not sure moving there because you know one person is the right thing to do."

Feeling a spark of annoyance, she said, "Then what should I do? Move back to California so I can be near my mother? Or Seattle, so Abby can see her father?"

Alec scowled at her. "Don't be ridiculous. That's not what I'm saying."

"Then what *are* you saying?"

"You shouldn't jump to make any decisions."

"Do you see me jumping?"

"If I hadn't asked you to stay for good reasons, you'd be on a damn plane by now."

Completely bewildered, she stared at him. It was oh, so tempting to think he didn't want her going anywhere and that's what he was upset about. But she wasn't dumb enough to go down that path. He couldn't possibly—

Her breath stopped in her throat and she almost gasped. Wasn't that what she *always* thought? What Molly had, not half an hour ago, chewed her out for thinking?

Was there a chance Alec really *did* want her to stay? He was definitely mad about something. But then, if he was interested in her that way, why didn't he say so? Could it have something to do with his ex-wife and his daughters?

This tension couldn't all be in her imagination, could it?

"I said I'd stay for now, didn't I? Shouldn't I be thinking about the future?"

Muscles in his jaw bunched. "Of course you should."

She threw up her hands. "Did you get out of bed on the wrong side this morning?"

He muttered a word under his breath that she was sure was a curse. Then he exhaled, a long, ragged sound. "Yeah. Probably. Don't listen to me. I don't know what I'm talking about."

They ate in silence for a couple of minutes. She tried not to look at him but felt so *aware* that her skin prickled. Sometimes she could suppress her physical response to him, but then there would be moments like this when tension rose between them and she was swamped by...oh, simplified, she would have to call it lust. Except she had a bad feeling it was more complicated than that.

As she went through the motions of eating, she focused on his hand, holding the fork or reaching for his glass. She remembered how his big hands had felt on her bare skin. He'd rolled up his sleeves, and she saw how the muscle in his forearm flexed at even a small movement. His shoulders were so broad, his neck strong, his jaw shadowed with the beginning of a beard and she speculated on how it would rasp under her palm if she laid her hand on his cheek. Without even looking at him, she saw the lock of dark hair that fell over his forehead, the clarity of his eyes when he flashed a wary glance at her. It was almost unbearable, feeling so much, wanting so desperately to touch and knowing she had to hide it all.

Then he commented about the beginnings of recon-

struction he'd noticed that day, and she realized the subject was firmly closed, the barrier between them set in
place. Which left her mystified about what he'd been
bothered about in the first place.

Alec wasn't an easy man to read. And she didn't dare
try, not now, not until this near-painful hunger for him
subsided to a quieter hum.

He surprised her again later, after they'd cleaned
the kitchen together and Abby had woken up. Usually
this was the point when he disappeared upstairs. She
couldn't help noticing that he made excuses whenever
she suggested he hold Abby, even for a minute, and her
nursing obviously made him uncomfortable.

But tonight, even though he made a point of not
watching, he poured himself a second cup of coffee
and sat at the kitchen table.

"I've been thinking," he said after a minute.

"Thinking?"

He sighed. "About the house. I don't know whether
I'm going to sell it or not, but it's ridiculous to be living
in two rooms. Especially with you here, too."

She waited. Even in profile, she could see the fur-
rows between his eyebrows. He was obviously struggling for what he wanted to say.

"I'm working my way up to asking another favor of
you," he said. "I thought maybe you'd consider tackling the living room. Pack up all the crap. I don't want
you to wear yourself out, but if you did a little bit at a
time— Sally has a garage sale sometimes. She could
sell everything."

"I know you don't like those figurines, but some of
them might be worth too much for a garage sale. They
should go on eBay, or you could get an appraisal from
an antique store or something."

"I can't be bothered with eBay. If you sorted the stuff as you went, I could take anything that you thought was valuable to one of the antique stores in Mountfort. Or, hell, get them to come out here. I'd like to get rid of some of the furniture, too."

"Like the two antique mattresses?"

Alec turned his head to look at her. His gaze flicked first to Abby, where she was latched onto Wren's breast. She was glad she'd carefully lowered her shirt to protect her modesty. Even so, there was something in his blue eyes when they met hers that brought a flush to her cheeks.

But after a moment he smiled crookedly. "I had the dump in mind for those."

"Good plan. I sat on both of them today. Kind of bounced a few times." She gave a cheeky grin. "I'm pretty sure I have a bruise on my butt now. Something *poked* me."

He laughed. "Dump, it is. If we're going to clean house, let's do it. I can tie them both on top of my Tahoe and haul them away Saturday."

To hide the pleasure his laugh gave her, Wren bent her head and smoothed the soft brown tufts of hair on Abby's head. "Are you sure you want me doing it?" she asked. "I mean, what if I ditch something that has sentimental meaning to you or your sister?"

Alec made a rude noise. "There's not a damn thing in there that holds any deep meaning for either of us." There was a pause, then he said abruptly, "I trust you. I suppose I'll need to sort the pictures. Otherwise, will you do it?"

Her eyes stung because he'd said *I trust you*. She retreated into the mundane. "Of course I will. Bring me some boxes. And whole bunches of newspaper, if you can find some, so I can wrap everything breakable. I'll start tomorrow with what I have."

"Good." His face had changed, she saw. Relaxed, as if having made a decision to clean out the house settled something in him. "You don't know how much I appreciate this."

"Oh, pooh. Quit thanking me. It'll be fun. Besides, nothing I can do will ever repay you for the amazing things you've done for me."

She could see he didn't like that. He hated it whenever she tried to thank him, which she couldn't figure out.

It was a long time before he said anything. When he did, he shocked her. "I like having you here," he said quietly.

While she was still staring at him, he pushed back his chair and rose. "I need to make some phone calls." After rinsing out his mug and setting it on the dish drainer, he left the kitchen without looking back.

Wren waited until she heard his footsteps on the stairs. Then she whispered, "I like being here, too."

CHAPTER ELEVEN

WREN WRAPPED a porcelain figurine in newspaper and carefully set it in the box she'd labeled Garage Sale. As she worked, she'd been chatting to Abby, who lay beside her on a blanket.

Closing the flap on the now full box, Wren felt a wave of satisfaction. In two days, she'd almost finished in the living room. She'd had fun. When she was growing up, one of the few things she and Mom had loved doing together was prowl antique stores. Wren couldn't absolutely swear she hadn't put something worth a small fortune into the garage-sale box, but she was reasonably confident in her decisions. It helped that Alec didn't seem very interested in whether he'd make any money from Pearl's possessions.

Wren felt good with the difference cleaning the house out seemed to be having on him. His mood had been lighter last night, as if she'd been packing away his unwelcome memories along with the overabundance of fragile collectibles. Tonight, she hoped he'd be willing to start looking at the photographs.

She'd made dinner simple the past couple of evenings, partly because she'd been busy and partly because, well, she could take a hint.

Tonight when they were done, instead of leaping up to clean the kitchen, Wren said, "Did you stop in the living room? I think my day's accomplishments deserve admiration."

"Has to beat my day's."

"Really?" He hadn't said much over dinner.

"Didn't get anywhere with much of anything," he said briefly.

"Does that happen a lot?"

His smile might be rueful, but it was a smile. "Yep. More common than not. Police work looks more exciting on TV than it is in real life. We spend a lot of time on the telephone trying to get information nobody seems to have." He followed her into the living room, and turned in a circle to take in empty shelves and end tables bare of ornamentation. "Wow. I'm impressed."

"I keep thinking I'm going to hear an echo when I talk out loud, though. Now it's too empty."

"I know what you mean, but there's still too much furniture. All these little pieces with skinny curlicue legs. Chairs that would collapse if I sat on them." He glanced at her. "I called around and found a guy who does appraisals. He's coming Saturday morning."

"No second thoughts?"

"Not a one."

"Do you want me to pack up the photos, or leave them be?"

He rubbed a hand over his chin. She could hear the rasp and had to squeeze her own hands into fists to quell the longing to touch him. After a minute he said, "The ones on the walls are going to have to come down, aren't they? I always hated the wallpaper in here."

Wren made an effort to focus. When she did, she couldn't argue; flocked olive-green stripes were divided by narrower stripes of mustard-yellow. "Maybe the colors have faded," she said doubtfully. "It could have been pretty when it was put up."

Alec gave a crack of laughter. "You want to think the best of Aunt Pearl, don't you? Or is it everyone?"

"Not everyone," she mumbled. Not James.

As if drawn to the display of his ancestors, he stepped closer. He touched a small oval photograph, unobtrusively nestled between larger, more ornately framed photos. "I guess I haven't looked at these in a long time. That's Mom's first cousin Newell. Edwina's youngest. He's the family black sheep. When he got drafted for Vietnam, he went to Canada and stayed. Nobody seems to know whether he was a pacifist or a coward. One of his other brothers, Bayard—" he pointed to another little boy in a family portrait "—he was killed in Vietnam. Left a pregnant girlfriend. Aunt Pearl didn't approve, but she did concede that it must be a comfort to Edwina to have Bayard's little girl once she was born. I'm surprised Pearl didn't delete Newell from her wall." His tone was dry.

He kept talking, telling Wren mildly scandalous and sometimes sad stories about the people so solemnly depicted in sepia. At one point, she said in surprise, "You know who they all are." She was seeing a new side to him that surprised her.

Alec shrugged big shoulders. "If Aunt Pearl had one consuming interest, it was family history. Did you see that big leather-bound book upstairs in one of the closets? That's the family tree, with notes about everyone. She was always making Sally or me listen to her drone on about Great-Uncle Hobart or some cousin we'd never met and never wanted to meet." He looked at Wren. "Doesn't your mother have some of these kind of pictures put away somewhere?"

She shook her head. Even though it wasn't her fault she had only her mother, it was one of the things that had always made her feel different from everyone else she knew. They had family; she didn't.

"Hardly any," she said. "I've seen a few of Mom's parents and her brother. I don't know how much she cared, but her brother got all the pictures after their parents died. Then he died and she doesn't know what happened to them. Antique stores always have these bins full of old photographs of people, and sometimes I'd wonder…" It sounded silly to say.

His eyes stayed keen on her face. "Whether that's what happened to yours?"

"I suppose. Or whether any of those faces I was looking at belonged to people who were my relatives." She'd never told anyone this. Not even Molly. "I wish Mom had this kind of record of where we came from. Doesn't it make you feel connected? As if you're a link between past and future?"

"I suppose it does." But he was looking now at the most recent family photo Pearl had on display, this one in color, and Wren saw that looking at it hurt him. She'd guessed when she studied it earlier that this was him and Sally with their parents. Alec hadn't been more than seven or eight when the picture was taken, tall and skinny, his brown hair so short a cowlick was obvious. Sally's grin showed off two missing front teeth. Wren felt a pang, seeing his father's big hand resting on Alec's shoulder and the way Sally gripped her mother's hand. Did he know how lucky he'd been?

"Maribeth looks so much like Sally," he said, only some roughness in his voice betraying any emotions.

Wren moved a little closer to him. She wished she had the nerve to reach for his hand, but he hadn't given her any reason to think he'd want a comforting touch. His constant air of solitude made her chest ache. "She does. You both look a lot like your dad, don't you?"

"Yeah, I guess we do. Mom wasn't short like Aunt Pearl or—" the corner of his mouth twitched "—like you, but she wasn't very tall. We got our height from Dad."

In contrast to the rest of the family, tall, handsome and dark-haired, his mom was a little plump and...cozy. Her smile for the camera was soft. She looked the way a mother should, Wren thought, then felt guilty. That wasn't even right, she knew; looks had nothing to do with how loving a woman was.

"Didn't your mother send Aunt Pearl your school pictures? I can't believe this is the last one of you she had."

"No, there are albums upstairs. I know she kept all those pictures. Mom started albums for—" the pause was so brief she wouldn't have noticed if she hadn't gotten so attuned to this man "—Sally's kids, and mine."

She longed to ask about his daughters, but she already knew what would happen if she did. She didn't want him to close himself off from her and make an excuse to retreat to his bedroom. So instead, she asked a few questions about his childhood, and he started talking, sounding as if the memories were rusty, but not as if he minded sharing them.

It all sounded idyllic to her. His dad had thrown the baseball with him on warm summer evenings and coached his Little League team. They'd fished together, and his father had patiently taught him to use woodworking tools in the garage. The whole family ate dinner together every night, when even the children were encouraged to talk about their days.

"I haven't thought about any of this in years. It's your fault." His scowl was half-kidding, but she was pretty sure it was also half-serious. He didn't know whether he liked the fact that somehow she'd inspired him to open up. She totally understood, since he had the same disconcerting effect on her.

He didn't clam up the way she expected, though. After continuing to frown into space for a minute, he said, "Mom and Dad were pretty traditional. I mowed the lawn, Sally helped Mom with the housework. She grumbles all the time about never having learned to change the tire on her car or how to use a drill or a jigsaw. Me, I didn't learn to cook until I was on my own and had to. Maybe Sally and I followed too much in their footsteps. Sally was a straight-A student going through school. She should have done more with her life. But all she ever wanted was to get married and raise her own family, like Mom did."

"That's not so bad, is it?"

"Her life isn't what I would have chosen for her." He stirred, finally breaking his stare from the photo. "But who am I to talk?"

She could see that he was starting to brood, which usually meant he'd make an excuse to disappear. Before she knew it, her mouth opened and she began chattering about her own childhood, the good and bad. Whether he really wanted to hear it or not. A secret part of her hoped he did, that he was as curious about her as she was about him.

The funny thing was, when she stole a look at him he did look interested.

Some of her memories were as rusty as Alec's. She'd

always hugged her loneliness to herself. She'd never thought about it, but maybe this was why Molly was her only really close friend. Trading stories was part of friendship, and she hadn't offered many.

It stung a little, imagining how different her life might have been if she'd had a family like his, with two parents who both wanted and loved their children, but to her surprise she found herself remembering happy times, too. Her mother had been a big reader, and that was a passion she'd shared with Wren.

"Mom read to me every night until I learned how. We'd go to the library once a week and pick out a pile of picture books. I loved sitting next to her and listening. If she was bored, she never showed it. That was when I felt closest to her."

Alec smiled. "She must like the idea of you becoming a librarian."

Familiar shame twisted in her stomach. "She couldn't understand when I said I was putting off starting grad school. Why would I waste a year?" Wren sighed. "She was right, except... If I'd insisted, I don't know what would have happened with James. And then I might not have Abby. I can't imagine anymore not having her."

As if she'd heard her name, Abby woke up.

"I'll clean up the kitchen while you take care of her."

Wren hoped that wasn't relief she heard in his voice.

Even though he was already opening the dishwasher and paying no attention to her when she lifted her baby from the bassinet, Wren carried her into the living room and sat on the hideously uncomfortable sofa to nurse. She didn't have to ask to know Alec would prefer she do it somewhere besides where he was. The memory of him gently helping Abby was beginning to seem dreamlike. Unreal.

Though she was talking softly to Abby, Wren could water running as he rinsed plates and washed the frying pan. From the sound of it, he was even drying and putting dishes away. She would have liked to have stayed in the kitchen. Her imagination wasn't nearly as good as watching him work would have been. There was something amazing and even incongruous in the sight of him doing domestic chores so competently. Maybe it was because she hadn't grown up with a father and therefore wasn't used to seeing a man in the kitchen or folding laundry or wielding a broom and dustpan, but Wren didn't think so. It was Alec—so *male*, big and powerfully built with that brooding air and the holstered handgun he wore all the time. The sight of him with a dish towel in his hands was startling.

Usually this was the time of night when he disappeared upstairs after checking that every window and door was locked. But tonight she was gently bouncing Abby and blowing raspberries on her tummy when he appeared in the living room with two steaming mugs in his hands.

The corner of his mouth lifted. "I thought you were supposed to play Mozart for babies."

She grinned at him. "This is more fun. Is that coffee?"

"Herbal tea for you. Was I wrong?"

"No. Coffee would keep me awake. Besides I don't know how much caffeine makes it through my breast milk."

At the faint horror on his face, she thought, *Uh-oh.* If he didn't want to watch her nurse, he sure wouldn't want to talk about it, either. But clearly that wasn't the direction was going. With a hint of humor, he said, "Maybe we should feed you soporifics instead."

Wren bit her lip. "Does she wake you up every time? I was hoping if I got to her quick enough you wouldn't always hear her."

"I'm a light sleeper." For a moment his gaze rested on Abby before he reached for his coffee, as if he needed another focus for his attention. "No, don't apologize," he said, even though he wasn't looking at Wren.

Her mouth had already been open. She shut it. Then opened it again. "But I *should*. Maybe Abby and I should sleep down here. I'm short enough for the sofa. This isn't fair—"

"Don't be ridiculous," Alec said brusquely. "I'm fine. I'm not the one who has to get up with her. And there's no way I want you downstairs by yourself at night."

Her pulse kicked up. "Do you mean— You think—"

"No, I don't think. But I'd rather be cautious than not."

"Maybe I've overreacted." Wren vocalized something she'd been contemplating. "James is a bully, not a killer. It's not like he hit me all the time. I wouldn't have stayed if he had. It was really just the once. He wants me back."

Alec's stare was hard. "*The once* was when you defied him openly. When he could see that his intimidation wasn't working."

"Well, I suppose—"

"Wren, you're a smart woman. You must have read about domestic abuse and stalkers. What James wants is control. He's okay as long as he has it. Men like him have manipulation down to a fine art. His problem isn't an explosive temper, where he lashes out every time he gets frustrated and violence is a release. He's different. He's likely to have a succession of tactics he uses to control the woman in his life." Alec paused, his intense gaze on her face. "I'm betting that when being nice didn't work anymore, he sulked."

She stared at him. That was exactly what James had done. His silences had been awful. It started about the time she'd realized she was pregnant and was feeling particularly vulnerable, so for a long time—months—she'd backed down to restore the peace. It was pathetic, how grateful she'd been to have him relax and smile at her again.

Inexorably, Alec continued. "Eventually, that quit working, too. So maybe he threw temper tantrums. Or he punished you by taking away what he saw as privileges."

Wren couldn't breathe. How did he *know?*

"He got angrier. You got more resistant. Finally, in his eyes violence was the only resort. He probably reasoned that it was like a parent spanking his kid. Unpleasant but necessary. Only, that didn't work, either. Wren, he *can't* lose control. The thought is unendurable. So what do you think he's going to do next?"

Alec's voice was still rock-hard, but she thought she saw pity in his eyes. She hated it. Hated that she'd been naive enough to not completely understand what he was telling her now. In one way she'd seen the progression, but it was far more clear-cut in retrospect than it had been while it was happening, each stage overlapping, her own responses complicated by her confusion about being pregnant by a man she no longer loved.

"Men like him kill when, in the end, that's the only way they can maintain control. James won't be able to live with the idea that you're happy without him. Abby's a threat to what he had with you. If he finds out you're living with me, he'll be enraged." Maybe it wasn't pity on Alec's face; maybe it was compassion. "Wren, the very fact that he's come after you means he's extremely dangerous. He must know that he's crossed a line. Saying I'm sorry and begging you to come back to him won't cut it. But he can't let you go and hold on to his belief in himself."

"No," she whispered.

Alec's expression softened. "Don't look like that. He'll show his hand, sooner or later. We'll find him."

"But what can you really do? You can't put him in jail and throw away the key. In fact, you can't even arrest him, can you?"

"We might be able to briefly, given that there's a record of him assaulting you in Seattle. But you're right. We can't keep him. What I can do is scare the crap out of him."

"Will that work?" She wished she didn't already know the answer. She might be naive, but not quite *that* naive.

Alec hesitated. "I don't know. Not all stalkers progress to the final phase. Some do give up eventually. They move on to another woman and start the cycle all over."

Wren gave a broken laugh. "I'd wish for that, except I don't want any other woman to go through what I did. There should be a way to *brand* men like that."

He smiled at her ferocity. His eyes held warmth again, as if he liked seeing her mad instead of wimpy. Well, she couldn't blame him. She liked herself better that way, too. Holding on to the mad instead of scared wasn't always easy, though.

Her arms tightened on Abby and she laid her cheek

against her baby's head. "Will I ever be able to stop looking over my shoulder?"

"We'll find a way."

Wren didn't let herself look at him. "You shouldn't make promises you can't keep."

He was silent for a long time. At last he said, "I'll do my damnedest to keep this one." He rose. "She's asleep, Wren."

The small body had gone lax without her realizing. "Yes." She cleared her throat and, careful not to jostle Abby, stood. "I'm ready for bed, too."

When she reached the doorway, Alec hadn't moved. She couldn't help herself; she paused and glanced back. His mouth was tight, his eyes dark and turbulent.

"I'm sorry for scaring you," he said.

"You didn't."

"I did."

She gave a little shrug.

"Thank you." He made an abortive gesture. "For what you did in here."

"I actually enjoyed it." Wren paused. "Do you want me to tackle the bedrooms, too?"

"If you're willing, I'd be grateful. Although there may be more up there you'll have to ask me about."

"Okay. Good night, Alec." She almost—*almost*—started to thank him again, but his eyes narrowed as if he'd read her mind and she stopped herself. Instead she nodded, feeling awkward, and hurried for the stairs.

ALEC HAD GOTTEN NOWHERE on identifying either of the two bodies left in the morgue. At first he'd assumed it was a matter of time; eventually it would become obvious which missing people were still missing. But as the days passed he wondered increasingly whether these two were men who happened to be passing through. It might not occur to family or employers that they had been in Arkansas at all, never mind that they could have been caught by the flood. He'd like to be hopeful that fingerprints would identify them, but the fact was that most Americans weren't in fingerprint databases at all. Why would they be?

The man who'd been shot was likelier to have a criminal history. But there were no guarantees. Alec hated the idea of ending up burying them in anonymous graves. It felt like a form of failure to him.

Saddler's Mill was not, at the moment, a pleasant place to live. For one thing, it stunk. The sludge had its own peculiar stench, not helped by the decomposing bodies of animals still left where they lay. No one had had time yet to deal with the sodden heaps of what had once been people's treasured—or not so treasured—possessions, either. Today Alec had paused behind the pharmacy at the sight of a bloated, dead cat tangled in black VHS tape still attached at one end to a cracked case. Beneath had been part of an upholstered chair, what he thought had been a blender, a Revere Ware pan made distinctive by its copper bottom, mangled, muddy books and too many things he couldn't even identify.

Then then there was the day-to-day refuse heaped in black plastic bags in alleys and at curbs. Garbage service hadn't yet resumed, although the need for it was growing desperate.

Hard times like this brought out the best in people, and the worst. Looting continued to be a problem. At the same time, even people who had lost everything were pitching in to help friends and neighbors tear out the damaged parts of homes and businesses and re-build. The shelters gradually emptied as folks found

somewhere else to go. There was talk of schools opening this coming week. They might be short on both
teachers and students, but neither the elementary school
nor the combined middle school/high school had suffered damage and the consensus seemed to be that the
kids belonged in them. Everybody wanted life to be as
normal as it could be.

Alec felt guilty leaving Wren alone so much. She
didn't show any signs of cabin fever, but she must be
feeling it. She hadn't left his house in almost two weeks
now. But when he said something Friday night, she
shook her head.

"I wouldn't want to be taking a newborn out much
anyway." She turned from the stove, her smile shy. "I've
actually been really happy. I enjoy cooking, and helping you work on the house was the perfect project for
me. I think it satisfied some kind of nesting thing." Her
eyes widened then, as if she hadn't meant to say that,
and color rose in her cheeks.

Nesting thing. Alec felt a dull thud of surprise. Was
that what had gotten him started on making changes?
Something about having a woman and a baby in the
house? Or was it because of this particular woman and
the confusion she seemed to be awakening in him?

Wren's back was to him, and, unable to help himself, he looked at Abby asleep in the bassinet only a few
feet from where he sat at the kitchen table. Most of the
time, he did his best *not* to look at her, but occasionally
he couldn't help himself. Every time he did, he felt a
painful mishmash of emotions.

Some had to do with her birth. There had been that
burst of relief and exultation and something too much
like a parent's instant love for this small being. His
hands had received her. He'd held her first. Cut her

cord. The effect might have faded faster if the three of them hadn't been trapped in that attic for days. As it was, he had been consumed by an intensely primitive need to protect both mother and baby.

The fact that she looked so much like her mommy bothered him, too, given his increasingly complicated feelings for Wren. Feelings that were churning in his belly right now.

Of course he couldn't help but think of India and Autumn when they'd been tiny and defenseless like this. He had loved them both so much from the moment they were born. It wasn't the same as what he felt for his parents, for Sally. For Carlene. The love for his two daughters was so powerful, he'd been helpless before it from day one. He'd known he would do anything—*anything*—to keep them safe and happy.

This was the first time he could remember that he was seeing Abby without the filter of a superimposed image of one of his daughters. Newborns did have a sameness, but her face was gaining character already. He stared at her, realizing she was her own self. Her mouth was her mother's, with a deep indentation in the upper lip that made him think of a pretty bow tied atop a wrapped gift. India and Autumn both had his dark hair, despite the fact that Carlene was blonde. Abby's was a soft, wren-feathered brown, but seemingly determined to stand straight up even though he remembered how fine and wispy it had been to the touch. Her face was squarer than her mommy's, her chin not so pointed and elfin. Of course, there were the ears. A smile tugged at his mouth. She was probably going to hate her ears, but he thought they were adorable.

Adorable? He almost lurched from his seat in horror. The chair legs scraped the floor.

What kind of word was *that?* Not one that should cross his mind. He couldn't afford to be tempted by a woman who, pretty clearly, had no intention of staying a day longer than she had to. Even if he was willing to try again. Which he wasn't. He couldn't be. The more he cared, the more he'd hurt when they left.

Some small movement in his peripheral vision brought his head around and he found Wren watching him. Her lips were slightly parted. He couldn't tell what she was thinking, but her brown eyes looked more all-knowing than he was comfortable with.

He returned her regard, willing his expression to be blank. He realized she hadn't been blinking when she finally did.

"Dinner's ready," she said, as calmly as if the air between them hadn't been shimmering with tension. "Why don't you grab a plate and dish up?"

"Thank you," he said, rising, pleased at how normal he sounded. "You've got me spoiled rotten."

The beef Stroganoff smelled so good, he told himself, that the churning in his gut might be hunger and not emotion. Relief swept him. He couldn't imagine ever wanting to love anyone again.

As things were, he could help Wren and her baby. Keep them safe. He'd meant it when he'd told her it was his job. Okay, he'd gone a little over and above for Wren, but that was natural given what they'd been through together.

Love was something different. Eventually he let down the people he loved, and hurt himself in the process.

Thinking a baby was cute didn't mean he loved her, any more than his struggle to keep his eyes from the luscious fullness of Wren's breasts or the subtle curve of her hips meant he was in love with her. The fact that all day long, all he thought about was getting home only meant he worried about her and Abby being here alone. And it was true that she was spoiling him. He did love walking in the door to the smell of dinner cooking. He loved the changes in the house, too, and having someone to talk to. He loved the new glow of accomplishment on Wren's face, the tenderness of her smiles for her daughter, the increasing strength he sensed in her.

Okay, he liked being able to do something for her. But that didn't mean he felt anything romantic for her.

He insisted on cleaning the kitchen after dinner and made his excuses soon after, reminding her that the appraiser would be there at ten the next morning. He'd check later that the house was secure. No reason to think it wouldn't be—Wren was scared enough to be ultracareful—but he felt better once he'd made a last check.

He sat in the easy chair in his bedroom pretending to read until he heard Wren's soft footsteps on the stairs and in the hall, a lingering whisper of a lullaby, followed by silence. Still he waited until she used the bathroom and finally returned to her—to Great-Aunt Pearl's—bedroom and shut the door.

Only then did he go downstairs, driven by a protective instinct so powerful it had taken him all evening to decide it didn't mean anything special.

CHAPTER TWELVE

THE APPRAISER CAME AND WENT Saturday morning, leaving Alec stunned at the value of some god-awful pieces. Who would *want* Aunt Pearl's sofa, even if it did date to the 1840s? They sure as hell wouldn't if they planted their butts on the cushions and tried it out.

Wren laughed at him for his surprise but pointed out that he wouldn't get anywhere near full value if he sold to dealers.

He shook his head. "It's not like I want to go into business."

"There's eBay."

"Too much trouble." He saw a gleam in her eyes. "You'd think it was fun, wouldn't you?"

"I would," she admitted. "But it's not as if I'll be here long enough to follow through. It would take a digital camera, and the time to write up descriptions, and then every single item has to be packaged carefully and mailed to the winning bidder." Her smile was quirky and a little sad. "And *you* don't have time."

No, he didn't, but he wished she did. She'd follow the bidding wars with glee. Alec imagined her greeting him at the door to tell him triumphantly that the ugly china shepherdess had sold for thirty-five dollars or the weird triangular table that fell over if he brushed against it had gone for a hundred and fifty. It wouldn't occur to Wren to wish she was making the money for herself; if he offered to pay her to do the work, she'd turn him down. But making a small fortune on Aunt Pearl's legacy for Alec would boost her belief in herself. He wished he could give her that.

Part of him wanted to say, *Will you do it for me?* Or even, *Maybe you can stay long enough to do it for me.* But that wasn't smart, was it?

No.

He cleared his throat. "I wish I had a better picture of James."

Her face pinched and he regretted not having chosen some other subject, but he would give a lot to be able to recognize James Miner if he saw him. The town was filled with strangers, and every time he encountered one in the right age range he'd find himself eyeing the guy and stacking him up against her description of the guy as well as the two, equally crappy photos he'd seen: a copy of Miner's Washington State driver's license that Lontz had faxed to Alec, and a group snapshot Wren had found on a friend's Facebook page. The trouble was, Miner was a common type: five foot nine or ten, dark blond to light-brown hair, hazel eyes that could, according to Wren, look green or gray or even blue depending on what he was wearing and the lighting, and a build that was neither extremely muscular, pudgy or skinny.

"He's really handsome," she'd concluded sheepishly because she had to know how useless that description was.

The problem was, hair and eye color were both easily changed. Alec had next to nothing to go on.

Now Wren ducked her head. "I didn't have a camera."

Or her own cell phone with a camera. She didn't

have to tell him. Wouldn't have mattered anyway, since they would have been swept away along with her purse and suitcase. And if she'd downloaded photos at home, they would have been on James's computer.

"You're not wearing your gun," she said suddenly.

"Yeah, I am." He hadn't realized she'd been so aware that he was constantly armed. "I have it in a shoulder holster."

She studied him, and he flipped his twill shirt aside to show her.

"Do you always have it with you? Isn't that kind of..." She hesitated.

"Paranoid?"

"I didn't say that."

"You didn't have to." He smiled. "No, I'm not one of those guys who won't go to the john without my gun. Usually I take it off the minute I get home." It was his turn to hesitate, but prevaricating wouldn't do any good. She wasn't stupid. "I'm keeping it close right now because of you."

He saw the quick dilation of her eyes, but she only nodded. He tried to think of what to say to ease the moment, but his cell phone rang. Looking at the number on the screen, he gave serious thought to not answering, but finally groaned and flipped it open.

"Sally."

"You sound so enthusiastic," she said dryly. "Be still my heart."

"Did you call to chat, or do you want something?"

"I called to invite you and Wren to dinner. And Abby, of course, although I don't have to feed her."

"You know I don't want to take Wren out." He glanced at her, afraid to find her looking hopeful. What he saw was worse. She'd retreated into that quiet place inside herself, as if she thought…what? That he would be ashamed to be seen with her? The idea enraged him.

"For goodness' sakes, who's going to see?" Sally said. "She must be sick to death of your company."

Gritting his teeth, Alec pointed out, "She's had yours already. Probably too much of it."

Wren was edging toward the door.

"You are such a jerk," Sally said. "Why don't you ask her what *she* wants to do?"

He *felt* like a jerk, even though he had no idea whether he was misreading Wren's body language entirely. He didn't know how to make this right.

Catching her gaze, Alec pitched his voice for her. "Would you enjoy going to Sally's?"

She gave him a startled, shy look. "If you don't think it's a good idea…"

"I don't know," he said honestly.

"There's no reason you couldn't go."

"You think I'd do that?"

As her gaze searched his, she caught her lower lip between her teeth. Why that was so damn sexy, he didn't know, but it was, and desire tangled with everything else he was feeling.

Her gaze became warier, and he wondered what she'd seen on his face. "Maybe this is a bad idea, but… if you don't think I should go out, what if we had them here for dinner?"

He'd forgotten his sister had been able to hear the entire conversation until her tinny voice came from the phone. "I heard that. Alec Harper, don't you dare say no just to be mean."

He was startled into a chuckle. His eyes lingering on Wren's face, which had relaxed, Alec lifted the phone to his ear again. "Here's an idea. Why don't you bring the kids and come over here for dinner?"

"And Randy."

Oh, hell. Was it too much to hope that his brother-in-law was dying to head to the tavern to shoot pool with his buddies tonight?

"And Randy," Alec said reluctantly.

They settled on six o'clock, and he'd no sooner ended the call than Wren was eagerly planning a menu. Her obvious pleasure made his chest cramp because he wanted to see her happy all the time.

Yeah, look what a great job he'd done making Carlene happy.

Wren fussed about what to serve, with him only pretending to listen. When she paused, he heard himself say, "Tell you what. I'll see if I can get some antique stores to take the furniture off my hands, and I'll hold off on the small stuff. If it looks like you're going to be here much longer, maybe you'd think about starting on the eBay thing."

"Really?" Wren's face brightened, instigating another throb beneath his breastbone. "We can pile those boxes out of the way easily enough. I was thinking you should give Sally a chance to look through them anyway. Maybe she can do that tonight. In case she does want something."

He couldn't imagine, but nodded agreeably to hide his dismay. Was he actually thinking that he would ask Wren to stay? It was crazy. She'd say no. She wanted to go to Florida to see her friend. His house was an involuntary way station for her, nothing more.

What if she said yes? Alec quit breathing.

God, he wanted her. He closed his eyes momentarily. He'd hurt her or himself or both of them if he let himself have her. And what about Abby? She almost scared him more.

Thankfully, Wren was taking something out of the freezer and hadn't noticed the shock that must have frozen his face. He eased from the kitchen before she had a chance.

Half an hour later, she'd settled in one of the bedrooms to look through more useless crap. Feeling restless, Alec wandered around appraising the general state of the house. Eventually, he even made himself care.

The wallpaper had to go throughout the house. He had a bad feeling that getting it off without damaging the plaster beneath was going to be an unpleasant job. He could peel off strips here and there, but most of it was stuck fast. He was dismayed when he did peel off a long strip in his bedroom only to see a different paper beneath.

Wren summoned him a couple of times to look at something. He'd managed to put a padlock on his unwelcome feelings and could stand close to her with no more than the inevitable stirring of his body. In between, he went online and read about how to steam wallpaper. What kind of shape would the walls beneath be in?

If he was going to go to the trouble to do all that work, then he'd need to do something about the moldings, as well. In keeping with the era of the house, they were stained a dark brown that added to the gloom. He imagined the walls a crisp white in some rooms and the tall trim along the floor and around windows freshly refinished in a warm chestnut or maple-brown.

Of course, the floors could stand to be stripped and refinished, too....

He swore out loud. Was he seriously thinking about

remodeling the whole damn house? And why? For sale? Real estate prices in rural Arkansas lagged behind the rest of the country. Unless he did the work himself— which he didn't have time to do even if he wanted to— he'd be better off financially to sell the house as is.

Was he thinking about keeping it? Turning it into someplace he'd actually like to live?

Someplace Wren would like to live?

Even the question closed his throat. Forget that— what about someplace he could have the girls? The idea of having them for an entire summer in Great-Aunt Pearl's oppressive house had seemed ludicrous. Cruel, even. He had hated most of his time here, and so would they.

There were other things, of course, stopping him from calling Carlene and insisting she ship Autumn and India to him the minute the girls' private school let out in June. The fact that he had to work, for example. Could he really ask Sally to take them on every day, all day, all summer? And he'd started thinking they might be scared. India especially was shy with him when he called. How much were they forgetting him? Would they *want* to come?

He was relieved when he heard Wren calling for him again. Was he really considering putting pressure on Carlene to live up to her end of the divorce bargain?

It's only December. I've got time to decide.

He found Wren in the bathroom changing Abby's diaper rather than sitting cross-legged by the boxes he'd piled in one of the spare bedrooms.

"I'm sorry," she said. "I didn't mean to drag you away from whatever you were doing. I wanted you to know I'm finished up here for now. Once I feed Abby I'll start baking some pies before I put dinner on." Wren smiled at him over her shoulder, then tickled Abby's belly. The legs were about all he could see, but they pedaled happily in response to the touch. He found his gaze riveted to those tiny, plump feet.

"Let me know if you want help," he muttered. "I can cook, you know. Or I can help wash up while you're cooking."

As if talking to her daughter, she said, "Detective Harper is an excellent dishwasher, isn't he? What do you say? Should we let him help?"

He snorted and retreated from the doorway, but discovered as he headed downstairs that he was smiling.

"WELL, DAMN. This place looks different. Doesn't it, pumpkin?" A typically dopey grin on his face, Randy swung his middle child so she hung upside down, her hair brushing the floor.

Amanda shrieked, but happily.

Alec followed his brother-in-law's gaze around the living room. "Yeah, I decided it was time to clear it out," he muttered.

"Wren helping you?"

"She seems to enjoy that kind of thing."

Randy made a typically male sound: not quite a grunt, not quite a sound of agreement. "Place could use some work," he observed as he swung Amanda upright then set her on her feet.

"I've been giving that some thought," Alec admitted. "Maybe come spring. Right now, anyone who can do construction is going to be busy."

"Uh-huh." Randy looked at his daughter. "Pumpkin, why don't you go find your mama?"

"Okay, Daddy." She beamed and trotted away.

"I hear the mill may not open until April or later," Alec said.

Randy took a deep breath. "Yeah, I hear that, too."

"Don't suppose you've been looking for a new job."

Randy faced him. "I've been working my butt off helping friends get back on their feet. You're a newcomer. Maybe you don't know what it's like here, but that's what we do. We help each other."

"I understand that, but I happen to believe your family should come first."

The other man's meaty hands curled into fists. There was no sign of a smile on his face. "You know, this crap gets old. You don't know me, you don't want to know me. What do you got against me, Harper? What did I do that was so bad you've never even been polite?"

"I've got eyes." Less than two feet separated them as they glared at each other. Alec kept his voice low, but he didn't even try to tamp down the aggression in it. "I see my sister living in a dump when you're adding on to some buddy's house. I call and she's alone with three children while you're down at the Blue Grouse having a pitcher with the guys. Never mind she was home alone all day with them already. I stop by and she's hauling wheelbarrows full of manure out to her garden while you're God knows where. And you think I should be thrilled that you're married to my sister?"

Bristling, Randy snapped, "You ever call on Monday or Wednesday evening?" He didn't wait for an answer. "No, you don't, because you know Monday night is Bible study and Wednesday is Sally's quilt group. First Thursday of the month is garden club. Bet you know better than to call that evening, either. Because you might have to catch me, home with my kids. Sally goes out as much as I do. More, some weeks. There's plenty of nights we're both home, too." He rocked back on his heels. "Why am I bothering to argue? You decided a long time ago I'm not good enough for your precious sister, and you're never going to hear any different."

Angry but mixed up, too, Alec looked past his brother-in-law's shoulder and saw Wren standing in the arched doorway to the living room, her eyes wide and shocked. Before he could react, she disappeared.

"Shit," he said under his breath.

"Maybe it'd be better if I don't stay." Randy started toward the now empty doorway. "Sally dug in her heels and insisted I come. You'd think she'd have given up, but she's a stubborn woman."

"Don't go." The surprise and disappointment in Wren's eyes had made Alec feel like scum. He had to clear some hoarseness from his voice. "You're right. Maybe I haven't been fair."

"What?" Still with his back to Alec, Randy stopped. It was a minute before he turned. "What do you mean, *you're right?*"

From between gritted teeth, Alec said, "I mean, I may not have always been fair."

"That about killed you to say."

Alec glared at him. "You aren't what I had in mind for Sally."

His brother-in-law gave a rough laugh. "You've got to be kidding me. What did you think, you could arrange a marriage for her? Maybe set her up with some nice doctor? Or—wait. No, it would have almost had to be with a cop, wouldn't it?"

"Not a cop." That response burst out before he could stop it. "We're not good marriage prospects."

He didn't like the way Randy looked at him with something that might have been pity.

"Do you know any doctors you could have set her up with?"

Alec's chest felt tight. "I should have been here to meet anyone she dated. Talk her out of being impulsive."

Randy met his eyes. "She loves me. I love her. That hasn't changed. It won't change."

Isn't that what I would have wanted most for Sally? The thought crept into Alec's head. *What Mom and Dad had?*

"I hope it doesn't," he said, in a voice that didn't sound like his.

"Why would it? Sally is…" Randy's shoulders moved. "She's beautiful and funny and always thinks she's right."

A choked laugh escaped Alec. "She'd tell you she *is* always right."

They exchanged grins. The moment of camaraderie was…unexpected.

A frown tugged at Alec's forehead. He felt as if he'd laid down his gun and stepped away from it. He knew he'd done it because of Wren. Because she'd looked at him as if *he* was the son of a bitch here, not Randy.

He didn't like wondering if she was right.

"Have you ever considered going into business?"

Randy looked at him, startled. "What do you mean?"

"As a contractor? From what I hear, you know what you're doing."

"Well, sure I do. I worked construction summers while I was in high school, and then for a couple of years after. But things got slow and I kept getting laid off. I married Sally and the mill seemed steadier."

"It's not so steady now. And my guess is you'd have more business than you knew what to do with."

Randy was already shaking his head. "I'd have to have a stake to start out. I'd need tools, equipment, someone to do the bookwork for me, enough in the bank to pay a couple of other guys to work for me."

"Don't you have money from Mom?"

"We swore we'd save that for the kids. If we have to use any, it'll be for a new roof."

"Maybe starting you in a new direction is more important right now." Alec hesitated then, although he didn't know what the hell was getting into him, said, "I could loan you some. Or hire you now to work on this place. If you think you could do what needs to be done."

His brother-in-law was flat-out gaping now. "You're serious."

Alec was in shock himself. Had he meant any of this? "I'm serious." He realized he was. Wren had given him a push, but it was one in the right direction.

From the kitchen came a call. "Time for dinner."

The two men ignored it.

"Because you don't think I take good enough care of Sally and this is your way of trying to fix that?"

Alec shook his head. "Because this is a good idea." He shrugged. He'd tried. The Randy he'd thought he knew would be too lazy to act on the suggestion. "Think about it. Talk to Sally."

"Wow." Randy scrubbed a hand through his shaggy hair. "Yeah. Okay."

Maribeth came into the living room. "Mommy says did you hear her?"

Her dad grinned at her. "We heard."

"Then how come you didn't come?"

"We were talking, munchkin."

Her serious blue eyes moved from one face to the other. "But you and Uncle Alec don't like to talk."

Randy gave a crack of laughter. "You said it, munchkin, but I'll bet your mom would scrub your mouth out with soap if she heard you."

She looked confounded. "I didn't say any bad words."

Even Alec was chuckling now. "Your dad is teasing you. All you did was sound like your mother. How could she be mad about that?"

Her face relaxed. "She'd never."

"There you go. Let's go eat."

Wren had set the table in the never-used dining room. When the two men walked in, both women scrutinized them with the same suspicion they might have employed for a pair of boys trying to sneak to the table without washing first. For once, Alec was amused by Randy's broad who-me? grin. Alec probably had one on his own face.

"Looks good," he told Wren, whose cheeks flushed with pleasure.

"Thank you," she said primly.

He found himself smiling easily at the interplay of kids and adults throughout dinner. The situation felt surreal, as though he'd stepped back in time. It had been so long since he'd been able to enjoy the family he had left. Tonight, this felt like family.

Because of Wren.

She'd baked a ham and scalloped potatoes that were simple enough to be acceptable to Maribeth, Amanda and Evan. The whole thing felt like a holiday meal, and finished with hot apple pie topped with big scoops of vanilla ice cream. They all ate until even Randy groaned. Sally happily bounced Abby for half the meal, after which Wren took over.

Now that they'd broken ground, the two men talked about reconstruction in town and rumors of who was planning what. Alec was amused by the suspicious way Sally's narrowed gaze moved from his face to her husband's.

At one point, seemingly at random, Randy said, "I wonder how safe the wiring in this place is."

Wren's eyes widened, but Sally said, "When Mom moved in with Aunt Pearl, she had it updated. And a new roof put on. You remember, Alec?"

He nodded. "They didn't do anything to the plumbing, though, did they? The pipes groan. The bathrooms need all new fixtures, too."

"Huh," Randy said.

The women stared.

"I don't know about the kitchen, but maybe."

"Huh," he said again.

Sally's mouth opened and closed a couple of times. Alec enjoyed the sight more than he should have.

Probably nothing would come of any of this. Randy would continue in his shiftless ways and Alec would end up selling the damned house exactly the way it was. But he was surprised to realize he felt good about his suggestion, even if he'd had to be shamed into it.

Sally wanted to stay to clean up, but the kids were obviously wearing down, so Alec insisted she get them home.

"Wren and I have a deal. She cooks, I clean."

Their eyes met and held; both of them were smiling. Alec was vaguely aware of Sally's raised eyebrows, but any conclusions she leaped to would die a natural death when Wren and Abby left.

A picture of him staying a stiff goodbye to Wren at the airport, watching her and Abby get swallowed by the lines at security, wiped the smile from his face.

What if he did ask her to stay?

But he had to be sure what he wanted, and he wasn't. A few weeks ago, he'd have sworn on a bible that he would never seriously get involved again.

By the time he came in from seeing his sister's family off, his mood had taken a nosedive.

Wren was already starting to clear the table, even though Abby, placed in her bassinet, was getting fussy.

"What are you doing?" Alec took the pile of dirty plates from her. "I meant what I said. Go take care of your baby."

He had a feeling she wouldn't have surrendered if not for Abby's escalating cry.

"You don't have to do it all," she said stubbornly.

Pretty soon he *would* be doing it all, cooking and cleaning. Because he'd be alone again. Thinking anything else was premature.

"Yes, I do," he said, and as if nothing was wrong began rinsing plates.

WREN DIDN'T HAVE A CLUE why Alec had gone from friendly to grumpy the minute Sally and the others had left. Had he been putting on some kind of act for their benefit? His face had suddenly looked so bleak, then closed into that expressionless mask that confounded her. It made her wonder if she'd done or said something.

The flutter of panic in her chest was all too familiar. The minute she recognized it, she squared her jaw. No way was she taking responsibility for Alec's moods. If he wanted to be sullen, she'd let him.

The living room seemed awfully lonely, though, and

the minute she started nursing Abby she realized the drapes at the front window were open. She reassured herself that nobody would be able to see her sitting here unless they were standing on the front porch, but still… Feeling uncomfortably exposed, she hunched a little and adjusted her shirt to better cover her breast.

Where was James? Was he in Florida wondering why she hadn't showed up yet? In the Bay Area watching her mother's house?

He'd know she had no one else to whom she could go for refuge. So if he wasn't in Florida or California, he was here. Either looking for her, or waiting. Until she went out? Or because he knew she was scared, and liked the idea of letting her sweat for a while?

That didn't ring true. James had never been very patient.

So where was he?

Once she'd put Abby down for the night, she thought about going to bed herself, but she wasn't really sleepy yet. Besides, she should at least check that Alec didn't need any help. And she wanted to see him. She wanted to know why he'd gone from angry to sociable and laughing to full-guard-in-place all in one evening. If he was still all closed off and it was obvious he wanted to be alone, she'd go read or something.

She found the kitchen spotlessly clean and the dishwasher running. Alec was leaning against the counter, apparently waiting for water to boil.

"Hi," she said hesitantly.

He looked up, his expression neutral. "Abby asleep?"

"Yes."

"Do you want tea?"

Would he rather be alone? She searched his face and couldn't tell. "Um, sure."

He nodded and grabbed another mug.

"Sally wasn't sure you and Randy could be civil all the way through dinner."

"We talked."

"Is that good?"

"I've been a jackass." He gave her a rueful look. "Again. I shocked you, didn't I?"

Almost whispering, Wren said, "You looked so furious. I've never seen you like that before."

"I scared you."

"No, not like that." She tried to think how to say this. "I didn't know. Although I guess I should have. I mean, you're a *cop*. So you have to be able to be..."

When she hesitated, he finished. "Violent? Is that what you were going to say?"

After a moment, she nodded.

"I can be, Wren." He sounded disturbed. Or maybe only weary. "I won't lie. But I would never hurt anyone defenseless. For me, it's always a last resort. Do you understand?"

She found herself nodding again.

"I would never hurt you."

"I know that." She crossed the room to him in a rush, because she could see that she'd wounded him. "I've never been afraid of you. I never could be."

His Adam's apple rose and fell. "Okay."

She stopped so close to Alec he could have reached out and touched her. She was embarrassed to realize how much she wished he would.

Somehow they'd come to be staring at each other. She got lost in how blue his eyes were, in the shape of his mouth when it softened as it was now. He straightened away from the cabinet so he was no longer leaning. Seemingly in slow motion, he took a step to close the small distance between them.

Wren's breath backed up in her throat as she kept looking at him. *Oh, please,* was all she could think.

"Wren?" His voice sounded raw.

She must be swaying toward him, because she could see every individual line radiating from the corners of his eyes, every dark eyelash, the texture of the stubble that shadowed his jaw.

He groaned, or she did. All she knew was that suddenly his arms had closed around her and she'd splayed her hands on his chest. His head bent, his mouth found hers, and he was kissing her. Not sweetly and gently, but so desperately she could tell he'd bottled up all his hunger as she had.

CHAPTER THIRTEEN

He was kissing Wren.

What in hell am I thinking?

He wasn't thinking. Couldn't. This felt too good. Too right.

Her mouth was unexpectedly lush, the taste everything good she'd ever cooked for him. Alec had started by diving in deep, his tongue startling hers into hiding. He cradled the back of her head so that he could angle it to please him. With the other hand he gripped her hips and pulled her tight against him. His erection pressed against her belly.

No subtlety. No decency. No romance.

He wanted her. That was all his blurry mind could wrap itself around. Wanting.

But he couldn't have her. Somehow he knew that, too. Newborn. She wasn't ready, even if he wasn't scaring or repulsing her.

His awareness grew, took in the fact that her mouth had opened to his and she wasn't fighting him. He loved the feel of her small hands spread open on his chest. His heart must be thundering against one of her palms.

But she wasn't kissing him back, either. She was holding herself very still.

Despite the fact that his blood all seemed to be in his groin, his brain regained enough function for her stillness to worry him. Had he *made* her afraid of him, despite what she'd said? He didn't want to know what he'd see in her eyes if he set her away from him.

Everything changed in that instant. He began gently massaging her hip and butt as his mouth became gentle. He licked her lips and nibbled at them, coaxed her tongue from hiding and played with it. Whispered, "You feel so good," between small, biting kisses.

She relaxed—*yes!*—and kissed him. Made a humming sound in the back of her throat that was so erotic he could go ballistic on her if he let himself. But no. *He couldn't have her. Newborn baby.* Kissing was enough. Listening to the song of her desire.

It was a long, long time before he could make himself gradually ease away. Stroke her hip instead of kneading it, move his hand up to the delicate small of her back. Relax his fingers in her incredibly silky straight hair. Take his tongue into his own mouth where it belonged, and brush tender, close-lipped kisses on her swollen mouth.

And finally, lift his head enough to see her face.

Her chin stayed tilted up to him and her eyes closed for seconds that stretched while his heart hammered in earnest. In apprehension. Then her lids slowly lifted to reveal the melted chocolate of her eyes, which studied him for a paralyzing moment.

She blinked several times in succession and took a step back. His hands dropped to his sides. He saw her swallow.

"You kissed me."

"Yeah." That came out hoarse. "Yeah, I—" *I what? I've wanted you like crazy since about twenty-four hours after your baby was born?* That would thrill her to hear. "I've been wanting to," he said at last, the closest he could come to what he really felt.

She absorbed his explanation. "Oh." Undecipher-
able thoughts caused little twitches in her expression.
"I didn't know."

"You didn't know?" he asked, disbelieving.

New color layered over already pink cheeks. "I
thought sometimes…"

Throat thick, he said, "I'm sorry if I've made you uncomfortable." He still had a raging hard-on. He didn't
dare glance down to see whether the loose twill shirt
disguised it. He could only hope.

"No. I mean…no." But now her eyes avoided his.

"I won't put any pressure on you. I swear."

She nodded.

Alec tried again. "I like having you here. I— Tonight
got to me."

"Your sister."

"And Randy." And the kids. The whole family thing.
Wren, most of all. The highs and lows had all hit him.

"I shouldn't have said that." Now she was looking
at him. "About you being violent. I know you wouldn't
have hit him. It's just that you looked like you wished
you could."

He rubbed his open hands against his jean-clad
thighs. One good thing, this particular topic was taking
care of his physical reaction to her. "It's probably good
that you interrupted when you did. I saw on your face
what an idiot I was being."

"That isn't exactly what I was thinking."

Surprisingly enough, he was able to smile. "It
worked anyway."

"The water is boiling."

"What?" He turned, startled, and saw that she was
right. It had probably been boiling for five minutes.
Swearing under his breath, he turned off the burner and

poured hot water over the tea bag in her cup and the scoop of instant coffee in his. He turned to her, mugs in hand. "Can we sit down? Talk for a few minutes?"

She moved ahead of him to the table and sat in what he'd come to think of as her place.

In dismay, he thought, *It will keep being her place, even after she's gone.*

He might have to quit eating at the table.

He watched as she stirred half a teaspoon of sugar into her tea, then waited.

"You know why I don't like Randy."

Her forehead puckered. "Kind of."

That said it all, didn't it? Yes, Randy wasn't exactly his dream brother-in-law. Whether he would have *liked* the rich doctor was another story.

I don't like Randy.

But maybe he could. A possibility that made him frown.

"If I'd been here for Sally to talk to when she first started dating him, she might have made different choices," he said. "I should have moved to Arkansas when Mom did. Dad would have expected me to take care of them."

"But you said that was ten years ago."

"Right."

"Sally must have been…sixteen?"

"Seventeen. I expected her to kick and scream when Mom dragged her here for her senior year, but she didn't. I thought she hated visiting Aunt Pearl as much as I did. But I guess not."

"So, she was almost an adult," Wren said slowly.

He could tell she didn't get it. "She was a teenager. At the worst of being boy-crazy. Mom had to take care of Aunt Pearl, so she wasn't paying enough attention to Sally. She took the SATs, then never applied to colleges." He grimaced. "She'd started dating Randy."

"How old was *he?*"

"Nineteen. Turned twenty before she graduated. Mom mentioned that she was dating someone, but not that he was older. I should have been paying attention."

"Alec. You're her *brother.*"

All too familiar anger rose in him. He bounced his fist on the table. "She doesn't have a father, does she?"

She stared at him for ages, her lips parted, her eyes no longer melted chocolate. Darker, thoughtful, possibly sad. "Why didn't you move with your mom and sister?"

"I had a job." It came out as a near snarl. "I'd gotten engaged."

"You had a life," she said softly. "Isn't that what your father would have wanted for you?"

He was having trouble taking air into lungs that felt compressed, and he didn't even know why. Why should something he'd believed for ten years now seem…unreasonable? He'd made a promise at his father's grave, and he hadn't kept it. It was that simple.

"So that's it. You feel responsible for everyone in your life. Your mom, Sally… Your nieces and nephew?"

He hesitated; nodded.

"Me," she whispered.

He could only nod again. Of course he felt responsible for her, and for the baby she'd named after him.

Something that might have been pain flared on her face and she pushed to her feet. The chair toppled backward to the floor, but she didn't seem to notice. "I don't want you to feel responsible for me. If things go wrong, you'll only torture yourself over me, too. I never meant for that to happen." Eyes huge and dilated, she pressed her hand to her mouth.

Alec rose slowly. "It's not the same." The calm voice came naturally; it was the one he used on the job, to soothe a hysterical victim. "You're different."

"How am I different? *How?*"

He loved her.

Hell. Damn. No.

He stared at her in shock. Thinking of asking her to stay so they could get to know each other better, toying with the idea of a future, that was one thing. Going under without even a chance to bob to the surface for a last breath... That was something else.

He was in such turmoil, he felt as though he'd swallowed battery acid instead of a gulp of black coffee.

Glittering with hurt or tears or maybe anger, Wren's eyes still held his. She was waiting for an answer.

Alec fumbled to say something. "You're not..."

"Family?"

"Maybe." That was a lie, Alec realized, still in the grip of that shock. She felt like family. *His.* And Abby felt like his, too, despite every effort he'd made not to let himself become attached to her. "No."

"Then you don't have to worry, do you?" she said in a cold voice he'd never heard from her before. "I guess you won't have to torture yourself after all, if something goes wrong."

Yes, he thought. He would. The way losing his father, his mother, then his girls, had come close to crippling him. But Wren... Oh, God, if James got to Wren— Alec didn't think he'd survive.

She wasn't different, he realized dully. She was more. It was crazy, given how short the time he'd known her, but the way his heart clenched was as real as his panic. He'd never felt this way about Carlene, which was why he'd suffered guilt after their divorce more than he had any sense of loss. No, the true grief was for losing Autumn and India from his life, not Carlene.

He couldn't afford to make an impulsive decision he'd regret.

"Why don't you ever see your daughters?" He didn't know what she'd seen on his face, but Wren's voice had changed. It was warm bath water instead of sharp-edged ice cubes.

"That's not really something we need to talk about." He managed to sound…remote. Facade safely pulled into place.

There was a long silence, neither of them moving. Then she made a funny sound, a gulp that, with horror, he realized might have been a sob, and she raced past him, striking the corner of the table with her hip as she went. Her untouched tea splashed, his cup rocked.

He spun. "Wren!"

Her footsteps were racing up the stairs.

Alec let loose of an obscenity and sank into his chair. Half an hour ago, they'd been friends. He hadn't known he was in love with Wren, hadn't ground his erection into her belly and thrust his tongue damn near down her throat. Hadn't told her he felt responsible for her.

Hadn't lied and implied that he didn't care in any personal way.

Hadn't screwed up his life even more than it was already screwed up.

He swore again, braced his elbows on the table, bent his head and ground the heels of his hands into his eye sockets.

IF ONLY THIS WASN'T SUNDAY, Wren mourned. Monday she could have stayed in bed until Alec left. He could have cold cereal for breakfast. That was undoubtedly what he did most of the time. Then she would have had all day to figure out what she would say to him.

Wren couldn't imagine what had gotten into her. Alec had been unbelievably nice, and what did she do? Turn into an emotional mess that must have astounded him.

How am I different? How?

What was the poor man supposed to say to that? *I worship and adore you?* Yeah, right. All he'd tried to do was be tactful and point out that she wasn't a member of his family, so of course, his sense of responsibility for her was different than what he felt for his sister or his mother.

Wren stifled a moan into her pillow. Yep, she'd gone off the deep end. How could he help but know how she felt?

In one way she wanted to march downstairs and tell him that she was leaving. Thank him for everything he'd done, but it was time she started depending on people who actually did love her and hadn't gotten shanghaied into taking care of her.

But she knew she couldn't do that to Alec. If she did that, and James hurt her or—God forbid—killed her, Alec would never forgive himself. He'd be sure it was his fault she'd gotten upset and taken off for Florida.

With a sigh, Wren tossed off the covers and got out of bed. Abby was asleep. She'd awakened and nursed about two hours ago, which should mean Wren would have time for a shower.

She took it hastily then made a face at herself in the mirror before she returned to the bedroom. She wished she had a hair dryer. With no makeup and her hair wet and slicked to her head she looked about twelve years old. Except—she glanced down at herself ruefully—her boobs were too big for that, and leaking, besides.

Abby was stirring, thank goodness, which gave Wren an excuse to put off going downstairs. She sat on the bed with her back to the headboard and let her daughter have a leisurely meal, then changed her and dressed her for the day. At last, with no more excuses to dawdle, she started downstairs.

The doorbell sounded before she'd gone down more than a couple of steps, and with a now familiar jolt of fear she stopped. Alec came out of the kitchen without noticing her and opened the door.

"Randy." He stood back and let the visitor in.

His brother-in-law was about the same height as Alec but with a rangier, less compact build, dark russet hair and big hands and feet. There was something unfinished about his body, Wren thought, but she found him disarming.

Without even a greeting, he said, "Sally liked what you suggested."

Knowing she was eavesdropping, still Wren didn't move.

"Hiring you to work on this house?"

"No. The idea of me setting up as a contractor. We're going to take a chance with a piece of her inheritance."

"Good." Alec nodded. "Does that mean you'll work on this place for me?"

"Yeah." The two men moved, and Wren saw Randy's grin. "Except I'm wondering if you'd mind waiting until spring."

"Spring?" Alec sounded surprised. "Ah…would you like a cup of coffee?"

"Sure." There was a bounce in the other man's step as they went into the kitchen.

Wren hesitated. Abby gurgled and managed to grip a fistful of her wet hair. With a giggle, Wren pried the fingers loose and smacked a kiss on her button nose.

Shoot. She wasn't going to lurk here in the shadows. Having Randy here would make seeing Alec easier. She should take advantage of it.

As she neared the kitchen she heard their voices. Randy was talking about having made a couple of phone calls that morning and already lining up a job.

"We're going to have to gut most of the first floor, maybe even lift the house off its foundation." His enthusiasm was apparent. Wren couldn't hear the next bit, but as she walked into the room he was saying, "Unless you're planning to put the house on the market, I figured you could wait. I want to jump on some of this other work."

"Makes sense." Alec turned to look at Wren, his blue eyes sharp.

She smiled vaguely in his direction, more directly at Randy. "Hi, you're up and about early."

He grinned in his engaging way. "People to see, things to do. Had to thank Alec here, first." He slapped his brother-in-law on the back hard enough to rock him on his feet.

Alec winced, but to his credit kept a smile on his face.

"Have you eaten?" Wren asked. "I thought I'd make pancakes if you'd like to join us."

Randy thought he'd like to. Alec started to protest that she didn't need to wait on them, but she ignored him, settled Abby in her bassinet and started cooking bacon. He gave up and, seeing that the coffee was ready, poured cups for the two men.

While she worked, he listened and made occasional suggestions as Randy talked enthusiastically about his fledgling business. They'd decided that Sally could do the books for now; she'd apparently done some book-keeping for a logger before Maribeth was born.

"She'll be my receptionist, too." Randy propped a booted foot on his knee. "Considering I won't have an office for the time being. Since we don't have a garage, I may have to rent someplace for equipment storage, though."

"I have a garage," Alec said. "I don't usually bother to park in it. Far as I'm concerned, it's yours as long as you save me an accessible corner for the lawn mower and garden tools."

"You're serious?" Randy looked incredulous then grinned again. "Damn. Okay. For now I'll take you up on it."

Wren put food in front of the two men. Even though he talked the entire time he ate, Randy was done by the time she sat with her own short stack of pancakes and a couple of slices of bacon. She acknowledged his thanks and said a cheerful goodbye when he left. She half hoped Alec would make an excuse not to return, but no such luck.

His expression unreadable, he busied himself replenishing his coffee. "Those were good pancakes. Did I see you putting applesauce in them?"

"Yes." She took a sip of her juice, then cooed at Abby to give herself an excuse to look elsewhere.

"I owe you an apology," he said quietly.

She shot him one quick, alarmed look and shook her head. "No, you don't. If anyone owes an apology, it's me. I guess the stress has been getting to me. Otherwise I don't know why I went off the deep end like that last night. You didn't say anything—"

"I kissed you." His voice was deep.

She felt a clench of misery. "Is that what you're apologizing for?"

"Uh…no, actually. Maybe I should, but no." He rasped his hand over his unshaven chin, the way he did when he seemed to want to give himself a moment. "What I'm saying sorry for is the way I've shut you down every time you've asked about my ex-wife and kids. I've been raw, but that's no excuse. God knows you've shared enough with me."

"That's not the same," she said. "I mean, I had to tell you about James if you were going to help me."

"I'd like to think we've become friends."

Friends? A word that should have made her happy instead increased her misery. "You don't have to tell me anything."

"You must have wondered."

She was mutilating her breakfast more than eating it. "Yes," she admitted softly.

"Carlene and I shouldn't have gotten married." His grunt was almost a laugh. "Probably every divorced person says the same thing. In our case, it's the truth. We should have dated longer. If I'd canceled enough of our plans, she would have lost interest. Instead we got married eight months after we started seeing each other. Mom and Sally had moved, and I was probably trying to fill a vacuum."

Wren knew that feeling.

"The first couple of years were okay. Things got worse when I was promoted to detective. She was enthusiastic initially, because in theory I was less likely to be killed on the job. Patrol is more dangerous."

"Really?" Wren said in surprise. "But as a detective you're dealing with murderers."

"Cops are in the most danger on a domestic disturbance call, serving a warrant or walking up to a car after a traffic stop. Detectives don't go unarmed, but mostly we're information gatherers."

"Oh." That made sense, she supposed.

"Unfortunately, the downside was that my schedule became less predictable. I worked longer hours. I couldn't quit at five because my wife was putting dinner on the table. I missed all kinds of occasions." He rolled his shoulders as if to release tension. "She was distracted for a while when she was pregnant with Autumn, but being home alone with a baby can be hard. India… When I didn't make it to the delivery room in time, our relationship was pretty much over even though we held on for almost three more years."

"I'm so sorry," Wren whispered.

He transferred his gaze to her face briefly. "I was, too. I'm, uh, ashamed to say I didn't mind my marriage ending. What I minded was her moving out with the girls. Sure, I worked long hours. But I could hardly wait to get home to see my daughters. I loved them." As if he'd heard the past tense, he said more softly, "I love them."

Wren wanted desperately to wrap her arms around him, but something in the way he sat, gripping his mug, staring out the window, held her back. He looked so solitary. And tired, too, as if he hadn't slept much last night. There was so much strain on his face.

He was quiet long enough, though, that she couldn't bear it. "Don't you see them?"

Alec scraped that hand over his face again. "At first we did the every-other-weekend thing, and I took them out for pizza or to McDonald's at least once a week. Carlene started to date someone pretty quickly. That actually worked out well for me, because she was happy for me to take the girls when she was going out, or, uh, spending the night."

Frozen, Wren stared at him. No matter what he said, it must have hurt to know his ex-wife and the mother of his daughters was spending the night with her boyfriend.

"I was living in a dream world, though. Carlene married the guy. Unfortunately for me, he's an executive with a corporation that does business all around the world. No sooner were they back from their honeymoon than Carlene was all excited on my doorstep telling me that he'd been transferred to Sydney. Half a damn world away."

"Oh, no. Couldn't you stop her taking your kids?"

"Wrench two little girls out of their mommy's arms? Argue that they were better off with me? Working the erratic schedule I did? How could I, Wren?"

He couldn't. She could see that, but...

"How long are they supposed to be there? In Australia?"

"Who knows. Two years? Forever?" A rough sound escaped his throat. "Maybe he'll get transferred to Berlin next. Beijing. Who the hell knows? And what difference does it make?"

"You're entitled to visitation." She hesitated. "Aren't you?"

"Yeah." He sighed. "Easier said than done, though." He seemed to have aged ten years while they were talking, the lines on his face etched deep, his shoulders

hunched as if braced against unbearable pain. "Do you
know how long the flight from Sydney to St. Louis is?
They're little girls, Wren. It's one thing to pop two kids
on a plane from Philadelphia to St. Louis under the care
of a flight attendant. It's another entirely to have them
travel that far by themselves. One of us could fly them
each way, but it's not cheap. And that's not the worst
of it." He looked at her, and she almost gasped at the
agony in his eyes. "They've been gone for a year and
a half, Wren. I call them, but conversations are getting harder and harder. With India especially. She was
barely five when they left. I wonder sometimes if she
really remembers me."

"It's not fair," she said fiercely. "You should insist
on having them. They're your children, too."

His face relaxed; something like a smile touched his
mouth. "You're right. They are."

She frowned, everything she'd learned from him
suddenly adding up in her head. "That's when you left
St. Louis, isn't it?"

"Yeah." He paused, renewed tension in his bearing.
"I knew Mom was sick, but how could I go that far
from the girls?" He gave a harsh laugh. "Then Carlene
moves to Australia."

"So you feel guilty because you weren't here sooner
for your mom."

He closed his eyes for a moment. "By the time she
was diagnosed, it was already too late for her. No, I'll
tell you what really eats at me. I might have saved my
marriage and my mother if I hadn't been so damned focused on my job. I could have moved my family here
way earlier. Even law enforcement is slower paced
in a rural county like this. I've been home for dinner
every night, haven't I?" His tone was harsh and getting

harsher. "I could have given Carlene what she wanted. I could have been here for Mom and Sally. But me, I was stuck on the fact that they all knew from the get-go who I was and what I wanted from life, and I was damned if I was going to give an inch."

Feeling bruised herself by his pain, Wren grappled with the knowledge that Alec was here in Saddler's Mill because he had been desperately trying to right everything that had gone wrong in his life and in the lives of the people he loved.

He had been trying—too late—to fix the unfixable. And of course he couldn't.

He was the kind of man who was used to taking charge, to finding answers and solutions for other people. He thought he had to be. She had this terrible picture of him at his father's funeral, watching the casket being lowered into the ground. At fifteen, he might have been as tall as a man, but he was a boy. She imagined him gawky and terrified, feeling the crushing weight of responsibility settling on his shoulders as his father was laid to rest. She knew he would have had an arm around his mother's shoulders, and that he would finally have pulled her to him and let her sob against his shoulder while his other arm encircled his bewildered sister.

He'd been the absolute worst age for a boy to lose his father. Especially since it didn't sound as if there had been any other adult male figure to step in. He'd never said anything about an uncle or grandfather, and his mother had obviously never remarried. No more than a freshman or sophomore in high school, he had become, in his eyes if not his mother's, the father figure.

Then his mother died and his sister married someone he didn't respect and his wife left him and took his little girls so far away he never got to see them.

And still, he had been willing to leap for that attic windowsill, risking everything because a pregnant woman he didn't know had needed him.

If she hadn't already been completely, totally in love with Alec, that was the moment she would have fallen.

As it was, she stood, marched around the table and hugged him.

He stiffened. In a belated agony of embarrassment, Wren almost withdrew. Was this the absolute dumbest thing she could have done? What if he saw it as pity? He'd already made plain that she was more of an obligation to him than anything. The friend bit, well, he was probably only trying to be nice.

But at the moment when she thought, *I have to drop my arms and step back*, Alec turned. There was a sound; a groan, maybe. He moved so fast she didn't have time to react. In something like a lunge, he clamped his arms around her waist and buried his face between her breasts.

Pressing her cheek to the top of his dark head, Wren held on tight.

CHAPTER FOURTEEN

ALEC HAD TAKEN COMFORT from her for only a minute, but he knew it had been a minute too long. He'd given away more than he'd ever intended.

The last time he'd broken like that was after Mom died. Dry-eyed, he dealt with the doctor and the funeral home, and comforted his sister, but when she was finally gone he had walked upstairs to his bedroom—*Mom's* bedroom—and punched the door frame. He'd had only enough sense, if you could call it that, to strike where he wouldn't do damage to the house. Only to himself. Over and over, he'd pounded until his knuckles were raw and he'd broken half a dozen bones. He remembered being blind with tears. The doctor who had plastered his hand the next day hadn't said much, simply looked at him with measuring eyes. By then he'd been able to sit calmly under the assessment. Alec had let Sally assume the injury had occurred on the job.

Behind the wheel of his Tahoe, he remembered the moment last night, leaning against another human being. Wren. At least he hadn't cried against her breast. He'd wanted to. Alec was humiliated at how close he'd come to sobbing. He didn't even know why. Why it had hit him like that. Why he had needed, more than anything on earth, to hold her and be held by her. All he knew was that, when her arms came around him, suddenly he couldn't help himself.

Thank God he'd been able to pull himself together quickly, to say, "Thanks, Wren," then stand and walk out of the kitchen. His voice had been hoarse; she wouldn't have missed that. But she hadn't said a word, merely stood there, her eyes dark with unhappiness, and had allowed him the dignity of retreat.

She'd made dinner later, as usual. He left the TV on while they ate and pretended to care about the news. About all he had actually paid attention to was the flood update. Disaster here in Arkansas had been true devastation farther south on the Mississippi delta. Cleanup was proceeding much as it was here, with governors asking for and receiving federal assistance and the people who could least afford to lose everything the least likely to actually get any meaningful help.

He made a few comments about the recovery; Wren asked questions. They managed civilized conversation. He'd made some effort to not meet her eyes, and he thought she'd done the same. The entire while all he wanted was to circle the table and snatch her into his arms. Or maybe beg her not to leave him. To say, what's Gainesville, Florida, got that Saddler's Mill doesn't?

The whole while, he grappled with the idea of love and all it entailed.

Their exercise in civility had lasted an excruciating hour before Abby woke up and he had a good excuse to suggest Wren go somewhere else while he cleaned the kitchen. She'd headed upstairs and didn't come back.

She'd gotten up early as always and made his breakfast this morning. Alec had felt like death warmed over and Wren looked worse, fresh bruises under eyes redrimmed as if she hadn't slept at all—or had cried.

Could he take the risk that he wouldn't hurt her, that

she wouldn't hurt him? If not, he owed it to them both to back off, before living together became unendurable.

But at the moment, he was pulling to a stop in front of the farmhouse where he'd been called, so Alec forced personal issues to the back of his mind. A dead man lay on the front porch, his wife sobbing inside a patrol car.

Two hours later, Alec had determined that the guy had slipped on sludge the flood had deposited in the barn, slammed his head against the sharp corner of a stall and somehow been able to stagger as far as the porch before he collapsed and died.

The tragedy was no less. The poor bastard's wife was left to wonder whether, if she'd been home, she would have been able to get him help in time. All the reassurance in the world would never make her believe there was nothing she could have done.

By the time Alec left, the wife's sister had arrived and taken her away, and the body was being bagged and carried to an ambulance.

He arrived at the station in a piss-poor mood. He'd pulled into a slot and was getting out of his SUV when a middle-aged deputy he knew slightly stopped his patrol car and rolled down his window.

"Detective, I hear you've got a couple of unidentified bodies at the morgue."

Alec walked over to him. "You heard right. You got something?"

"We found a car this morning. Looks like it went off the road and tumbled into the river. Wedged there against an old snag. Nobody in it, but I could see from the plates that it was a rental."

Alec felt the faint buzz that told him he was about to hear something important. "Did you call the company?"

"I did. It was Enterprise, and they hadn't gotten any accident report." He reached for a notepad that lay on the passenger seat, lifted it and squinted. "The driver was a guy named Miner. James V. Miner. Washington State license plate."

The buzz became something more. Son of a bitch. Was there any chance one of his two stiffs was Wren's James? That he had indeed been here in Saddler's Mill all along, but had been dead? Very likely drowned by the time Alec delivered Wren's baby?

"They're faxing over a copy of his driver's license and insurance card," the deputy said. "I told them to send it to your attention."

Alec thanked him cordially. As he walked into the building, his brain was working with a speed and precision he hadn't yet managed today. Why hadn't it occurred to him that both the unidentified bodies fit the general description of James Miner?

Because they fit the general description of a quarter of the male population of the United States, that's why. Brown hair, eyes of the indeterminate shade that could be labeled hazel, brown, gray, green, even blue. Average height, average build, no distinctive identifying feature. Alec wanted to excuse himself but couldn't entirely.

Was James likely to be the gunshot victim? What if he'd thought he had found Molly's house and bullied his way in? In these parts, most home owners had guns and were prepared to use them. Still, this guy had been shot in the back, which might explain why it hadn't been reported.

Maybe. But if the car had tumbled into the river it seemed likelier that Miner was the drowning victim.

They could wait and identify him by fingerprints.

Ignoring the normal hubbub of the cramped police station, Alec walked to the fax machine and found that the one he wanted had come in. He'd already seen the driver's license photo, of course. Wren had admitted it didn't look much like James. *He's way better looking,* she'd insisted. Alec had shrugged. The guy might not photograph well, or he'd been particularly unlucky that day at the Department of Motor Vehicles. Hell, most people were unlucky when it came to license photos.

Alec stared now at the black-and-white faxed copy and tried to reconcile that face to either of the corpses at the morgue.

It was possible.

What should he do? Contact Seattle P.D. and try to get a quick fingerprint match? Or subject Wren to the horror of looking at the faces of dead men in hopes of identifying one of them as the father of her child?

He knew what she would want. As reluctant as he was, Alec felt respect for her, maybe even pride in her. She was a lot gutsier than she believed herself to be.

Swearing, he found his lieutenant and explained where he was going and what he had to do. Then he drove home although it was barely two in the afternoon.

WREN HAD BEEN halfheartedly rooting through a box filled with miscellaneous papers, separating potentially interesting items such as photographs or what looked like a stock certificate from copies of ancient utility bills and bank statements. Her attention kept straying. She knew what she wanted to do.

"Enter not into temptation," she muttered.

Oh, what would it hurt if she *looked?* As long as Alec didn't catch her?

Wren scrambled to her feet, leaving the piles she'd

created where they lay, and hurried into his bedroom. The relatively new-looking album was on the shelf in his closet. Maybe it would turn out to hold more old family photographs, but he *had* said his great-aunt Pearl had kept his and Sally's school pictures, and Wren couldn't imagine that his mother hadn't also kept pictures of Alec's and Sally's kids.

Standing on tiptoe, she took the album down and lowered herself to sit cross-legged on the floor. Feeling even more guilty, she opened it to the end rather than the beginning. The last few pages were as yet unused. She kept turning back until—

Maribeth's school picture was darling. She was a lovely girl with vivid eyes and a bright smile. Beside it, Amanda's showed a pudgy girl with hair that hadn't wanted to stay in the pigtails her mother had undoubtedly braided so carefully that morning.

Wren flipped the page back, and quit breathing. The collage of photos could only be of Alec's two little girls. They were so beautiful; both had his eyes and his dark hair. The older girl laughed in one picture, her arms flung out with dizzying confidence. Her younger sister's smile was shyer; Wren had the sense that she looked at the world with more trepidation. Wren pressed her hand to her chest as though she had heartburn. *Oh, Alec.*

Slowly she worked her way through more pictures of Sally's family that included glimpses of Alec's mother, and then, finally, there was *his* family. All of them together in a posed photo that might have been taken for Christmas. He wore a dark, formal suit, white shirt and red tie, his wife had on an elegant, form-fitting black dress and both girls were clearly delighted by their red velvet dresses, the bows in their hair, the lacy white socks and patent-leather shoes. Wren stared and stared at that photo, her gaze going from face to face. She felt horribly guilty, as if she'd sneaked into someone's house to go through their things, but she couldn't stop herself.

His wife was a stunning woman with hair the color of honey and eyes as blue as his. She was tall, long-legged and curvy. Her makeup was perfect, her smile serene and her ears didn't stick out.

Wren wanted to cry. She should be jealous; probably she was. But mostly she was sad for Alec. Neither he nor Carlene had been happy in their marriage by the time the family had sat for this photograph. Sexy, handsome man, poised, beautiful woman, a darling pair of girls. The perfect family. Yet the illusion was soon to be shattered.

No wonder he didn't keep this photo framed at his bedside. It must hurt terribly to look at.

She heard the engine of a vehicle outside and tilted her head to listen. Was it passing? Or—

With a gasp she closed the album, leaped to her feet and shoved it on the shelf. She had barely made it across the hall into the other bedroom when the key scraped in the lock. Oh, dear heavens. What if he'd caught her being so unforgivably nosy?

Then her heart took an uncomfortable bump. What was he doing home so early?

It *was* him, wasn't it?

She tiptoed to the bedroom doorway and poked her head out. She couldn't see downstairs from here.

"Wren?" he called.

She closed her eyes for a moment in relief and guilt and probably a hundred other emotions then hurried to

the head of the staircase. "Alec? Why are you home
so early?"

He looked up, his face somber. His expression was
enough to make her heart bounce over a couple more
speed bumps, neither of which slowed her pulse.

"Alec?"

"Is Abby asleep?"

Wren nodded.

"Can you come down? I want to talk to you."

She had a death grip on the banister. It took her a
moment to pry her fingers loose, and start down. His
eyes never left her face. Two steps up from him, she
stopped.

"Alec?" She couldn't seem to say anything else. Not
even something sensible like, *What is it? Why are you
looking like that?*

"James's rental car was found today in the river."
He spoke quietly, even gently. "From what I'm told, it
wasn't more than a mile or two from where you had to
abandon yours."

He had been that close behind her? No, Wren
thought, hadn't that police officer in Seattle said he'd
disappeared the day after she fled? So, he hadn't liter-
ally been right behind her.

"Was he in the car?" she asked, her voice almost
steady.

He shook his head. "He'd gone off the road, though,
and the car likely rolled several times before it went
in the river." He seemed to hesitate. "The chances are
good he's dead."

It was very strange to realize she couldn't quite
decide how she felt about that. There was relief, a
breath away. But she was unexpectedly shocked, as
well. And…upset?

"I should have considered this possibility before," he said, sounding grim, "but I'm now wondering whether James isn't one of the two unidentified bodies we're holding in the morgue."

"But you saw his picture. I mean, I know it wasn't very good—"

"It was worse than not very good. And—" He paused, obviously uncomfortable with what he had to say. "Both of these bodies were battered in the river. They'd been in the water a while, too."

Okay, now she felt a little bit queasy, even though she didn't consider herself squeamish.

"Wren, we can wait for fingerprints. Or you can see if you can identify him. I'm going to leave the decision to you. You don't have to actually view the bodies. We can have you look at some photos."

"No. If it's him, I want to see him. I *need* to see him and know—" She stopped. "Just, um, let me put some shoes on and— We'll have to take Abby, won't we?"

"Why don't we drop her at Sally's? I know she won't mind. You might need a few minutes after..."

After she looked closely at the faces of two very dead men who might be perfect strangers. Yes, she might indeed need a few minutes.

She could stay calm. She'd survived giving birth in unbelievably primitive circumstances with a man she hadn't known kneeling between her legs. This couldn't possibly compare to that.

Alec waited while she put on socks, the gardening clogs and a heavy canvas coat that had belonged to his mother, then bundled Abby against the cold and collected a few necessities for her.

Alec escorted her with a reassuring hand on her elbow. She could feel his worried glances as he drove the half mile to his sister's house, which was small and shabby. He parked and was the one to unbuckle the car seat and carry Abby in to Sally's house.

"Of course I don't mind watching her," she assured them. But then she stared. "You're going to *what?* Girls," she snapped, her parental antennae having quivered, "please go into the living room."

"I'll be fine." Wren smiled. "Thank you for helping."

Alec didn't let Sally have time to undermine Wren's resolve. He hurried her out and they drove in silence to the hospital. As they walked the short distance across the parking lot, several people called greetings to Alec.

"We've given ourselves away," she said. "If this isn't him..."

Alec didn't have to say anything. He thought one of the bodies was James.

What will I feel if it is? she wondered.

The pathologist wasn't there. An attendant was available to usher them into the morgue and pull out one huge stainless-steel drawer at a time. It was chilly in here; of course it would have to be, to prevent the bodies decomposing. By this time, Alec's arm had come around Wren and he held her close. She felt mostly numb, but his warmth soaked into her.

The body was draped with a green cloth that looked like the same fabric surgical scrubs were made out of.

"At a bigger hospital, you'd be shown a video feed," Alec said. "I'm sorry that isn't available here, Wren. Are you sure you wouldn't rather start with photos?"

"I'm all right," she said, unsure whether she meant it or not. She held herself rigidly and waited.

With a practiced flick, the attendant folded back the sheet enough to reveal a man's face. Wren's breath hitched. His color was...horrible, like spoiled milk.

There were obvious contusions. She stared blankly, thinking, *Oh, God, no wonder Alec couldn't be sure.* What if this was James and she didn't recognize him?

"Is— Is this the man who was shot?"

"Yes."

"Oh." She gulped and stared.

Alec's arm tightened. "You're breathing too fast," he murmured. "Relax. Take your time. Look at the hairline, the way his ears lie, his nose, the ridge of his eyebrow. Focus on details."

Yes. She closed her eyes for a moment then opened them again. She could do this.

After looking carefully for a minute, she shook her head. "No. It's not James."

"You're sure?"

"Yes. This face is broader. The nose is too flat across the bridge. And see how large his earlobes are?"

"All right." Alec nodded at the attendant, who recovered the face and slid the drawer silently into place.

They moved a few steps. He pulled out the next. An identical green drape covered this body, as well.

The moment he folded it back, Wren knew. A sound burst from her.

"Take your time," Alec said again, his voice unbelievably kind.

She was sure, but she looked carefully anyway. She knew his nose, the angle of his cheekbones, his mouth. She would never in a million years have imagined him looking like *this*, but... "Oh, his poor mother," she whispered.

Though he appeared utterly focused on her, Alec somehow signaled the attendant and the drape was whisked over the face. Even before the drawer closed, Alec urged her out of the room.

"He's dead." That was a truly dumb thing to say, especially since James looked really dead, no embalmer's art giving his face a semblance of life. "I've never seen anyone dead before," she said, her voice too high.

"You did great, Wren." Alec kept her moving, into the elevator that rose from the basement, through the hospital lobby and out into the chilly winter air of the parking lot. "It's normal to be shaken by seeing a body. Especially when it's someone you knew."

"I don't know if I did," she said. "He was never who I thought he was. He represented something. I let myself be fooled."

They'd made it to Alec's black SUV. He opened the passenger door, but instead of bundling her into the seat he gently turned her and drew her against him. They were shielded by the bulk of the vehicle and the open door as well as the pickup parked in the next spot. For this moment they were in their own small world, utterly alone. She leaned against him, closed her eyes and breathed in the scent that was distinctly Alec. He was talking quietly, but she didn't even try to take in the words, only let his low, kind rumble join the comfort of his strong arms and the big hands moving in soothing circles on her back and shoulders.

"He's dead," she mumbled against his down vest.

"Yes. You're safe. He can never hurt you again."

She wondered why she wasn't crying. Shouldn't she be? It wasn't as though she was *happy* that James had been killed, although maybe eventually she would be. What she'd done had been surprisingly traumatic. And yet anticlimactic, too. These past few weeks, she'd imagined a thousand times a confrontation with James, scripted what he'd say and do, what she'd say and do. Girded herself to be strong. Now she didn't have to be.

He'd cheated her of the chance to stand up to him—to know that she could.

Most of all, though, she felt shell-shocked.

"How are you doing?" Alec asked.

"I—I think I'm okay." Wren thought about it and decided she really was. Summoning her dignity, she drew away. "Do I have to go to the police station with you, or can we go home?"

He smiled, although his eyes were watchful. "We'll pick up Abby and go home."

She nodded and got in the SUV with only a small boost from him. She'd already buckled herself in by the time he got in on his side.

Once again they drove in silence. On the way, she had been oblivious to her surroundings, but now she looked around and saw how awful the town looked. But amid the mess were signs of healing—piles of fresh lumber, work happening on half the buildings they passed, people shoveling the icky-looking sludge into wheelbarrows and Dumpsters.

"Do they do this every time it floods?" she asked.

His gaze flicked her way. "This was what's called a hundred-year flood. One this bad hasn't happened in any of these people's lifetimes. The folks along the river do get flooded on a regular basis. You'd think they'd give up, but—" He shrugged.

"Is there anything I have to do? About James, I mean?"

"No. We'll confirm your identity with fingerprints. If you know his mother's name and hometown, that would help speed things along. She could start making arrangements."

"We don't have to tell her what he was doing here, do we?"

Even without turning her head, she could feel him looking at her. "That's up to you. We can leave you out of it completely. It'll be a mystery to her why he was in Arkansas."

"That's what I'd like to do. There's no reason now for her to know what a creep her son was." She was quiet a moment, not moving even though Alec had pulled to the curb in front of Sally's house. "I know they say you love your own kids no matter what, but I wonder if she might not be a little bit relieved, too."

Alec set the emergency brake and turned off the engine, then shifted in his seat so he was facing her, one arm draped over the steering wheel. "You said he wasn't very nice to her."

"No. He was pretty awful when he talked to her."

"Was James her only child?"

Wren nodded. "I do feel sorry for her."

Alec gave one of those smiles that invariably made her heart somersault. Warm, tender, intimate. "You have a kind heart, Wren Fraser. James was the biggest idiot on earth."

Her sinuses burned and, even as she mumbled, "Thank you," she fumbled for the seat-belt release. He meant well, she told herself. And she valued kindness. She did. She'd thought often enough that *he* was kind. But right this minute, she ached for more. For him to be unhappy that her identification of James meant there was no more reason for her to stay in Saddler's Mill.

Scrambling out of the Tahoe, she thought fiercely, *I will not cry. I won't.* She owed Alec so much, and she wouldn't repay him by clinging. Think how lucky she was—not only was her baby healthy and darling, but there also wasn't even a whopping big hospital bill for the birth. She'd escaped James and never had to worry about him again. She could think about whether she wanted to tell his mother that she had a granddaughter. Molly would be excited to hear that she was coming, and she would get to be there when Molly's baby was born.

Considering the desperation she'd felt when she fled Seattle—never mind when she'd battled to escape the car she'd driven into the flood-swollen river—life was good now. Really, really good.

She wouldn't let herself think about how, once she left, the odds were she would never see Alec again.

CHAPTER FIFTEEN

THE AFTERNOON WAS advanced enough that Alec chose not to return to work. Instead, once they were inside he excused himself to go upstairs. When he came down a minute later, he'd changed into jeans and a sweater and no longer wore the holstered weapon or badge at his belt.

His assessing glance was sharp enough to *be* a weapon. "You haven't moved," he said.

He was right. She hadn't. She stood in the entry hall holding Abby, both of them still bundled against the cold, and the past couple of minutes were a complete blank. Abby was beginning to fuss, which meant... She was hungry or cold or hot or wet or something. For the very first time since she'd been born, Wren felt incapable of determining what that something was.

"Will you take her?" She thrust Abby at Alec. "I need— I need—" His reluctance was obvious but for once she couldn't honor it. "I'm sorry." The moment he accepted Abby from her, Wren bolted for the stairs. She knew he was staring in astonishment as she fled.

She shut herself in her borrowed room then sat on the edge of the bed. She was shaking. Why was she shaking? She hadn't lied when she told Alec she was all right. Why would she suddenly fall apart now?

There was a rap on the door. "Wren? Are you okay?"

She hugged herself, swallowed and said, "Yes. I need

a few minutes. Please." The last came out as a whisper, but she suspected he heard her anyway because he went away.

She didn't cry, or even feel like crying. All she did was indulge in a teeth-rattling panic attack and try to figure out what was wrong.

Nothing was her eventual diagnosis. Somehow her life had gone terribly askew, and she didn't know how to fix it. It wasn't James anymore, although seeing him…

Don't think about that.

It was Abby and Alec and Molly and Mom and…

Gradually she became calmer. She knew what her choices were now, and Alec wasn't one of them. She could go visit Molly or she could stick a pin in the map and set out to build a new life in a strange place where she knew no one. Being near her mother—not an option.

Of course she wanted to see Molly. She'd been dreaming of that for months.

So, buy airline ticket. Thank goodness she had the money, although if she were to buy it online she would have to ask Alec to put it on his credit or debit card, and she'd give him the cash in payment. No reason he'd mind.

A glance at the clock told her it had taken her only a few minutes to overcome the unpleasant attack of doubt and fears. So that was good. She'd be fine.

To prove how fine, she went downstairs. It wasn't fair to leave Alec in charge of Abby when he so obviously didn't want to be.

She found them in the kitchen. Alec sat facing the bassinet, which hadn't been moved from its usual corner on the other side of the table. He didn't look very happy. In profile, his expression was, if not grim, at least bleak. She would have been willing to bet he'd put Abby down the second Wren was out of sight. Now he was dreading the possibility that she might start crying and he would have to do something.

For the first time, Wren had some sympathy for his ex-wife. He said he loved his kids, but maybe he had been a lousy father. Maybe he was the kind who wasn't willing to get up at night with them, who thought men didn't change diapers.

Yet she remembered his gentleness with Abby during those days in the attic. The deft, experienced way he'd handled her, that big hand always cradling her head. His creativity in coming up with diapers. His grin when she suggested submitting his designs to a survivalist magazine.

Even though she hadn't made a sound, he somehow knew she was there. His head turned and his expression changed. "Wren."

She was too muddled to guess what he was thinking. She took a few steps into the kitchen, enough to see Abby, who was awake but seemingly contented as she gazed up at the mobile that was turning above her. Alec must have wound it up.

Wren caught an odd whiff and was distracted. Diaper? No. Oh, dear God. She smelled like the morgue. *That's* why Alec had changed clothes the minute they walked in the door. The scent had seeped into her clothes. Maybe even into her hair and her skin. The rational part of her knew she was probably imagining this, but— Panic returned full force. "I need a shower." She retreated toward the hall, her voice rising. "I need to get clean."

His eyebrows rose and then his face softened. "Go ahead, Wren. We're fine."

Of course they were. Even if Abby did start to cry, she'd survive for ten minutes.

It took longer than that, though. Wren scrubbed and scrubbed. It was as if she had to get every inch of herself. Finally satisfied, she put on clean clothes from the skin out.

Maybe, she thought, she could dump the clothes from the hamper directly into the washing machine without touching them.

Downstairs again, she discovered that Alec had apparently moved far enough to grab the newspaper—he must have heard it thud onto the front porch, because it wasn't there when they'd gotten home earlier. He was in the same chair—as far from the bassinet as he could get and still sit down in the kitchen—with the sports page spread out in front of him. Abby had begun to get vocal—she was probably hungry.

"I'll feed her then start dinner," Wren said brightly, going to her daughter.

His head came up and he looked searchingly at her. "I can cook tonight if you'd rather."

"No. If you don't mind, I'd prefer to stay busy."

"Okay," he said slowly.

"After dinner, I wonder if I could borrow your credit card and buy my airline ticket. I can pay you with cash."

He went absolutely still. Was that shock she saw on his face? "There's no hurry for you to go."

"No reason to stay, either, is there?" She sounded positively blithe. *I'm excited about the future,* her tone said.

His dark eyebrows drew together. "Wren…"

Abby squawked.

"Let me go feed her."

He didn't argue. Wren carried her baby to the living room and sat on that hideous sofa. The minute she lifted her T-shirt and opened the front of the bra, Abby latched on with a ferocity that suggested Mommy had been trying to starve her.

Wren felt as if her heart was being crushed inside her chest. It was that painful.

By the time Abby was satisfied, the sensation had eased, if not gone away. Wren was afraid she was going to keep hurting for a long time, especially when she let herself think about Alec.

Maybe forever. Which was ridiculous, considering she'd known him such a short time.

She refastened her bra and went to change Abby's diaper.

Alec still had the newspaper spread in front of him when she returned to the kitchen, but he looked at her so quickly she wondered if he'd actually been reading. He watched as she laid Abby on her back and tucked a blanket around her.

"Anything happening in the world?" she asked casually, going to the refrigerator.

"Murder, mayhem, white-collar crime and world unrest. Nothing out of the ordinary."

"I remembered where James's mom lives. It stuck in my mind because it's such a strange name for a town. Boring. Boring, Oregon."

Alec laughed. "You've got a point." He was silent for a moment. "We should have fingerprint confirmation by tomorrow. I'll call her then."

Wren nodded. She knew she hadn't made a mistake.

"I didn't have very inspiring plans for dinner. How does homemade macaroni and cheese grab you?"

"Good."

They didn't talk much until she put the casserole dish into the oven, although she knew he was watching her even if he did occasionally turn a page.

The moment she closed the oven door, Alec said, "Come and sit down."

"I need to make a salad."

"You've got plenty of time."

She hesitated then went to her usual place. There she folded her hands on her lap and waited.

"You really intend to leave right away." His tone was strange.

"You must be eager to have your house to yourself again."

He leveled a look at her. "You're kidding, right?"

Feeling suddenly uncertain, Wren said, "Well, no."

"You've made this house into a home." Alec's expression was oddly vulnerable. "I…like having you here."

He'd said that before. Could she believe him? And what did he mean by it? Rather flatly, she said, "You could hire a housekeeper."

"That isn't what I'm saying." His voice was low, the words more halting than usual.

"Isn't it? You love coming home to find dinner ready to go on the table. And I'm glad you appreciate the help I could give you clearing the house out. But—" Oh, this was so hard. "I think it's time I get on with my life. I shouldn't keep leaning on you, Alec. That's probably not healthy for me."

"You did a lot less leaning than you think you did, Wren. You've shown amazing strength. I know you have a hard time believing that, but it's true. You had to be scared to death when I found you in that attic, but you never complained, barely even groaned when you were in labor, and once Abby was born you managed to laugh despite being hungry, cold and anxious about her. The truth is—" His mouth twisted. "What little leaning you've done, I liked."

She had to be gaping at him. "You...liked?"

"Nobody's needed me for a long time."

She didn't know how she was going to survive this. "Your daughters still need you."

He moved his shoulders uncomfortably. "Maybe."

"Definitely."

"Okay." His faint smile twisted. "That doesn't have anything to do with the fact that I'd like you to stay."

Despite a gigantic ball of emotion in her throat, Wren managed to say, "As what? The never-ending guest? A paid housekeeper? A—" She couldn't say it. *A lover?*

His forehead furrowed. "I think...a wife."

Maybe it was the wrong reaction, but she was suddenly mad. "You *think?*" Her spine had gone ramrod-straight.

He pushed back his chair as if to stand, but he didn't. "I know I'm being clumsy. I hadn't planned how to do this. Maybe I should have let you go without saying anything. But I need you, and you need me." His voice was thick. "I've been hiding how much I was feeling because I thought you weren't ready."

"You mean, because *you* weren't ready."

He stared at her. It was an age before he said, "Maybe that, too."

What really hurt was the hint of shock she could see in his eyes. He really hadn't planned to say any of this. Wren wanted—so much—to believe she was what he truly wanted, but she couldn't. She thought he had liked having her here, and maybe he didn't want her to go, but how likely was it that he'd fallen madly in love with her, Wren? A Wren who had disappointed her mother? A Wren who hadn't so much as caught the eye of another man until James, and, wow, look how that turned out. James, who she now understood—to her shame— had seen a weakness in her that he knew could exploit to meet his own need to dominate.

Having her here had probably made Alec realize he was lonely. She needed so much more than that, and maybe she'd never find it, but— She wouldn't settle for less. Never again.

"What about Abby?" Her tone was so uncompromising she shocked herself. "You can hardly bring yourself to look at her."

A muscle jumped in his cheek and his gaze flicked toward the bassinet then returned to her face. "That's... not as easy for me, Wren. But I know she's part of the deal. If you'll give me time..."

Deal?

"You feel sorry for me. That's a ridiculous reason to propose to a woman." If that's what this had been.

"No. I don't feel..."

When he floundered, Wren said, "Well, at least you can't bring yourself to lie."

He shot to his feet so abruptly, Abby startled in her bassinet. Then he pushed the chair aside and strode across the kitchen before swinging back to face Wren.

"How can I not feel bad after hearing about the way your mother treated you? Not to mention that son of a bitch lying in the morgue? That's compassion, Wren, not pity. Was I supposed to listen to you and not feel a goddamn thing?"

"I didn't say that."

"You did." His throat worked. "Obviously you don't feel the same way I do. That's okay. Let's not end on a sour note."

For the first time, her eyes filled with tears.

"I'm sorry," Alec said hastily. "I never meant… Oh, hell. I'll leave you in peace."

A second later, she heard his footsteps on the stairs. Stunned, Wren sat at the table and thought, *What did I do?*

The right thing.

If he'd said, *I love you*… But he hadn't.

She should be glad he'd asked in a way that made it impossible for her to stay. If he'd said, *I like having you here and you need some time and space to figure out your life,* she would have been terribly tempted to accept. But if she stayed any longer, all she'd do was fall deeper and deeper into love. So deep she'd never surface again. It was much better to end this now.

She felt as if she'd been hit by a car. Standing was an enormous effort, but somehow she did it. She'd go on the same way she had since she'd stolen out of James's apartment pulling her suitcase and caught the light-rail train to the airport in Seattle. She would think about nothing but the next step.

Make a salad.

ALEC TRIED TO KEEP his attention on the highway. Abby was buckled into the backseat, Wren beside him. He'd insisted on driving them to St. Louis rather than letting them take a bus the way she'd wanted. His impression was that she was as miserable as he was, but he didn't have it in him to beg.

He heard himself say haltingly, *I think…a wife.*

Even in retrospect, he winced. Okay, he could

have done a better job of persuading her that he really wanted her to stay. He could have told her that the idea of going home without her made him feel as if he was plunging down into a pitch-dark coal mine, utterly alone.

No, he should have told her that he felt things for her he never had for a woman before. That sometimes he thought of her as a campfire on a dark night, casting generous heat and a golden glow. He'd been cold for years until he had held out his hands to her warmth.

But it was more than that. She was funny, smart, sweet and loving in a way he had never experienced. He knew she didn't think she was sexy, but she was. She was…delicate. Completely feminine. He loved her small, competent hands, the fragile line of her collarbone, her freckled, pixie face. Her curves were all subtle except for her breasts, especially lush right now. Her feistiness turned him on, her vulnerability tugged at something almost forgotten in him. He didn't want to keep her dependent, but he liked the idea of her knowing, completely and without doubt, that he was there for her if she needed him.

He could have offered to move to St. Louis or wherever she needed to go when she was ready to start grad school. But everything had happened with stunning speed—James was dead and Wren packing to leave while Alec was still stumbling over his own feet.

He was beginning to think Wren wouldn't have given him a real chance no matter what he'd said.

He tried now to work up some anger, but apparently the ache beneath his breastbone wasn't the right kind of tinder.

They talked only fitfully during the drive. Things had been awkward since last night. How could they be anything but? He'd come down to eat dinner, afterward offering her his credit card. She had very politely returned it twenty minutes later and told him she'd booked a flight for the next day.

She'd accepted the gift of one of his mother's suitcases. "I'm sure Sally can find someone else who can use the bassinet," she'd said, and he'd nodded.

The couple of hours that morning before they left were hell. They'd realized that she wouldn't be allowed on a flight without a picture ID, so he took her to the DMV, where she applied for one using his address. They'd sat side-by-side during the wait in complete silence.

Traffic became heavier the closer they came to the city. He was glad to be able to bypass downtown on Highway 570, which delivered them almost directly to the airport.

"You can drop me at departures," Wren said.

He hated that idea as much as he did the idea of watching her and Abby be swallowed by the crowds at security.

"You've got too much to juggle. You need help until you check your bags."

Out of the corner of his eye, he saw her struggle with that, and her eventual concession in the form of a nod.

He parked and took the suitcases out of the back, then opened the passenger door to unbuckle Abby's car seat. Her knitted beanie hat was clutched in one chubby fist. She stared at him with eyes that no longer had that unfocused, newborn look. It was as if she *saw* him.

Damn. He felt as if he had a boulder in his chest.

Unable to help himself, he lifted a hand and skimmed it over the fluff of her hair before he gently pried the hat from her hand and tugged it over her head, making sure her ears were tucked in. She watched him as if his face held all the secrets of the universe. His eyes burned.

He kept his back to Wren while he gritted his teeth and waited for the desolation to subside. Then he lifted the car seat, closed the door and hit the door lock on his key chain.

"I can get one of those suitcases," he said. Wren had already hoisted the diaper bag they'd bought only that morning after the visit to the DMV and was gripping the handle of the larger suitcase.

She cast a look at him in which he read despair.

Don't go. He didn't say it.

As they walked in, he asked, "Will you let me know you've arrived safely? And that you've found your friend and everything's all right?"

"I have your email address."

"Okay." His throat wanted to seize up. He cleared it. "Good."

She'd already printed her boarding pass. Baggage check was ahead.

Maybe he could beg.

He was fairly certain that wouldn't sway her. Either she didn't think she could ever love him, or she needed desperately to prove to herself that she could be self-sufficient. How could he blame her either way?

They stood briefly in line, not talking. She produced her boarding pass and her shiny new Arkansas identification. Her suitcases went on the conveyor belt and Wren turned to him. "I can take Abby now."

"I'll walk you to security."

After a moment, she gave a stricken nod.

The line was short for late afternoon flights. He held

the car seat while Wren unbuckled her daughter and
lifted her out.

"Wren." His voice was hoarse.

Her eyes met his and he felt as if she'd punched him.

The timing couldn't be worse—he knew that—but
the words crowded their way out. "I should have said
this before. You probably won't even believe me, but...
I love you. Wren." Desperate, he finished, "Come back
to me. When you're ready."

She squeezed her eyes shut, and he saw that her
lashes were wet. She made a hiccupping sound then
opened eyes swimming with tears. "I wish I thought—"

"Thought what?"

"I have to do this."

Alec swallowed and stepped back. No touching.
Touching would be his downfall. "Then do it," he said,
knowing he sounded harsh but unable to help it.

Anger, finally, began to blast away the pain.

"Goodbye," she whispered, then turned and hurried
away.

He watched as she presented her boarding pass and
ID again. When she toed off the clogs and bent awkwardly with Abby in her arms to pick them up, he
turned his back, unable to take any more.

THE PLOD TO BAGGAGE CLAIM at the Orlando airport
almost killed Wren. Abby whimpered and the car seat
felt as if it weighed ten pounds more than it had when
they left St. Louis. Wren's *feet* felt as if they weighed
more than they had any right weighing. *We're both
tired, that's all,* she told herself.

Thank goodness Molly's husband was there to meet
her. She liked him on sight. Tall and thin with curly
dark hair and friendly brown eyes behind wire-rimmed

glasses, he had a gentle smile. Better yet, he made her grin when he said, "Molly was mad I wouldn't let her come. She's undoubtedly wearing circles in the carpet waiting for you."

"I'd almost forgotten how much she hates waiting for anything." Molly might not be happy to stay home, but considering her due date was barely a week away, it was probably a good thing that Sam had insisted.

Once on their way, they chatted for a few minutes, before he said, "You look done in." He glanced at his rearview mirror. "Abby is over and out. Maybe you should do the same."

Gratefully, Wren followed his suggestion and was mildly shocked when she woke to a hand gently shaking her shoulder and his voice saying, "We're here." Dazed, she looked around, but with it dark she couldn't see much except that the house seemed small. "I'll get Abby and then come back for your suitcases," Sam said.

Still operating on autopilot, she climbed out as the front door opened.

"Wren?"

"Molly?" A burst of emotion hit her and she hurried to the porch. The two women all but collided, Molly's huge belly between them. Wren was crying for the second time that day when they retreated to arm's length to look at each other. "You're really pregnant."

Molly giggled. "I told you. Didn't you believe me?"

"I did, but I guess I couldn't picture it."

Sam arrived with Abby and Molly cooed and admired her while he brought everything into the house. Two hours passed in a blink while they talked and laughed and occasionally hugged again just because they could. Sam was the one to say at last, sternly, "You two both need to get some sleep."

They'd put Abby in the crib already set up for Molly's unborn baby.

"We took down the bed that was in here," Molly said apologetically. "I wasn't sure you were coming and I feel like such a whale, I keep expecting to go into labor any minute. But we have a pull-out couch."

"Tonight, that'll feel like a luxury," Wren said firmly.

There were two bathrooms, thank goodness, and the house boasted a cozy dining room as well as the kitchen and living room. Wren knew she couldn't stay forever, but maybe for a few weeks.

She punched the pillow into a shape that suited her then lay looking at the darkness and listening to the muted sounds of an unfamiliar city. She wanted, quite fiercely, to be in Aunt Pearl's bedroom in Saddler's Mill, knowing that Alec was across the hall.

She heard his voice, low and rough. *Come back to me.* And, *You probably won't even believe me, but I love you.*

She had come so, so close to flinging herself in his arms and saying, "Please take us home." Pride had stopped her. Pride...and fear.

Feeling as if she'd had open heart surgery without anesthesia, Wren asked herself if there was any chance at all that he really had meant it. That the pain she'd seen in his eyes was real, as was the tenderness in the way he touched Abby when he thought she couldn't see.

Had he been waiting for her email? She'd sent one from Sam's Droid phone, saying simply:

We made it. All is well. Thank you, Alec.

Despite her tiredness, sleep eluded her. She could now make out the light from a street lamp seeping through the blinds. A distant siren grew in volume then faded. Somewhere a dog barked. A car with major muffler problems passed no more than a block away.

Maybe in a few days she'd call him. She'd give him the phone number here and see whether he called her.

After he enjoyed a few uninterrupted nights of sleep, he might decide to be grateful she hadn't taken him up on his offer.

But what if he did love her? What if tonight he was hurting, too? What if *she'd* hurt him?

Oh, God, Wren thought. *What if I made a horrible mistake?*

CHAPTER SIXTEEN

NO MATTER WHICH WAY Alec read Wren's email, he couldn't make it say *I'm sorry* or *I miss you,* or discern even a hint of a desire to stay in touch. That *thank you, Alec* sounded damn final to him. Would he ever hear from her again?

Maybe it would be better if he didn't. He drew on his anger, although it felt more like despair. He thought of how impossible it was trying to be any kind of father to Autumn and India via telephone and email. He *couldn't* cut loose from them, however much it all hurt. If Wren wasn't ever coming back, he couldn't imagine how he'd make conversation with her should she phone only to chat. What was he supposed to do, say, "How great" when she told him Abby had crawled or said "Mama" for the first time?

He went through the motions of his day. When he got home he finally decided he had to respond to Wren's email. He sat down at his computer, opened his account and read what she'd written another five or ten times in hopes he'd missed something.

Nope.

Reply. Fingers unmoving on the keyboard, he stared at the monitor. He wanted to ask her if she really felt welcome there in Florida. Was the friendship as powerful as she'd believed it to be? Would she be able to find a job before her money ran out? He would have offered to help, but he knew how welcome that would be. She'd come right out and said that leaning on him wasn't healthy for her. He understood why she felt that way. He did. But accepting a helping hand wasn't the kind of dependence she feared. Accepting love wasn't.

She had to recognize that herself.

He swore and started to type.

Thanks for letting me know you made it. I called James's mother today. She sounded so shocked I couldn't tell how much she'll grieve. She supposed he was in Arkansas on business and I could tell she was confused but she didn't ask any questions except about how to bring his body home. Here's her contact info, in case you decide to tell her about Abby.

He included the name, phone number and address. He briefly told Wren that they'd given up on identifying the last body in the morgue and buried it. Gruesome, maybe, but Alec figured she'd want to know. She wouldn't forget that face any more than she would James's.

He thought of a hundred ways to conclude the email, finally settling on:

I'm here, Wren.

Then he tapped Send.

A week passed. He couldn't seem to rise above his misery. Alec couldn't decide if this was worse than the weeks and months after he'd said goodbye to his children knowing how long it would be before he would see them. Did it matter?

He avoided his sister beyond informing her that if she knew someone who could use the bassinet, he'd be glad to drop it off wherever she told him. Unfortunately, it was impossible to avoid Randy, who was taking over

Alec's garage. Alec had taken to parking on the street so that his Tahoe wasn't in the way when Randy needed to load sheets of plywood or unload a table saw. His brother-in-law wasn't growing on Alec, exactly; it was more that he was becoming inured to him, like developing a callous on his heel where a boot rubbed. He did have to admit that Randy was taking his change of career seriously, which would have once surprised him but now didn't. He went so far as to invite the guy in for coffee a couple of times, when they discussed Randy's current job, the two buddies he thought he'd take on as soon as he was sure the workload would justify it and the priorities when it came time to tackle Alec's house.

It struck him that he did think of it as his house now, instead of Mom's or Great-Aunt Pearl's. The idea of selling felt wrong. Wren was right. There were ties here. As alone as he felt, hanging on to those ties with the past seemed important. And maybe it was a hope for the future, too, however thin it sometimes seemed. With Wren here, this house had been a home. It could be again.

In SOME DREAM WORLD, Wren had imagined going to the hospital with Molly and maybe taking turns with Sam being at her side, but of course she couldn't. What would she have done with Abby? So when Molly, after a night and half a day of intermittent contractions, was sure she was really in labor, Wren could only give her a last hug and say to Sam, "Call me the minute the baby's born."

During the long wait, all Wren could think was how much she wanted to talk to Alec. She missed him so much, it was an ever-present ache.

I'm here, Wren.

Not letting herself have second thoughts, she picked up the phone and dialed, then sat tensely listening to the rings. Maybe he wasn't there. Maybe when he didn't recognize the phone number he'd think it was some kind of solicitation. Maybe—

"Hello?"

"Alec?" she said, heart pounding. "Um, it's Wren."

"Is something wrong?"

"No! No." She felt her face form a funny, crooked smile that expressed the bittersweet emotions that poured through her, hearing his voice. "I wanted to say hello. Molly and Sam are at the hospital. She's having her baby. And I kept thinking about you."

"Because childbirth brings me to mind?" Was he smiling? "Aren't you glad you didn't have to be bothered with monitors and doctors and, hey, a bed with metal stirrups?"

How had he known what she needed from him? Only a little huskily, Wren said, "I wouldn't have liked the metal stirrups, I know that."

"Actually, birthing rooms are homier than that."

"But not as homey as our attic."

They were both quiet for a minute.

"No," he said finally. "I think about it sometimes."

"Will the house get torn down?"

"Yeah. I don't know if there's any family to see to it, though. It may have to fall down on its own."

Why did that feel so unbearably sad?

Because we were happy there, that's why.

"Will anybody rescue the quilts?"

"I can, if you want. I can let Josiah know I have them."

"Yes, please." Once, those quilts had made a bed for the two of them. No, the three of them. She took a deep breath. "I didn't really have anything to say. I guess all I wanted was to hear your voice."

"You wanted to hear my voice," he echoed, so slowly she wondered what he was thinking.

I miss you. Oh, I miss you. "Yes," she whispered.

"Okay," he said after a minute. "Wren, I'm here if you need me."

Somehow she said *thank you* and *goodbye.* Tears were pouring down her cheeks when she ended the call. It was supposed to make her feel better, and instead she felt worse. So much worse.

She'd forgotten to give him Molly's phone number. That was going to be a test, and she'd forgotten.

It occurred to her that she'd had Molly's phone number in the first place only because *he* had given it to her. So, he'd had it all along, and he hadn't called.

But she was confused to realize she might not have liked it if he had, not after he'd asked her to stay and she'd said no. It was the kind of thing James would have done, putting pressure on her under the assumption he could change her mind. Alec hadn't done that. He'd said, "Come back to me," and "I'm here," but he'd let her go because she'd said she had to. He had respected her decision.

Was it him she hadn't trusted, or herself?

Wren was still sitting there in the quiet kitchen trying to decide when the phone rang again and she grabbed it eagerly.

"We have a little boy," Sam announced jubilantly.

ALEC WASN'T SLEEPING MUCH anyway, so tonight he wouldn't bother going to bed. Or, at least, not until he'd spoken to his daughters. That was one of the difficulties he'd faced: the awkward time difference. To catch them at six in the evening, he had to call at three in the morning. Early evening was about the only time he could successfully get them on the phone. In school full days, they seemed to be extraordinarily busy the rest of the time, too.

It had been a month or more since he'd called. The intervals between talking to them had been growing. His fault, but guilt didn't grab him by the throat the way it usually did. He was ready to do better, make sure he was a part of their lives.

Alec had a cup of coffee while he watched the ten o'clock news. His upholstered rocker and the TV were now in the living room, all by their lonesome. One of these days Alec guessed he'd have to go furniture shopping, but so far he hadn't felt inclined.

He picked a sci-fi novel almost at random from his unread pile and opened it, but he couldn't make himself focus.

He found himself thinking instead about the Alec he'd been before his father died. About the days after. The grief, which time had muted. What hadn't been muted was the sense he'd had that, in the blink of an eye, he'd assumed a terrible burden. It had been almost physical; he'd locked his knees to be sure they didn't buckle beneath the weight he'd felt descend on his shoulders.

Mom's death was different, but no less painful. When he gently closed her eyes, he'd been dimly aware of Sally sobbing in the background. Inside, he'd felt anything but gentle. He'd been enraged. His mother shouldn't have died of cancer that was now so treatable. Somebody had failed. *He* had failed.

The night crawled on. He turned pages, but didn't know what he'd read. Instead, he saw himself walking in the door from work to be met by Carlene saying, "We have to talk."

It wasn't really a talk she wanted. She'd already packed, waiting only to tell him face-to-face that she wanted a divorce. He never even knew what had precipitated her to make the decision that day. Not ten minutes later, she'd called two subdued little girls from their bedrooms, let him hug them and then driven away with them to stay temporarily with her father. Alec had been left standing in front of their house, shocked in a way he wasn't sure he'd been before or since. He'd felt…lost.

Sitting here now, in the silent living room, he realized that somewhere along the way, love had come to be synonymous with a crushing sense of responsibility. He had to take care of the people he loved. If anything went wrong, it was his fault. Always his fault.

No wonder he had been afraid to love again.

Almost from the minute he had laid Wren down in that attic and talked her through a contraction, he'd quit feeling lost.

I might fail her. Or Abby.

The alternative was living without them. Pain swelled, and he knew he was ready to take any risk.

If only he'd known sooner, not given Wren such mixed messages.

Alec rocked and let himself remember the few times he'd held Wren. He thought about things she'd said and not said, and wondered if it would have mattered had he gone after her openly from the beginning. His conclusion was: no. His gentle Wren was filled with self-doubt. He would have sworn she had grown in confidence while she was here; maybe having a baby had done that for her, made her understand that she could be a lioness for Abby's sake. He hoped he'd made a difference, too. But in the end, when she said she had to go, Alec understand that she'd meant it. After James, she couldn't trust another man until she believed in herself and her own strength.

Great. Good to know his massively inept interpersonal skills weren't responsible for driving her away. But this new understanding might drive him crazy. Waiting for someone else to come to a decision and take action didn't sit well with him. Feeling powerless reminded him too sharply of his father's funeral, of sitting at his mother's bedside and watching her suffer, of standing in front of his house as Carlene drove away with his girls. And now he'd admitted to himself that he had no control over Wren's decisions. There was a strong possibility that she would indeed come to believe in herself—but *wouldn't* come back to him. He'd said, "I love you." She hadn't.

He never did get very far with the novel.

At two-thirty in the morning, he placed the call.

Carlene answered. When he identified himself, she said, "Oh, I'll get the girls."

"Wait." He was surprised to realize this was really why he'd called.

"What is it, Alec?"

She sounded far away. That was another thing that made these phone calls so difficult. There was a hint of a delay between speaking and hearing, a faint echo that blurred words. Sometimes he couldn't understand what one of the girls was saying, and had to ask them to repeat it. He knew they didn't catch everything he said.

With sudden, explosive anger, he wondered why Carlene couldn't have married a man who lived in Madison, Wisconsin, or Chicago or, hell, Providence, Rhode Island. Other divorced men he knew got to *see* their kids.

"I want the girls for the summer," he said bluntly.

For the summer, his own voice whispered back to him.

Carlene wasn't in any hurry to say anything. When she did, it was, "They're really young to make the trip."

"If necessary, I'll fly over to get them."

"What would they *do* all summer, with you working your usual ridiculous hours?"

"I don't work ridiculous hours anymore." For the first time ever, he didn't feel guilty because now, too late, he'd changed his life enough to be able to say that. His marriage had been doomed no matter what. He hadn't loved Carlene the way he should, and Alec suspected she hadn't loved him much toward the end, either. They'd jumped into marriage and Autumn had come along before they recognized they had made a mistake. Some of it was his fault, but not all of it. "You know Sally is here," he said. "The girls will have a great time with their cousins."

She was quiet again. He braced himself for an argument. But to his surprise, what she finally said was, "I think maybe they do need to see you. Autumn cried the other day because she was afraid she was forgetting you."

Autumn, he thought, stunned.

"A year is a long time in her life," Carlene pointed out.

"I want them every summer, Carlene. I can afford the airfare."

Again she surprised him. "We'll pay half of it."

They had an unexpectedly civil discussion about the

details, after which she went away for a minute and finally he heard a small, timid voice on the phone.

"Daddy?"

He was smiling, but, damn it, his eyes were wet, too, when he said, "India. Honey."

HE REALLY DID SUCK at waiting.

At least every couple of days, Alec went online and priced airline tickets to Florida. He wanted to go in the worst way. To show up on her doorstep and say, "Damn it, I love you, and you're coming home with me." No matter how short their time together had been, no matter how arrogant it made him, he couldn't believe she didn't love him, too. He remembered the way she'd kissed him, the delight on her face when he came home every day, the things about herself she'd told him that he knew she never talked about. The way she'd wrapped her arms around him and held him so tightly. With such love. It had to be with love.

Alec kept thinking of things he could have or should have or would have said, including "I love Abby, too." In the end he knew none of them would have made any difference. Wren had a soft heart and he could have begged or played the you-owe-me card, but the truth was, he didn't like the idea of her staying because she felt sorry for him, or obligated to him. He hated the idea of her staying because he'd manipulated her in any way.

And that's why he didn't buy the ticket. Wren had to come to him of her own free will.

The fact that she stayed in touch gave him hope. First it was very occasional emails that over the weeks became more frequent. His heart sank when she found a place to live, but he was encouraged by the fact that she was only temping and didn't mention interviews for permanent jobs. She *was* managing, though, and that was good. She'd needed to know she could cope on her own. If she'd stayed with him, she would always have wondered. Maybe he would have wondered, too, whether she was with him because she knew he would take care of her and Abby.

More and more, Wren's sense of humor crept through, as did her curiosity. She wanted to know about Randy's business, about whether the two men liked each other any better. She asked about the house, and whether Alec had bought any furniture. She scolded him when he said no. He told her he would eventually, but it had become symbolic for him. He wanted them to buy everything together, so it was their home, not his. Alec had a bad feeling that the day he bought a sofa was the day he gave up on her. And he was a long way from ready to do that.

Wren was pleased that his girls were coming for the summer. She told him that she and her mother were talking more often, that her mother wanted a new picture of Abby at least weekly.

When Alec replied, he asked if she'd email him a picture of Abby, too.

She didn't respond for two days. Then:

Do you mean it?

His reply had been:

Isn't her name Abigail Alexa?

That same night she sent a brief email with several photos attached. When he opened the first one, he felt as if he'd taken a blow to the solar plexus. Abby was smiling.

He'd missed her first smile.

He stared for the longest time, and that was when he came closest to despairing.

Alec sat in his nearly empty living room, wondering if he should buy the damn couch.

UNTIL TONIGHT, Wren hadn't heard from Alec in days, not since she'd sent him the photos of Abby. Not a word.

But she and Molly had renewed their friendship, big-time. That made Wren happy.

And she and her mother had had a conversation that shook her. Her mother had actually said, "I wish you'd felt you could turn to me." And then she sent a really big check and a note that said:

> It was scary when you were little and I didn't have anyone to ask when I needed help. I don't want that for you.
> Love, Mom.

Wren stuck the note on the refrigerator with a magnet and reread it at least once a day. She couldn't quite make herself believe she'd been wrong her whole life, that her mother really did love her and wasn't ashamed to have a plain daughter. Disoriented, Wren had to consider the possibility that Mom merely wasn't comfortable cuddling or even touching. That maybe some of her ambition on the job had to do with the fear of not having any support if she failed. That maybe she'd done her best.

The worst part of Wren's new life—well, the next-to-worst part—was having to leave Abby every day. Wren trusted Molly to take care of her, but that didn't keep her from feeling a horrible wrench every morning when she handed Abby over and had to hurry out the door. She missed her so much all day, she ached. All that saved her was knowing that when she got off work at five she would be able to hurry to Molly's and sweep Abby up into her arms.

No, the absolute worst thing about this new life was that Alec wasn't there at the end of the day. Every time she thought about him now, her rib cage seemed to have contracted, not leaving quite enough space for her heart and lungs.

She didn't like Florida all that much. Except that wasn't fair. The problem wasn't Gainesville or Florida. It was that she didn't want to be here. She could be in Saddler's Mill, helping Alec remodel Pearl's house and make it his. No. *Theirs.*

Then tonight Alec had called her. Mostly he waited for her to do the phoning, but not this time. After she hung up, she realized she didn't even know why he had. He hadn't actually said that much. When she asked if he'd gotten the pictures, he said, "Yes," and then was quiet for a minute before he asked her something about her latest job. He'd encouraged her to chatter, and he might even have been smiling at the end when he said, "I'm glad things are going so well for you, Wren."

Except, she hung up the phone and knew that he'd been feeling sad. She remembered the time she'd told him she wanted to hear his voice. Tonight, Wren thought, all he'd really wanted was to hear hers.

Her mouth opened in a silent, horrified cry. Oh, God. Was she letting something as petty as *pride* keep her from Alec?

The pain was terrible. She tried hard to remember all those good reasons she hadn't stayed in Saddler's Mill in the first place.

Yes, she'd been afraid of replaying her dependence on James. But she knew now that she wasn't the same person she'd been then, and Alec certainly wasn't anything like James. She'd told herself there weren't any job openings in Saddler's Mill, and probably no available rentals, either, and that she couldn't let Alec step in where James had left off and take care of her. It had really mattered to her to prove she could manage on her own. Mom's money had gone straight in the bank to provide backup. Wren was earning enough herself to pay her minimal bills. Regaining her pride had seemed all-important.

Was her pride that important?

It was a while since Alec had said, *I'm here, Wren,* but he hadn't had to. Wasn't that exactly what she heard from him every time he emailed and on the rare occasions they talked, like tonight, on the phone? Yes, Detective Alec Harper was so sexy it had been hard for her to believe he wanted her, but couldn't she feel his loneliness? Almost from the beginning, she'd known that he was a complex, guarded man hiding a whole lot of pain. As damaged as he was, he'd let her in, which wasn't easy for him. It might have happened because of those days in the attic, or because he'd seen her physically and emotionally naked and that made him feel safe enough to reveal his own vulnerability. It didn't matter why, she realized now in wonder, only that he had.

Abby was three months old today. Alec hadn't seen her in two months. Maybe he'd been afraid to let himself love her—maybe he still was—but he asked about her in every email and every time they talked. He'd wanted pictures of her. If Wren was patient, he wouldn't be able to help himself but love Abby, too. Not once he knew Wren and Abby both were there to stay, that they wouldn't leave him again. Convincing him of that was essential. Too many people he loved had left him, in one way or another.

She could only imagine how much she had hurt him by coming to Florida.

All of a sudden, she broke into a smile, and it was huge and wobbly.

What could be more powerful than the simple words he'd chosen?

Come back to me, Wren.

I'm here. He'd said that over and over.

There was nothing in the world she wanted more than to go home to Alec.

She barely slept that night. Come morning, feeling light and ridiculously happy, Wren dropped off Abby for the day and, instead of going right to the office where she was temping as a receptionist, she stopped at the library, went online and bought her ticket. The price was once again ridiculous because she couldn't seem to plan her journeys in advance. *Mom,* she thought, *thank you.*

OVER DINNER AT SALLY'S, Alec talked to his nieces and nephew about their cousins and how they would be spending the summer. He was living for the day. June 18, he would meet them at the airport in St. Louis. Carlene had decided to combine bringing the girls with visiting her father and sister. Alec would fly to Sydney with them at the end of the summer.

Having something to anticipate kept his despair at bay.

This week a milestone had passed: it had been three months since he'd delivered Abby. Such a short time, and yet forever. He had changed.

Sally refused his help cleaning the kitchen after

dinner. He kissed her cheek, hugged the kids and even exchanged a few words with Randy before he walked out to his SUV.

A block away from home, he saw a strange car sat at the curb in front of his house. He could think of reasons someone might have parked there—a neighbor could have had a bunch of guests earlier, for example, and this car belonged to a straggler. Still, he was a cop, and the fact that someone had chosen to park there of all places made him wary. He pulled up behind the car, a new-looking compact, and realized the driver was sitting behind the wheel.

Waiting for him?

If this had been a traffic stop, he would have left his headlights on. It wasn't, and the street lamp was only half a block away. He turned off the engine, hesitated, then got out and walked forward. He'd almost reached the car when the door opened and a woman jumped out.

"Alec?" His name came out as a strangled cry. "I didn't think it was you. Why didn't you pull in to the driveway?"

He stopped dead, his heart going into overdrive. "Wren?"

"It's me." Suddenly she sounded shy.

"You're here," he said stupidly.

"Yes. Maybe I should have called, but, um, I guess I wanted to surprise you."

There they stood, a good eight or ten feet separating them, neither moving. He felt as if the soles of his shoes were stuck in the asphalt of the street.

"Where's Abby?"

Her hand fluttered. "In the car. She's asleep."

He wished he could make out Wren's face better, tell

what she was thinking. Did her arrival mean what he hoped it did?

Light-headed, he realized he'd forgotten to drag in the next breath. "I'm not dreaming?"

The dim light caught a new shimmer in her dark, shadowed eyes. "You kept saying, *I'm here*." Her voice cracked. "And, well, now so am I."

Released from his paralysis, Alec didn't think he'd ever moved faster. He had her in his arms, his face buried in her hair as he mumbled, "I tried to believe you'd come. I've been hanging on by my fingernails."

Her laugh was choked. Probably they were both remembering that moment when he'd done exactly that, dangling above the turbulent floodwaters with her grip on his wrists helping keep him from falling. She was holding him now, too, every bit as tight as he was holding her.

"I missed you so much," she whispered.

"I've only been half-alive."

"Me, too. But I had to go."

"I know you did. I do know." He lifted his head to look hungrily at her. "Please tell me you're here to stay."

"If you really want us." She tried to smile, but her effort was shaky. "I packed everything. I had to leave a crib behind. Poor Abby, she can't hold on to a bed."

"Her bassinet is still right where you left it. Sally found someone who wanted it, but I made an excuse."

Those big brown eyes were drowning. He stopped the overflow with his thumbs.

"You do want me."

"Oh, yeah," he said hoarsely.

"I love you." Wren unwrapped her arms from around his waist only to fling them around his neck instead. She rose on tiptoe and sought his mouth. "I love you."

He closed the small remaining distance and kissed her with all the urgency he'd tamped down. Their tongues tangled and their teeth scraped and their bodies strained together. He was shaking, or she was. Maybe both of them. They stood in the middle of the street, kissing as though there might never be another chance.

What happened then was out of character. He wasn't an optimistic man, but suddenly he knew: there would be plenty of other chances. A lifetime of them. And joy swelled in his chest until it burst open like the fireworks on the fourth of July, startlingly beautiful in a sky that had been all darkness until now.

He dragged his mouth away long enough to say, "I love you, my beautiful brown-feathered Wren," and kissed her again, but with all the tenderness in the world this time.

"I won't leave again," she promised, when they came up for air, and he believed her.

Against all the odds.

He'd been lost but found again. In her need, Wren had given him her trust, and he had to do the same in return.

"I still haven't bought any furniture," he murmured against her throat, where he strung kisses like pearls.

"Why not?" Wren asked in a strangled voice.

"Because I was waiting for you."

"No more waiting," she whispered, and he smiled, filled with that completely insane and absolutely convincing joy and faith.

* * * * *

COMING NEXT MONTH

Available November 8, 2011

> You can find more information on upcoming
> Harlequin® titles, free excerpts and more at
> **www.HarlequinInsideRomance.com.**

REQUEST YOUR FREE BOOKS!
2 FREE NOVELS PLUS 2 FREE GIFTS!

Harlequin

Super Romance

Exciting, emotional, unexpected!

YES! Please send me 2 FREE Harlequin® Superromance® novels and my 2 FREE gifts (gifts are worth about $10). After receiving them, if I don't wish to receive any more books, I can return the shipping statement marked "cancel." If I don't cancel, I will receive 6 brand-new novels every month and be billed just $4.69 per book in the U.S. or $5.24 per book in Canada. That's a saving of at least 15% off the cover price! It's quite a bargain! Shipping and handling is just 50¢ per book in the U.S. and 75¢ per book in Canada.* I understand that accepting the 2 free books and gifts places me under no obligation to buy anything. I can always return a shipment and cancel at any time. Even if I never buy another book, the two free books and gifts are mine to keep forever.

135/336 HDN FC6T

Name _____ (PLEASE PRINT) _____

Address _____ Apt. # _____

City _____ State/Prov. _____ Zip/Postal Code _____

Signature (if under 18, a parent or guardian must sign) _____

Mail to the **Reader Service:**
IN U.S.A.: P.O. Box 1867, Buffalo, NY 14240-1867
IN CANADA: P.O. Box 609, Fort Erie, Ontario L2A 5X3

Not valid for current subscribers to Harlequin Superromance books.

**Are you a current subscriber to Harlequin Superromance books
and want to receive the larger-print edition?
Call 1-800-873-8635 or visit www.ReaderService.com.**

* Terms and prices subject to change without notice. Prices do not include applicable taxes. Sales tax applicable in N.Y. Canadian residents will be charged applicable taxes. Offer not valid in Quebec. This offer is limited to one order per household. All orders subject to credit approval. Credit or debit balances in a customer's account(s) may be offset by any other outstanding balance owed by or to the customer. Please allow 4 to 6 weeks for delivery. Offer available while quantities last.

Your Privacy—The Reader Service is committed to protecting your privacy. Our Privacy Policy is available online at www.ReaderService.com or upon request from the Reader Service.

We make a portion of our mailing list available to reputable third parties that offer products we believe may interest you. If you prefer that we not exchange your name with third parties, or if you wish to clarify or modify your communication preferences, please visit us at www.ReaderService.com/consumerschoice or write to us at Reader Service Preference Service, P.O. Box 9062, Buffalo, NY 14269. Include your complete name and address.

HSR11

Harlequin® Special Edition® is thrilled to present a new installment in USA TODAY *bestselling author RaeAnne Thayne's reader-favorite miniseries,* THE COWBOYS OF COLD CREEK.

Join the excitement as we meet the Bowmans—four siblings who lost their parents but keep family ties alive in Pine Gulch. First up is Trace. Only two things get under this rugged lawman's skin: beautiful women and secrets. And in Rebecca Parsons, he finds both!

Read on for a sneak peek of CHRISTMAS IN COLD CREEK. *Available November 2011 from Harlequin® Special Edition®.*

On impulse, he unfolded himself from the bar stool. "Need a hand?"

"Thank you! I..." She lifted her gaze from the floor to his jeans and then raised her eyes. When she identified him her hazel eyes turned from grateful to unfriendly and cold, as if he'd somehow thrown the broken glasses at her head.

He also thought he saw a glimmer of panic in those interesting depths, which instantly stirred his curiosity like cream swirling through coffee.

"I've got it, Officer. Thank you." Her voice was several degrees colder than the whirl of sleet outside the windows.

Despite her protests, he knelt down beside her and began to pick up shards of broken glass. "No problem. Those trays can be slippery."

This close, he picked up the scent of her, something fresh and flowery that made him think of a mountain meadow on a July afternoon. She had a soft, lush mouth and for one brief, insane moment, he wanted to push aside that stray lock of hair slipping from her ponytail and taste her. Apparently he needed to spend a lot less time working and a great deal *more* time recreating with the opposite sex if he could have sudden random fantasies about a woman he wasn't even inclined to like, pretty or not.

"I'm Trace Bowman. You must be new in town."

She didn't answer immediately and he could almost see the wheels turning in her head. Why the hesitancy? And why that little hint of unease he could see clouding the edge of her gaze? His presence was obviously making her uncomfortable and Trace couldn't help wondering why.

"Yes. We've been here a few weeks."

"Well, I'm just up the road about four lots, in the white house with the cedar shake roof, if you or your daughter need anything." He smiled at her as he picked up the last shard of glass and set it on her tray.

Definitely a story there, he thought as she hurried away. He just might need to dig a little into her background to find out why someone with fine clothes and nice jewelry, and who so obviously didn't have experience as a waitress, would be here slinging hash at The Gulch. Was she running away from someone? A bad marriage?

So...Rebecca Parsons. Not Becky. An intriguing woman. It had been a long time since one of those had crossed his path here in Pine Gulch.

Trace won't rest until he finds out Rebecca's secret, but will he still have that same attraction to her once he does? Find out in CHRISTMAS IN COLD CREEK. Available November 2011 from Harlequin® Special Edition®.

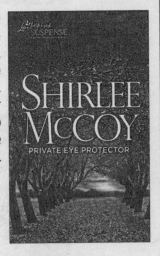